EMERGENCE

R. H. DIXON

CORVUS CORONE PRESS

Front cover by Carrion Crow Design.

A CIP catalogue record for this title is available from
the British Library.

ISBN: 978-1-9997180-0-8

Corvus Corone Press

For Derek, Marvin & Delilah

Other books by R. H. Dixon:

A STORYTELLING OF RAVENS

'Whoever fights monsters should see to it that in the process he does not become a monster.' **Friedrich Nietzsche**

R. H. DIXON

1

As he adjusted the black tie around his neck, John's throat felt closed and his fingers stiff. He pulled at the knot and looked at his reflection. The face staring back didn't seem familiar; it was lost within the dark surface that looked like a film of crude oil on top of still water. He was trapped behind a slick veil where there wasn't much clarity and he didn't feel real.

The blue-green pigmentation of his eyes appeared greyscale, lifeless and devoid of optimism, as if the cheerful colour had been washed out with every tear issued from the bottomless well of grief within himself. And yet the glossy sheen of the black coffin lid showed up the dark crescents beneath his eyes well, betraying his secret of sleepless, wine-guzzling nights. His skin had a sickly pallor. He doubted he'd ever look or feel normal again.

Black shadows pirouetted around him in the funeral parlour's chapel of rest and the ceiling spotlight was caught next to his own reflection like a snared seraphim, peeking over his shoulder. He watched as his own hand reached out, shaking, moving in slow motion. There was no sound as he inched the lid open, increasing the unnerving silence of the room. And it was this silence, this cold, massive nothingness, that was worse than the coffin itself. The sheer lack of noise filled his head with the harsh intensity of neuralgia, numbing his face and further serving to displace his sense of identity, making him subconsciously question his capability to carry on, his want to continue.

He knew that once the coffin and all it was taking with it had disappeared behind burgundy velvet curtains this same unbearable level of quietude would return. Awkward conversations at the wake would follow, where nobody would know what to say to him because death offers no true opportunity for consolation, no words to sugar-coat the finality of a shortened life or, indeed, make allowances for genuine predictions of happier times ahead. Once all of the fish paste vol-au-vents and corned beef slices had been eaten and everyone had sloped off to resume the mostly undisturbed routines of their own lives, that's when John knew the silence of oblivion would latch onto him with firm resolve and follow him home. To linger whenever he took a bath or tried to read the newspaper, whenever he cooked a meal or washed the dishes. And despite all his best efforts to drown this soundlessness out with the noise of the television or radio, it would remain ever present until he learned how to blot it out with a new routine, a new life established after the fallout from his old life had settled like cold ashes around his feet.

He couldn't even begin to imagine when that day might be and he couldn't understand his own contribution to the quietness of the chapel of rest right now. His sense of mourning felt like it should have a sound all of its own. A weighty, palpable thing that he expected might be able to exist outside of his body, to be heard like the lonely cry of an orca in the deep dark. Lost. Alas, the unpredictability of grief surrendered him to horrific silence.

His head buzzed with thick nothingness and his chest ached with a feeling of complete ineptitude. The coffin lid was fully open and there inside, lying on a bed of silver satin, was Amy. His wife. Her ash blonde hair was neatly styled and she would have looked angel-serene had it not been for the absurdity of her makeup. Her cheeks were displaying more rouge than she'd have put on herself and her lips, also, were too red for the occasion. There was a time when the shade would have denoted passion, frivolity and playfulness, but in the wake of tragedy and the onset of misery it looked abhorrently wrong. The crudeness of it all made her look like a life-sized doll that a little girl – *their* little girl – had been playing dress-up with, and there was a waxy, unreal quality to Amy's skin that suggested she'd never been alive – a denial that the little girl had ever been a part of her.

Amy was wearing her favourite blue dress, the one she'd worn on the evening of their wedding. To John, the soft billowy material retained no evidence of the happy moments of laughter, kissing and slow dancing. Now it was a dress that signified loss, heartache and end.

The mortician's arrangement of his wife's body – left hand laid across her stomach, right one on top, elbows tucked down by her sides – reminded John of the way she'd often held herself when she was pregnant. Three years ago. Caressing her belly and protectively holding it. Now, sadly, the child she'd given birth to wouldn't get to play with her makeup or enjoy motherly embraces. Except, perhaps, in dreams.

Deep down in the depths of John's waking awareness he knew *this* was a dream, a crassly embellished re-enactment of one of the worst days of his life. He knew how it would pan out as well, because it was the same rendition each time. Still, he reached out and touched the back of Amy's hand. And, still, his breath caught. She was cold and unwelcoming. No warmth or softness left in her pianist's fingers. The slender, ivory digits which had stroked his skin and sought his affection during the best days of his life were nothing more than white corpse fingers.

His own fingers became tense and he flattened his palm against the back of her hand in an attempt to warm it. Death had taken her from him much too soon, but when she failed to react to the warmth of his touch he knew it had no plan to give her back. There was no hope her passing had been a case of mistaken identity that could be rectified and he knew he could win this fight of fate no more than she could. Not even for just one night, because his own subconscious was rallying against him, denying him any solace from the possible oblivion of sleep-induced fantasy. His most sadistic inner-self was determined to relive this day over and over. Again and again. With no deviation from the well-rehearsed script his subconscious had created.

Tears welled up in his already raw and puffy eyes. He wished for the umpteenth time it could be the other way round – he wished it was him lying in the coffin and that Amy was standing where he was, alive. He gripped her hand tight, afraid to let go, and told her through wet lips that he loved her. He hoped this time the dream would be different, that the story might change and she'd wake up and embrace him. But as he looked upon her face again he saw that it was the usual nightmare: her expression not quite right. A wry smile had crept to her plastic-red lips. A sneering smirk.

Recoiling, he snatched his hand away and watched as her eyes blinked open.

She looked at him, cold blue.

Her shiny mouth parted.

And with all the wispy coarseness of coal-dust she said, 'John, it's just you now.'

2

John awoke, sweat-drenched. The bedroom window was cracked open but there was no air circulating, just the balmy stagnancy of summer clinging to his bare skin. There was a constant sizzle of rain outside and the threat of thunder hung in the air. Water coursed down the drainpipe at the side of the house, lashing out onto the gravelled garden below like a drunk relieving his bladder. At the insistence of the sound John felt an instinctive need to pee, and with this urge came a heightened sense of alertness that broke through the remnants of his troubled sleep. His mouth was parched and his teeth felt fuzzy against his tongue. Clamping a hand to his clammy forehead, he groaned and rolled over onto his side.

The glowing red numbers of the digital alarm clock on the bedside table showed it was three a.m. (half an hour later than he'd awoken the previous morning, twenty minutes earlier than the one before that). He pushed the damp sheets away and swung his feet to the floor, patting the carpet roundabout with his right foot, trying to locate his slippers. As he did so he became aware of the distant whirring of an engine somewhere outside. It grew louder and more distinct over the continuous hiss of rain till eventually a car sailed past the house, the road's surface water spraying noisily beneath its tyres as it glided by. The engine sound then receded to a faraway hum again and John thought the driver of the car might as well be on a different planet. Other people seemed to go about their business as though there was nothing wrong with the world while he merely existed in a long-term state of grief-induced zombification. He felt disconnected from everyone else.

When his big toe hooked the edge of a slipper he pulled it closer, and a small voice behind him said, 'Dad?'

John started, his whole body becoming tense. 'Christ, Seren, you're like creeping bloody Jesus!'

His daughter was standing just outside the open doorway watching him, the lenses of her purple thick-rimmed glasses spellbound ink-black by the night's gloomy hues. She was clutching Geller, a large plush triceratops, beneath her left arm, and the first four buttons of her pyjama jacket were undone. Her blonde hair was a disarrayed halo against the artificial light that shone in through the landing window. It looked like she was putting in a hard night as well.

. 'I can't sleep,' she said, her voice hushed and dream-like in the pre-dawn murk.

'Why not, kidda?' John stood up and reached for his fleecy bathrobe, which was a heaped black mound on the floor by the bed.

'The rain.' Seren looked to the curtainless window of the landing, her expression strangely solemn. 'I don't like it.'

John finished securing the robe's belt around his waist and rubbed his face with both hands before going to her. 'Since when?'

She shrugged.

'Don't you feel all snuggly knowing that you and Geller are tucked up in bed safe and dry?'

She contemplated this for a moment then shook her head. 'Rain means someone in the sky has lost their way, they can't get to where they need to go so they're crying.'

'People don't get lost in the sky, kidda.'

'How do you know?'

'I just do.' John reached out to smooth her hair with

his fingers, sighing inwardly as he did. A sourness lay heavy in his stomach, creating an acrid taste in his mouth, and there was a dull throbbing at his temples, no doubt working up to a full-scale headache. This was a conversation he didn't feel like having right now. He had a busy schedule later that morning – teleconferences to attend, meetings to set up, reports to write – so his own bad dreams teamed with his daughter's middle-of-the-night randomness were not things he wanted to be dealing with.

'Come on,' he said, taking hold of her upper arm and guiding her towards her own room. 'Back to bed with you, you've got school tomorrow. Nobody's crying and nobody's lost, okay? The rain comes from the clouds, that's all.'

She fixed him with wide eyes, the kind reserved for invoking pity. 'Can I sleep with you?'

John shook his head, resolving not to give in to any guilt-inducing acts of piteousness. If he let her sleep in his bed tonight she'd expect it every other night. He ushered her back into her own room. 'Nice try, kidda, but no.'

Seren's bedroom was bound in greyness. Blackout curtains at the window barred any light from entering and the streetlight glow from the landing was weak beyond the open doorway. Clustered silhouettes of toys and furniture made the room feel smaller than it was. John switched on the nightlight, on top of the bedside table, swathing the room in a soft, dreamy radiance. He sat down on the single bed and patted the dinosaur-print duvet, motioning for Seren to climb back under it, which she did without argument. Once she was lying down, her blonde hair contrasted with the red and green pillowcase and she watched him with steely blue eyes that were tired but ever alert.

'No more gloomy thoughts, okay?' John said.

'Okay.'

He leant over and kissed her on the forehead. 'Do you want me to leave the light on?'

Seren shook her head.

'Sure?'

'I was sad, not scared.' She wrapped an arm around Geller, her eyes still imploring.

'Alright.' John stood up. Not prone to unnecessary pandering, he was sure she'd fall asleep again. 'Night night then, trouble.' He turned, stooping to switch off the nightlight.

'*Dad?*'

With his finger poised at the base of the lamp, John looked round, surprised. 'Yeah?'

'What's a bellend?'

Unsure if he'd heard correctly, he found no words with which to reply. He stood there gaping, while her expression remained neutral to his quiet, but surely all-too-obvious, shock. Was this some deliberate challenge? A new ruse, he wondered, to see how far she could push him? When he didn't respond, she explained, 'Yesterday Harry Dalton said that Mr Crampton, our head of year, is a bellend. What does it mean?'

As much as he was inclined to agree with Harry Dalton, John made a stern face. 'And where did Harry Dalton hear that word?'

'His big brother. He says most teachers are bellends.'

John puffed his cheeks and exhaled wearily. 'Sounds to me like Harry Dalton's big brother has been making up silly words.'

Seren looked almost disappointed. 'So Mr Crampton isn't a bellend?'

'No! And don't ever let me hear you say so.'

'But Harry Dalton says…'

'Harry Dalton and his big brother can say whatever they bloody well like, but I don't want you using that word again, young lady, you hear me? In fact, if I catch you saying it again you're in seriously big trouble.'

Seren nodded sheepishly, her cherubim mouth downturned, but John caught a gleam in her eyes that was too deliberate not to be founded upon mischief. 'Now go to sleep,' he said, snapping the nightlight off.

When he got to the door she called out to him again. He leant against the jamb, his back to her, and sighed. 'Seren, it's late.'

Ignoring his complaint, she asked, 'Do you think Mam misses us?'

John was quiet for a moment, his face falling into a frown. He looked back towards the silhouette of the single bed and was unable to see his daughter amongst the moleskin shadows. 'Of course she does,' he said. 'Why would you even think otherwise?'

'Because Petey Moon says she never visits us so she mustn't care.'

'Well Petey Moon obviously doesn't know what he's talking about, does he?'

Petey Moon was Seren's imaginary friend. A nine-year-old boy with red-hair and skinny legs. John had never had imaginary friends during his own childhood, so at first when Seren had relayed imagined conversations with Petey Moon to him he'd been concerned about his daughter's development, or lack thereof. But after extensive online research he'd discovered that actually it was fairly common for kids to have make-believe sidekicks, creative even. So the fact Seren spoke about Petey Moon as though he was a real boy didn't necessarily mean she was neurotic or schizophrenic. As far as John could tell it was nothing more than a phase she'd eventually grow out of. The sooner the better.

'Wherever your mam is now I guarantee she misses you with all her heart,' John reaffirmed. 'So you can tell

Petey Moon to put that in his pipe and smoke it. Now go to sleep, it's late.'

He didn't hang around waiting for a reply. He shut the door behind him and made his way to the bathroom, by now desperate to relieve his aching bladder. Standing in front of the toilet he thought about his late wife. What Seren had said was true. Amy had never visited them. Not once. No whispery voice blowing in through an open window, telling them how much she missed them. No misplaced ornaments or flickering lights to let them know she was near. No invisible arms to hold him at night, to reassure him he wasn't alone. Just shitty nightmares that weren't even a good representation of how she'd been.

What if she *was* lost; frantic and alone in the starlit vastness of the sky?

John shook his head. Amy would find her way home blindfolded and in the dark, he was sure of it. He remembered the time she'd navigated through central London at the height of rush hour. One-way systems and other road users had tested his patience to the point of wild frustration, but she'd remained calm throughout, directing them to the A1 northbound with her good sense of direction and skilful, old-fashioned map reading. So, no, he refused to believe that Amy Leigh Gimmerick might be lost on some celestial highway in the sky. She had an inbuilt homing device. And if not for him, she'd definitely come home for Seren. If there was a way.

After flushing the loo John washed his hands and looked at himself long and hard in the vanity mirror above the basin. His face looked pinched, his skin too pale like it needed a good dose of vitamin D. And it was this sickly pallor that made him look older than he should. His light blue eyes, striking in vibrancy, had once served as his most powerful pick-up tool, but now they lacked a certain appeal. Surrounded by bloodshot whites they made him look more like a vampire who was on the turn than the approachable heartthrob of his former glory. Dark patches plagued the pouchy areas beneath his eyes and his hair was an unruly mop of darkest brown in dire need of a cut.

You look like shit, mate.

In the first few months after Amy had passed away, simple tasks like brushing his hair and cleaning his teeth had become beautifying rituals that John no longer felt inclined to perform. Personal grooming just hadn't seemed important anymore. Three years on and he was coping with the basics well enough, but the tormented look in his eyes was always there – sleep or no sleep – and more often than not he sported stubble that was auburn in colour and bordering on scruffy-looking.

This didn't, however, mean he was a complete lost cause. Over the last twelve months he'd been out on a handful of dates. Albeit nothing more consequential than awkward, guilt-inducing sex had ever transpired from these encounters. He still wasn't ready for anything too emotionally engaging and couldn't be sure he ever would be. Not while Amy clung to his thoughts to such an all-encompassing degree. All he could do was take things one day at a time.

Reaching for the bathroom cord he clicked the light off and stood in darkness, deliberating as to whether a shot of Southern Comfort might help to slow the barrage of thoughts running through his head. He often imagined his skull was an opaque glass jar filled with poltergeists that wanted to rest but didn't know how. Some days he expected the glass would break, thus releasing all of the trapped negativity, along with his sanity, into the aether. It was bound to happen.

Making his decision, but not without guilt, he crept downstairs to the kitchen and poured a generous measure of whiskey liqueur into a glass tumbler. He swished it round a couple of times then swigged it down in one go. As the sweet amber liquid coated his throat with a warmth that would soon fill his belly with acidic fire, he rested against the counter and berated himself. Then when he went back to bed he lay with his eyes open and listened to the rain. He wondered if his life might return to some semblance of normality. Sometime. Ever. And he was still awake when the angry buzzing of his alarm clock signified yet another day for him to take on the chin.

3

Sissy Dawson's paper-thin skin was covered in raw bed sores and it felt like it was filled with nothing but stiff joints and brittle bones. The mattress she was lying on provided no sense of cushioned comfort whatsoever and felt unduly harsh against her fragile frame. Despite the disrepair of her body Sissy still had all of her sensory faculties intact (although some would beg to differ), which seemed a cruel jape to add to her endless excruciating purgatory.

It was now, during night time hours, when life became most unbearable. Unable to shut down, Sissy could sense most things that went on within Eden Vale as though the building was an extension of her being. Each sound, smell and vibration tormented her. Cars came and went, their drivers slamming doors, revving engines and tuning radios. Other residents moaned and called out during agitated sleep, sometimes bidding good riddance to mortal existence. Members of staff snuck into the communal gardens for cigarette breaks and banter, making for a long-running soap opera that Sissy couldn't switch off. As a result she knew that Lesley, head of the kitchen, was worried her son might have got a girl who was barely out of school pregnant, and that Charlotte, one of the trainee care assistants, was having doubts about marrying her fiancé because she suspected he was sleeping with her so-called mate, who happened to be a man. Then there was Donna and Julia, both laundry staff, who were concurrently fooling around with Eden Vale's manager, Rob Fairhart. Neither woman knew about the other's involvement with him, and nor did Rob's wife Lisa.

Donna, a plump divorcee from out of town, whose whites never looked white when they came out of the wash, was a malicious troublemaker. Her rabble-rousing, mostly incited by boredom and a keenness to screw people over, meant that every Tuesday and Thursday afternoon she'd blow Rob behind the juniper bushes with a hope that Gerard the caretaker would catch them together. Gerard was an ill-tempered man with wiry grey hair, big hands and green corduroys. He tended the gardens (plants being just about the only thing he seemed to care about), did odd jobs around the nursing home and occasionally fucked Donna in the store cupboard. Their trysts were always hard and fast. He'd take her from behind and not utter a word before, during or after. She'd given him her private number three times, but he'd never called. She often wondered what he'd do if he found her trampling his begonias with the boss's cock in her mouth. It was something she was keen to find out.

Julia, on the other hand, was a pernickety single-mother who wore Marks & Spencer twinsets and went to water aerobics classes in her spare time. She looked the prissy type who would most likely make love like they did in the cosy romance novels she was so fond of reading, yet in the privacy of Rob's office she'd do all kinds of crazy shit to him that would warrant her having to stuff her knickers in his mouth to stop him from bellowing like a stag when he'd eventually come. It was during these times that Sissy could feel the heat of their lust and taste the zingy sweat of their bodies from all the way up in her first floor room.

Unsurprisingly, these frequent episodes of debauchery sickened Sissy to her stomach and made her wizened flesh burn. She could do nothing but lie there and hum to try to block it out. But no matter how loudly she did this, or how stridently she sung hymns in her head, she was still right there – bent over the office desk or squatting behind bushes – hanging thick in the air along with a profound level of deceit and yearning and the smell of sex.

Tonight there had been no goings-on of that nature, so she'd been spared the feelings of shame and blasphemy. Sissy, a deeply religious woman who'd attended church regularly in the days she'd been deemed able-bodied and sound of mind, held onto the hope that God might be as forgiving as Jesus said He was. She tried to have faith that He was merely keeping her here while she paid her dues. Because He alone knew she had a lot to pay.

On the wall above her bed the slow scrape of the clock's second hand kept a nauseating synchrony with her heart. She wished it would stop. Dawn was slowly approaching with tendrils of grey and the shrill rage of a blackbird and the only positive she could take from this was that she must be one day closer to death.

From elsewhere in the building canned laughter carried on fusty air, travelling down corridors straight to her door. Someone else was having trouble sleeping, she supposed, and the sound of laughter itself, she thought, was very sinister. Nauseating like vertebrae grinding together, bone on bone. Demented like the hysterical noise Rob's wife Lisa would make when she eventually found out about her husband's infidelity. And disingenuous like most people, she found.

4

It was mid-afternoon when the landline started to ring, dragging John's concentration from the spreadsheet he was working on and irritating him to the point of cursing. He expected it would be a cold caller because time-worthy calls seldom came through direct to the house, but when he picked up the cordless receiver he saw his mother's number displayed in the caller ID window. His immediate thought was that something must be wrong.

'Mam?'

'Hi love, how're things?' Judith Gimmerick's voice was calm and casual, not what he'd expected.

'Is everything okay?'

'Yeah fine, love. Sorry to disturb you while you're working.'

'Don't worry about it.' John wafted his hand, a dismissive pardon as though she might see. 'I needed to start wrapping up anyway. Got to pick Seren up from school.' He checked his wristwatch, alarmed to see it was later than he'd thought.

'I'll not keep you long in that case. How *is* my gorgeous granddaughter anyway?' There was a certain amount of concern attached to his mother's voice that ruined the intended upbeat spontaneity of her query. It was a thinly veiled question that suggested she wanted to provoke conversation about what Seren had been up to and other such trivialities, but John knew it was a ruse to detect whether or not he was taking care of his daughter properly. It was all in the tone. Over the past three years he'd become well accustomed to *that* tone, and unfortunately such doubting concern, however well-intended, wasn't exclusive to his mother.

Staring at his laptop screen, John directed the cursor to the white cross in the top corner of the spreadsheet and jabbed at the left mouse button a little too hard. 'She's okay, Mam. We're both okay. Now what was it you wanted?'

'That's good to hear then,' his mother said, her voice slightly strained. 'That you're both doing well. And yes, of course, I'll get to the point. See, the thing is, I'm in a bit of a quandary. You know, I wouldn't usually ask such a big thing of you but I need a massive favour…' Her voice trailed off and an uneasy silence ensued. John imagined she was cringing on the other end of the line, waiting for some sort of positive reaction from him, some gesture of encouragement that would give her the go-ahead to ask whatever it was she wanted, whatever it was that was making her feel so uncomfortable. He took the bait and prompted her. 'Go on.'

'You know how it's mine and Norman's tenth anniversary of being together next week?'

John hadn't, but didn't say as much. 'Er, okay…?'

'Well, the soppy bugger went to the travel agents' yesterday afternoon without me knowing and booked us onto a last-minute cruise.'

'Great.'

'I know! Four weeks sailing round the Med, can you imagine? Even got a drinks package chucked in. Oh and an upgrade into a cabin with a view as well. I thought he was winding me up at first, you know how he is, but…'

'Right, okay, I'm with you so far, Mam,' John said, flipping his laptop screen down now he was aware of the time. 'It sounds great but what's it all got to do with me? I'm a bit far away to be doing an airport run surely?'

'Oh no, love, we don't need a lift to the airport,' she said, a nervous laugh denoting it must be a comparably big favour that she needed to ask. 'It's the dogs. We've got nobody to watch Otis and Mindy.'

John's brow furrowed. 'I still don't see…'

'It's just, I thought maybe you could bring Seren and stay here during the school holidays. Change of scenery for you both…'

'You want me to stay at your house for a month to watch the dogs while you're away?' John was beyond incredulous. He picked up a blue stress-ball from his desk and squeezed it in his fist, watching as bits of rubber expanded between his fingers. 'I do work you know…'

'Yes, but you'd be able to work from my house just as well. Norman's had that super-duper broadband malarkey put in and you can use my phone as much as you need to.' Her voice had risen in pitch, marking her desperation. 'Listen, love, like I said, I wouldn't have asked if I wasn't in such a fix…'

'What about kennels?'

'Oh come on,' she scoffed, 'Otis and Mindy wouldn't like that at all, they're too used to their creature comforts. They enjoy lying on the couch and having peanut butter on toast suppers. Besides, Pamela Tanner left her little Jack Russell in kennels last year while she went to Ibiza and the poor thing came back with fleas and gastroenteritis. He was never the same again after that. And neither were Pam's carpets.'

'Who the hell's Pamela Tanner?' John scrunched the stress-ball again, watching the veins in his wrist bulge.

'Lady five doors up.'

John rolled his eyes and sighed. 'What about Chris or Nick, can't you ask either of them to do it?'

'Chris and Laura are taking the kids to Florida in three weeks' time, so the cruise clashes with their plans. And Nick's expecting to have to travel to Dubai for work, so he can't commit.'

'What about Norman's daughter? Can't she have

them?'

'No. She's got one of those little Shih Tzu things and he's not keen on other dogs. Besides, I was hoping to get the house watched too, there's been a spate of break-ins round here lately.'

'Couldn't she just open and close your curtains every day, make it look like someone's home?'

'Her car isn't on the road at the moment, the radiator's bust, and they won't have the money to fix it till next month.'

'So why can't she just walk?'

'Oh John, I can't exactly ask her to walk all the way down Yoden Way with the three little 'uns twice a day, can I? It's a good two miles there and back at least.'

'Yet you can ask me to travel eighty miles?' His response was snappier than he'd intended, but he wasn't about to back down. 'Look, Mam, you're just going to have to get Amanda to sort it.'

'Who's Amanda?'

'Norman's daughter.'

'Miranda.'

'Whatever. There's your neighbour as well, can't Miranda and Pamela Tanner work something out between them?'

'God no, Pam's alright for a bit of a chinwag now and then, but she's not the type I want mooching about in my house…'

'It'll have to be Miranda then,' John said, slamming the stress-ball against the wall opposite. 'Listen, Mam, I'm gonna be late, I have to go for Seren. I'll call you later, okay?'

'Oh. Alright then.' Judith Gimmerick's voice sounded small and dejected, all of the pre-holiday excitement she'd conveyed moments before now gone.

As soon as he hung up John cursed himself for being such an uncaring and uncooperative, lousy shithouse of a son. Then he cursed his mother for asking and expecting too much of him in the first place, thereby making him feel the way he did. And then he cursed himself some more. His mother seldom asked anything of him.

5

John scowled behind mirror-tinted aviator sunglasses, still trying to make sense of why his mother thought it would be such a great idea for him and Seren to move into her house for a large chunk of the summer. Surely there was a better solution. He'd left Horden almost eighteen years ago when his parents were going through the proceedings of a nasty divorce and he hadn't been back since.

His father, Billy Gimmerick, had torn the family apart, triggering matrimonial warfare by having an affair with one of the young barmaids, a girl not much older than John himself, from the local Working Men's Club. Billy might have got away with the brief fling too, had the barmaid not fallen pregnant. The bitter-sweet irony was that when Judith Gimmerick kicked him out of the family home the barmaid had decided she didn't want him either. The younger woman had resolved to keep the baby, but concluded that Billy Gimmerick was much too old for her after all.

It was John's older brothers Chris and Nick who had supported their mother throughout the whole ordeal. John had upped and scarpered. He'd had his own issues to deal with, stuff he still didn't like to think or talk about, stuff he wasn't proud of to this day. So, on top of that, he hadn't had the emotional capacity with which to cope with his parents' marital crisis.

He'd left Horden in the summer of '97, moving to Manchester to find work and create a new life for himself. He spent nine years there in total. Long weekdays being an IT consultant were offset by short weekends living it up. The social aspect was an energised blur of liver-crippling benders, decadent sex and Class B drug dabbling – incidentally, none of which had made him feel remotely better about himself. All had been temporary fixes that made him descend into a different kind of low. Eventually work had seen him relocate to Leeds and that's where he'd changed his recreational pursuits and met Amy Howard, a vivacious blonde who was originally from York. They'd shacked up together within months, got married a year later and set to creating their own family unit straight away – a small taster of true happiness that had lasted John a mere five years.

Now he was back to being a lone adult, but without the free-falling energy of his youth. His six-year-old daughter was enough to curb any antics that might have led him back to a debauched way of life, but these days he wasn't much interested anyway. He didn't take drugs, apart from prescribed ones. He was extremely lucky if he got laid once every quarter. And alcohol…well, two out of three wasn't bad going, all things considered.

As he drove, air blew through the dash vents, brushing John's knuckles with a constant air-conditioned chill. Despite having his sunglasses on, he reached up and flipped the car's sun visor down. The sun's glare was fierce and there was an energised hotness to the day that he couldn't recall from summers past. The temperature gauge on the dashboard display indicated it was a massive thirty-two degrees Celsius outside. West Yorkshire was onto its fifth consecutive day of sunshine. It was hardly surprising the housing estates he drove past were epitomising British summertime.

Ballgames were being played in the hot tarmacked streets: footballs bounced off kerbs and basketballs were pitched through hoops on driveways. Most players wore vests and shorts, a good percentage of them revealing post-winter skin. Front doors were flung wide,

England's answer to residential air-con, and deckchairs and sun-loungers in gardens were positioned sun-facing. Paddling pools on lawns were filled with hosepipe water, squealing children and dead midges. Bassy beats thudded from car sound systems and the continuous loop of an ice-cream van's jingle confirmed that summer was in full flow. The media would declare a national crisis of some sort sooner or later, John thought, most likely a hosepipe ban, because according to the forecasts it was set to hot up to the mid-thirties in time for the first few days of the school summer break.

In order to make the most of the favourable weather front, before the jet stream got its mad up and pummelled the country with an onslaught of cold, wet misery, John planned to get some barbecue supplies after picking Seren up. If he left it any later he imagined the supermarkets would run out of charcoal and crates of lager.

It would be a nice treat for Seren, he thought, for the pair of them to have dinner alfresco on Friday evening to mark the start of the summer holidays. They could enjoy burgers and sausages in the garden, then light the chiminea when it got chilly, because no doubt Seren would want to stay up late. He'd been secretly collecting money-off coupons from the back of Frosties boxes so that he could take her to Alton Towers, because she'd been harping on for ages about wanting to go. He was going to wait till Friday evening and then tell her they'd be riding Nemesis and all the other rollercoaster rides whenever he could schedule some time off work. Perhaps even as soon as two weeks into the holidays, if he could finish preparing the auditing documentation he'd been working on for the past month.

By the time he arrived at St Philip's Primary School there was already a long queue of cars waiting to get out of the car park, road works further up the street seeing to it that they were filtering from the junction at a painfully slow rate. Knowing he'd be going nowhere fast once he pulled off the main road, John grumbled a few choice expletives, indicated right and turned in through the school gates.

Seren was standing on the kerb near the school's rear entrance, waiting. She kept thrusting her navy gym bag up into the air and kicking it with her plimsolled foot on its way back down. Her hair, which John had secured into a neat ponytail that morning, was a dishevelment of lose strands framing her face. Her white polo shirt was a stubborn mess of rough-and-tumble dirt, and her legs were like two spelks sticking out the bottom of her knee-length grey skirt, the hem of which was grazing an assortment of new and old scabs. Next to Seren was a taller, mousy-haired girl who exuded a neatness that belied her age and whose name John couldn't recall. Behind both girls was a thin, angular woman whose chestnut hair shone glossy and artificial in the daylight. A distinct level of concentration on the woman's face made her look serious and tight-lipped as she worked the keypad of a mobile phone with nimble thumbs. John presumed her to be Seren's friend's mother.

Pulling his black Honda Accord into a vacant spot, he gave Seren a wave to let her know he'd seen her. As he hitched the handbrake up he turned to look out of the rear window to see if she was coming. She wasn't. She was smiling and gesturing with her hand for him to go to her.

'Shit, Seren,' he groaned, dashing his palm off the steering wheel. Nothing irked him more than schoolyard banter with the other kids' parents. Feigning interest in upcoming birthday parties, or chatting about Disney bloody Princesses or Peppa sodding Pig was not his idea of fun. Reluctantly he switched the engine off, stepped from the car and stalked towards the waiting trio.

As he drew nearer Seren's friend's mother looked up, stuffing her mobile phone into the front pocket of her straight-leg jeans. She moved forward to greet him. Her red suede trainers seemed to insinuate some boldness or daring about her character, however nothing else about her appearance backed up this claim. Her even-toned complexion was makeup-less, indicative of a no-nonsense practicality, and her shoulder-length hair was straighter than straight and boring in style. When she fixed him with a smile, John died a little inside – her brown eyes sparkled with much more of a keenness to socialise than he would have liked.

'Hi, I'm Paula, Grace's mum,' she said, pointing at the mousy-haired girl who was now looking up at him with wide-eyed interest.

John offered Paula a reciprocal smile and nodded his head, already beginning to feel the first twinges of awkwardness. 'Hi. John.' He reached out his hand, unsure if a handshake was wholly appropriate, but unsure what else to do.

The gesture seemed to please Paula. She accepted his hand, smiling all the more widely for it. 'Nice to meet you, John. Seren's told Grace a lot about you. It's good to put a face to the name at last.'

Paula's hand was rough against his, her fingers and palm calloused. She smelled of fruity yoghurt and continued to stare at him in that way people do, which made him feel uncomfortable. 'Er, yeah.' He smiled again, moving his sunglasses to the top of his head.

For a fleeting moment Paula's eyes widened a fraction as though she was surprised by what she saw.

John gritted his teeth. 'So. Was there anything in particular…?'

'Yes. Yes, there is.' Paula tucked the front sections of her hair behind her ears and, as she did, John saw there was a pink rawness to her fingers that was indicative of eczema or contact dermatitis perhaps. 'What with the girls breaking up from school on Friday,' she said, 'me and Ian, that's my husband, we've been thinking about taking them on a camping trip. A week in Scarborough maybe. Or Filey.'

John's eyes narrowed. 'You mean Seren?'

'Yeah. That is, if it's alright with you? I think Grace would really...'

'No.' John was already shaking his head and glowering more than was polite. 'I don't think so.'

Paula looked stunned by his abrupt retort.

'Why not, Dad?' Seren asked, her blue eyes appealing to him. 'Paula says there're fairground rides in Scarborough and a beach I can make sandcastles on.'

'I'm sure there are, but you're not going,' John insisted, shaking his head some more.

'But *why?*' Her eyebrows bunched up in disappointment, making him feel somewhat mean. But he was too vexed by Paula's short-noticed, overly confident presumptuousness to back down. Besides, the idea of letting his little girl go off for a week with people he didn't even know made him feel nauseous. She was only six, still a baby.

He fixed her with a stern look. 'Because I said so.'

'Look, I'm sorry,' Paula said, a faint look of apology creasing her forehead. 'Perhaps I jumped the gun. It was just a suggestion, okay? I just thought...I dunno, I thought it'd give you a bit of a break.'

'A bit of a break?' John didn't attempt to hide his bemused annoyance. 'What's that supposed to mean? A bit of a break from what? My own daughter?'

'That's not what I meant,' Paula said, raising her hands to calm his rising temper. 'It's just...I hear you work hard.'

'*Really?* And what else do you hear?' He stuffed his hands into his front pockets, imagining he'd probably been the target of much schoolyard tittle-tattle amongst nosy mothers over the past couple of years.

'You've misunderstood…'

'You don't know a damn thing about me, okay?'

'Hey, chill out.' Paula's face flushed so it was the colour of her sore hands and she adopted a defensive stance, arms crossed tightly over her chest and feet shoulder-width apart. 'You're twisting my words. It's just what Seren's told Grace, that's all. She said you work long hours. I'm not implying anything or disrespecting your…situation. I just thought it might be helpful if Seren joined us for a week or two…'

'Well you thought wrong. I'm capable of looking after my own kid during the summer holidays, thank you very much.'

Paula nodded resolutely, her thin-lipped mouth pinching together more tightly and her eyes becoming a lot less friendly than before. She took hold of Grace by the shoulders. 'Okay, if that's how you feel, I'll let you get on with it. It's just a shame, what with all the other kids in the girls' class going places over the summer and Seren saying that…well, never mind.'

John closed his eyes and sighed.

Had he overreacted? Was he being paranoid? Overly protective even? He squeezed the bridge of his nose, feeling increasingly stressed by the way the conversation had turned out. This was the reason he tried to avoid social situations wherever possible. He always said the wrong things or ended up misconstruing people's intentions. Defensive by choice, though he hadn't always been that way. Now he knew he'd be regarded as the shittest dad ever once Paula told all the other schoolyard mothers about this little episode. They'd be even more intimidating in their daunting little cliques. All of them emotional scavengers just waiting to pick him to pieces with their cold, watchful eyes. Only this time maybe they'd have good reason to judge him. After all what *did* he have planned for Seren? A barbecue on Friday evening and a day trip to Alton Towers whenever he could find the time to take a holiday from work? Talk about a lousy effort.

He ran a hand over his face and groaned. 'Hey, look…I'm sorry we've got off on the wrong foot, Paula. Really. I acted like a bit of a tool just now. I mean, it was really kind of you to offer to take Seren away, it's just…the thing is…I've, er, I've got stuff planned for her myself.'

'Oh. I see.' Paula's demeanour relaxed a little, but she didn't look completely appeased. 'If that's the case then you should have just said in the first place. But I'm pleased to hear it, it'll be good for her.'

'Yeah.' John placed a hand on Seren's shoulder. She looked up at him curiously, squinting against the sun. He winked at her. 'Yeah, it will.'

'Alrighty then, in that case I guess I'll get going.' Paula's eyes widened to emphasise her newfound awkwardness with the situation. 'I hope you have a lovely summer and, um…maybe I'll see you about.'

'Yeah. Maybe.' John nodded, though he knew it wasn't likely to happen. Not if he could help it. 'And same to you. Have a good one. Enjoy Scarborough. Or Filey. Whichever.'

'Cheers.' Paula forced a final smile and nudged Grace in the direction of a newish, cream-coloured Mini Cooper that was parked with its left wheels on the pavement.

Seren watched till they were seated and belted, then waved goodbye. Craning her neck, she looked up at John and asked, '*You've* got stuff planned? Does that mean we're going away?' Her eyes sparkled with quiet excitement; a nervous-joyful energy that was carefully kept in check in case it turned out to be unwarranted.

John took hold of her small hand and led her to the Honda. 'That's right, kidda.'

'Where to?'

'Where would you most like to go?'

'Hmmm.' She closed her eyes, thinking. 'Somewhere with a beach.'

'I thought you wanted to go to Alton Towers. Or Flamingo Land?'

Shaking her head, she said, 'No, I changed my mind. I want to go to the beach. Lucy Dale's going to Spain and she says the hotel she's staying in is right next to the sea. How splendid's that?'

'*Splendid?*' John looked at her quizzically, a bemused smile on his lips. 'You been reading Enid Blyton, kidda?'

'Enid who?'

'Never mind.'

Seren nudged her glasses over the bridge of her nose with the knuckle of her forefinger and shrugged. 'Petey Moon says splendid all the time. It's a good word, isn't it?'

'Suppose it's better than what Harry Dalton and his big brother say,' John said, quietly amused. 'So, about this beach…'

'Yes. Lucy Dale says she makes sandcastles and plays in the water the whole time.'

'Suppose it does sound splendid,' he said with a wink. He dug the car keys out of his jeans pocket.

'We should go there. And I'd have an even better time than Lucy Dale.'

'Why would you think that?'

'Because her mam and dad argue lots.'

'Oh. That must suck.'

'Yeah. Her dad likes to drink beer and look at topless women. Her mam doesn't.'

John made an involuntary chortling noise in his throat.

'Yes, well, maybe we can do that next year. Go abroad that is. But I don't think we can manage it this summer.'

'So where *can* we go this summer?'

'How about a few day trips here and there? That way we can do theme parks *and* the beach.'

'Day trips?' Seren's shoulders sagged, she dropped her gym bag to the floor with a huff.

'Yeah, it'll be cool.'

'No it won't. It means you'll be working all summer and that we're not *really* going anywhere. Not properly anyway.'

Seren's despondency saddened John. Given the choice he suspected his little girl would go camping with Paula and Ian, whoever the hell they were, in a heartbeat without giving him as much as a second thought. This made him feel insignificant, something of a failure. Hunkering down so they were eye to eye, he put his hands on her shoulders and took a deep breath. 'Listen, what if I told you we can stay near the beach for *four whole weeks?*'

She scowled, studying his face and trying to determine if he was setting her up for further disappointment. 'But you just said…'

'Forget what I said.' He swatted the empty space between them with a dismissive hand.

'You mean we can *stay* near the beach for four weeks, not just go there on day trips?'

'Yep, that's right.'

Again she regarded him suspiciously. 'Just you and me?'

'No.' John allowed himself a sly grin. 'You, me and…two dogs.'

Seren's eyes widened. 'Are we getting *two dogs?*'

'No! No, we're bloody not. We'd be looking after them that's all.'

'Where?'

'Gran's house.'

'We're going to visit *Gran?*' This time her excitement gushed out, unstoppable, and she punched the air with both fists.

'Well, not exactly. We'll be staying at Gran's house with Gran's dogs but she won't be there.'

'Where will she be?'

'On holiday.'

'Oh.'

'But,' he was quick to add, 'if you really like it at Gran's house we could stay a little while longer so that we get to see her when she gets back from her cruise.'

Seren nodded and John could tell the beach in Spain was forgotten about.

He didn't dream about Amy that night. Nor did the black dog that was prone to nightly visits come howling at the back door of his subconscious to be let in. Instead an all-embracing blackness blocked out all thoughts and worries, allowing him to sleep through until morning. And when he rang his mother after dropping Seren off at school, he was more than confident he was making the right decision.

6

The day of transition started off warm. Low clouds above the North Sea banded the horizon like great albatross wings; a storm gathering, readying to fly inland. For most of the two hours it had taken John and Seren to travel from Leeds to Horden Seren had chattered excitedly, wanting to know if crocodiles are dinosaurs (and if so why aren't they bigger), if Roseberry Topping is classed as a mountain or a hill (and at what point does a hill become a mountain) and why the Tees Flyover smelt like eggy farts as they drove over it. John had been concentrating on the high volume of traffic while they talked, yet still managed to miss their turn-off. He came off at Murton instead, joining the A19 southbound then backtracking for three miles to Easington. When he pulled off the dual carriageway they followed a long slip road till they arrived at a roundabout. Unhindered by other traffic now, John came to a complete stop and pointed off to the right. 'See over there?'

Seren looked, trying but failing to see anything of particular interest. Apart from fields, trees and a large grey chequerboard building, which looked out of place in the largely green setting, there was nothing but a rook hopping about at the kerbside and a strip of black polythene snagged on a fence post, its tattered strips flapping in the breeze like corvid wings.

When she didn't answer, John announced, 'That's where I was born.'

'*In a field?*' Seren made eye contact with him in the rear-view mirror, clicking her tongue to let him know she wasn't being fooled by his smart-arsed japery.

John laughed. 'No, silly, I'm being serious. There used to be some buildings, right there. Thorpe Hospital.'

Her eyebrows rose with piqued curiosity and she took another look. 'Why's it not there anymore?'

The corner of the field where the hospital once stood showed no obvious signs of it ever having been there. Green foliage bowed inwards, concealing a small lane that ran alongside it.

'I dunno,' John said, releasing his foot from the brake and pulling out onto the roundabout. 'It was knocked down years ago.'

Seren carried on looking at the field's empty corner as they moved off. The rook, seeming to sense her interest, jumped onto the fence and watched her with beetle-black eyes. She raised a hand and waved goodbye. It cawed and spread its wings in return.

When John announced their imminent arrival into Horden, Seren fell into a quiet, thoughtful concentration, her gaze alternating between the side window at the back and the windscreen up front. Every now and then she would lean to the right and look between the two front seats, her high ponytail bleached blonder by the last few days of sun and her nose and cheeks dappled with freckles. She was wearing her favourite new top: a white t-shirt with a purple tyrannosaurus rex printed on the front. John had bought it from the boys' section in Next. It coordinated well with the frames of her glasses and she'd insisted on wearing it that morning. John gathered it was a feel-good emblem to mark the beginning of their month-long adventure together and wished he could share her enthusiasm. As they drove along Thorpe Road he was feeling increasingly anxious though. He thrummed his thumbs against the steering wheel, a surge of nervous energy forming a repetitive rhythm on the plastic. Questions and fears resounded in his head like quick-fire assaults: *What if it doesn't work out? What if she hates staying here? What if I hate it even more?*

Air blowing in through the dashboard vents brought with it the smell of Walkers, the nearby crisp factory. The pleasant cooking aroma of thinly cut potatoes failed to appeal because John's breakfast was sitting uneasily in his stomach. He shifted in his seat, agitated, tugging absent-mindedly at one of the rolled-up sleeves of his checked shirt. And his face began to itch, the memory of the razor's kiss earlier that morning starting to irritate him with some degree of psychological prickliness. He rubbed at his jawline, the skin smooth beneath his fingertips.

If either of us doesn't like it then we'll go back home, for chrissakes, he told himself with angry resolve. *And we'll take the damn dogs with us.*

There, he felt marginally better.

Up ahead a young woman was pummelling the pedals of a pushbike, her tanned calves muscular below cropped leggings. As she rode past on the opposite side of the road John openly stared at her exerted face before eventually deciding he didn't recognise it.

Did you really expect to?

He had no place in this ex-colliery village anymore, didn't know a damn thing about its residents or street-life. He felt he was little more than a ghost coming back to haunt the setting of his youth, coasting along on a different plane to the one he'd known. Little pockets of recollection opened up with every tree and grass verge he passed, but this initial reacquaintance with Horden seemed to command an altered, perhaps harsher, clarity through his thirty-eight-year-old eyes. He felt overwhelmed and underwhelmed all at the same time.

The Dewhirst factory units, where his mother had worked as a machinist during the seventies and early eighties, were no longer there. In place of the corrugated buildings was a derelict stretch of wasteland and rubble.

Directly opposite was the cemetery, now almost full. Oddly, this resting place for both of John's maternal grandparents, with its neatly lined rows upon rows of gravestones, cherubim, flowers and greenness, looked thriving compared to the ruined site of Dewhirst's across the road. He supposed the cheaper manufacturing of clothing had been sourced elsewhere, but business would never be short when it came to burying the dead.

Just past the cemetery rape fields stretched out to the left, a vibrancy of aureolin yellow that contradicted the sky's bad mood. Further off in the distance the sea was brooding, conspiring with the sky to generate one hell of a rainstorm. It was only now, when confronted by it, that John could say with some modicum of sincerity that he'd missed the sea in his absence, its invisible pull instantly causing a renascent longing, a link to his heart. And maybe it was, he thought, no coincidence that he'd been lured back to his place of origin. There was something weighty and unseen in the air all around him. A sense of foreboding as unnerving as the North Sea at its darkest, and it was calling to him in the persuasive, hypnotic tongue of the sultriest of sirens.

It was the silent cry of nostalgia.

What else could it be?

A homecoming after almost two decades had passed was bound to cause a conflict of emotions. This sense of wistfulness, or whatever it was, was as thick as lightning-charged static, filling every bit of the Honda and making John feel as though he was encapsulated within a dream – and not a very good one.

Down an embankment, immediately to the left of them, was a cluster of houses and farm structures, and further back leafy trees sheltered a larger, stone building clad in ivy with a vacuous black doorway that yawned through a row of stone pillar teeth.

'Look, Dad!' Seren said, breaking the silence inside

the car. 'A haunted house!'

John smiled, pleased to be distracted from his own thoughts before his mood dipped below reform. 'Hey, you might be right, kidda. That's Horden Hall. It's been there since around the sixteen hundreds.'

'Wow, that's even older than Petey Moon.'

'I should say so, he's only nine isn't he?'

'Yes, but he's been nine for like forever.'

'Of course. Silly me.' John looked in the rearview mirror and saw that Seren had directed her attention to the empty seat next to her.

'Actually, he wants to know if anyone lives there?' she said, before swivelling her head and stretching round in her seat for a continued view of the portentous building that was Horden Hall.

'I'm not sure, kidda. I expect so. When I was your age your granddad used to tell me tales about there being tunnels in the cellar that went all the way down to the beach.'

'Cool. Does that mean the people who own the house own the beach as well?'

'No.' John smiled. 'The tunnels, if there ever even *were* any, were allegedly used for smuggling.'

'What's that?'

Checking the rearview mirror again, he saw her blue eyes staring back, waiting to be enlightened. 'Er, let's see. It's when people fetch things they shouldn't into the country.'

'Things like what?'

'Oo I dunno, lots of things. Cigarettes. Alcohol. Perfume…'

'But why?'

'To avoid paying tax. Then when they sell the goods on, they make more money for themselves.'

Seren's brow crumpled and she looked thoughtful for a moment. 'Lucy Dale's dad fetches cigarettes back from

Spain. He sells them to his mates at the pub, does that mean he's a smuggler?'

John laughed before he could stop himself. 'Suppose it depends how many he fetches back, kidda.'

'Lucy reckons he only takes two sets of clothes to last him all week so's not to take up much space in his suitcase, then before they come home he stuffs it full of Superkings. He must fetch quite a lot back.'

John was both astounded and amused by his daughter's matter-of-fact tale-telling. 'However many he fetches back,' he said, 'it sounds to me like Lucy Dale says *way* too much about her dad. I dread to think what you must tell the other kids about *me*.'

Seren shrugged, pushing her glasses up even though they didn't need pushing up. 'Not a lot really. There's not much to tell.'

'Gee thanks.'

'It's true. You work all the time and you're always tired.'

'Surely there must be more to me than that?'

'Hmmm. You drink too much mucky beer and don't shave as much as you should.'

Ouch!

'Cheeky little sod, you mean to say you never liked my beard?' John rubbed his hairless jawline.

Seren caught his reproachful glare in the mirror and giggled into her hand. 'Nuh-uh, it's horrible. Makes you look like an old man. You look much better today.'

'Well, I'm pleased that today I have your approval.'

'And I'm pleased that today you're making an effort.'

'Good, then we're both pleased.' John became aware only now that his freshly shaven face was just as symbolic as Seren's t-rex t-shirt. On some subconscious level, without him having realised, he'd made the effort to clean himself up with a view to starting afresh.

They passed along Sunderland Road and John saw

four teenagers in caps and skinny jeans standing about in a Perspex bus stop, all of them interacting on smartphones instead of with each other. He remembered being that age only too well. Leaving school with a handful of decent grades and going steady with the girl he thought he'd marry and regular band practice in his mate's parents' garage, because he was going to be a rockstar someday. A life full of opportunities had stretched out before him. How quickly things had changed.

On the other side of the road, opposite the bus stop, an expanse of green passed by. The pony field. John could remember whippet racing and football games taking place, but in all his life he'd never seen a pony tethered there. It was during Horden's industrial heyday that the field had been used for keeping pit ponies on, way before his time, but the name had stuck and was passed down through the generations. He could vaguely recall the demise of the coal-mine in the mid-eighties, but even that was long after ponies had been swapped out for machinery. Nowadays the pony field was still as pony-less as he'd ever known it, overlooked by elevated red-brick, semi-detached houses that had been built in the seventies. With matching white fascia boards and jaunty, narrow windows, synonymous with style at the time, the uniform houses weren't ageing too badly, but neither were they retro-cool just yet.

Further on, straight over the mini-roundabout, John was surprised to see The Bell: a large public house with Tudor-style façade. In his late-teens he'd spent many a weekend there, it being one of many stop-offs for him and his mates on their infamous Saturday evening pub crawls. Suffice it to say there'd be no shenanigans of that type going on this time around. The only inebriated crawling John was likely to be doing was to and from his mother's kitchen, either side of the witching hour.

Approaching the traffic lights outside Memorial Park, he shot a glance down Blackhills Road and saw the impressive stone bulk of St Mary's. It was the same warm, oatmeal biscuit colour he could remember, and the green-grey tint of its slate roof was now complemented by a shiny new golden cross. The church looked as grand as ever, yet John felt nothing but emptiness and a certain despondency towards it.

When red flashed to amber he pushed the accelerator pedal down and cruised past the clock tower on the left, which still stood white and proud amidst pristine lawns in the park itself. He remembered playing there as a kid: blocky and footy with Stuey Griggs and Daniel Homestead on and around the green, sometimes knocky-on-nine-doors up Park Terrace where they'd knocked on random doors and run like hell. He also remembered lying on the sloped green opposite St Mary's with a girl called Maria – her face more memorable than her surname. She'd had long wavy auburn hair and the colour of her eyes, strangely, had reminded him of the underside of a crocodile. The pair of them used to roll from the top of the bank to the bottom, then lie there with their fingers interlocked. They'd watched clouds roll by overhead, dreaming up shapes as well as their futures. That was in a time before kissing involved tongues and life became complicated. A time now untouchable, save for such fleeting, dog-eared images of his mind's rosy eye.

Ah Maria.

He wondered what had become of her.

The motorbike shop at the top of Cotsford Lane and the Chinese takeaway on the corner of Third Street soon passed by on his left, then the Comrades Social Club and Kingy's coal yard on his right; all of them markers of his youth in one trivial way or another. The instant recognition of each seemed to imbue a deeper sense of melancholy within him, which in turn brought with it a dose of guilt and shame. These buildings from the past had stood through so much and all remained impartial to the worst of Horden's secrets and scandals. They didn't judge, they were nothing but bricks and mortar after all, but their being there made John judge himself. He'd been away for so long yet they had continued to exist. They were all testament to the idea that without him the world could, and would, carry on unabashed but also that past problems would continue to exist for as long as he did. Not for the first time John felt as though he was drowning in a void of black-dark insignificance, with nothing to grab onto. Not even sentimentality, because that didn't belong to him. Not here.

By no means was his downward spiral in mood an indulgence of self-pity, or even a type of pity reserved for Amy, his dead wife, without whom the world and everything in it was still spinning. These feelings of regret simply provoked a caustic question to arise within him. A question that had all the ferocity of acid reflux and had burned a hole – a deep, empty, growing chasm – in his core and plagued him most days: *What's the point in all of this?*

'Dad are we nearly at Gran's yet?' Seren was peering between the two front seats and her voice disrupted John's thoughts, prompting the answer to his own question.

She was the point.

'Yeah, sweetheart,' he said. 'Here we are.'

7

John slowed to a stop near the end of the street then steered into a tight parallel park outside his mother's house. By now the rain had started, a fine drizzle that stippled the windscreen. The strengthening wind ruffled the bushes in the neighbour's garden and buffeted their wooden gate back and forth. Before turning the ignition off John knocked the wipers on and looked straight ahead to the North Sea. The great body of cold water, which consisted in equal measures of danger and allure, was exactly as he'd left it.

Seren sat with Geller on her knee, fiddling with the pleated ruffles around his head. She was uncharacteristically quiet and suddenly looked about as excited as John felt. He couldn't help but wonder if it was Horden or the weather that was a disappointment to her already. Or if he was being paranoid.

'Okay, so here we are,' he said, forcing a smile.

'Is that Gran's house?' Seren pointed to the semi-detached house at the end of the drive which had remarkably white UPVC window frames and front door. To either side of the door were hanging baskets with a citrus burst of pansies.

'Yep, that's it.'

'Is she in?'

'No, kidda, I already told you. She and Norman have gone on holiday. They left a few hours ago.'

'Are Otis and Mindy in?'

'Yeah, they'll be waiting for us.'

'And we're going to stay here for a whole month to take them for walks and feed them?'

John nodded and suppressed a sigh. Being on his

mother's doorstep with Seren summarising their responsibilities to such a simplified extent suddenly made the whole idea seem so very lame.

Well done, mate, round of applause. Some bloody holiday this is, you've really excelled yourself.

'Can we go in and meet them?' she asked.

'I think we'd better,' he said. 'They might be sitting with their legs crossed by now.'

Seren giggled and unclipped her seatbelt.

Outside the wind caught John's bare forearms with needle barbs, reminding him how the north-east coast reserves the right to expel its own cooler weather front. Northerly chills and errant showers had been making obnoxious rebellions against Horden summers, with about as much predictability as Tourette's, for as long as he could remember. In fact probably since time began. Sometimes on the hottest of days the creeping chill would remain exclusive to shaded areas, but no matter what day of the year it could always be found. The smell of rain was never too far away either.

'What's down there?' Seren was now standing on the pavement, seemingly unfazed by the light rain. She swung Geller in the air to indicate the end of the tarmac road. The road gave way to a stony dirt-track which, in turn, led to a railway bridge.

'See the allotments across the bridge?' John pointed to a large cluttered area of wooden outhouses, corrugated roofs, tall fences and glass-panelled greenhouses. 'If you cross the field behind them you'll reach the top of the beach banks.'

'The top? How do we get to the bottom?'

'Don't worry,' he said, smiling, 'there are some steps. Or if we're feeling adventurous we can climb down, I used to know an easy way. For now, though, let's get you out of this rain, the beach can wait.' He motioned her towards the gate then looked up at the house, which seemed to be silently daring him.

To enter.

To reacquaint.

To remember.

How could I forget?

Tense with apprehension and gooseflesh, John shivered. The fragile equilibrium that existed between his heart and mind rendered him emotionally unstable, he knew. Internally he felt as though he was standing on some dangerous, dark precipice where anger, grief and a distinct lack of faith were trying to push him over the edge. Usually it was his dogged will to survive and the unconditional love he had for Seren that prevented him from falling, but right now he felt light-headed with a sense of vertigo. Coming back to this place, painful memories he didn't want had repositioned themselves at the forefront of his mind, insistently reminding him of the things he was least proud of. He felt self-loathing for those things he'd done, and regret for the things he hadn't. Of course, he'd been a different person back then – young, immature and out of control – but that wasn't altogether excusable. He'd continued to hate himself and being here again served to amplify those feelings.

As if detecting her father's unrest, Seren reached for his hand. 'What's the matter, Dad?'

He closed his eyes and shook his head, imposing a smile of enthusiasm. 'Nothing, kidda, just thinking.'

'About stuff when you were a kid?'

'Yeah, something like that.'

She squeezed his hand and he followed her into the garden, letting the gate swing shut behind him. The metal sneck bounced against the latch without catching and the gate sprang open again with a resounding *clank*. Wood against wood. Venetian blinds twitched in the house two doors up.

After retrieving the key his mother had hidden beneath

some potted geraniums at the side of the house, John unlocked the front door. Frantic dog paws clawed UPVC on the other side, and when the door opened inwards a flash of grey and beige hurtled past his legs. Otis, a grey lurcher, leapt about on the lawn before relieving himself on a purple and yellow lupin, and Mindy, a sand-coloured whippet/Bedlington terrier cross (or whipplington, as his mother insisted), licked Seren's hands and face, her tail wagging with all the curious enthusiasm of an elderly dog. While Seren and the two sighthounds became acquainted in the drizzle, John stepped into the dry, boxy hallway of his mother's house.

Here we go.

The first thing he noticed was the white blown vinyl wallpaper of his childhood was gone. The walls were now smooth stretches of nondescript cream. Blank canvases lacking the build-up and residue of bygone years. The second thing he noticed was that the house smelt of his mother. A sweet, musky fragrance: roses and talcum powder, perhaps, with all the cleanness of fabric softener. John hadn't consciously realised, till now, that his mother had her own scent. It was lingering like a ghostly extension of herself and made him feel strangely comforted. He breathed in deeply and smiled.

After ushering Seren and the dogs into the house, out of the rain, he unloaded the car by himself. By the time he was done, having made eight journeys up and down the garden path in total, his hair and clothes were more than a bit damp. He left the pile of holdalls and carrier bags, containing clothes, shoes, toys and work stuff, in the hallway at the bottom of the stairs and went to the kitchen.

Simple oak units and cream marble-effect worktops complemented rustic terracotta floor tiles, all of it refurbished since the last time he'd been there. A small, unfamiliar dining table was pushed against the wall so that only two of its four accompanying chairs were readily accessible. On top of the table, held down by a jar of peanut butter, lest he forget about the dogs' supper, was a note from his mother wishing him and Seren a happy stay. He rummaged in cupboards and found teabags and a mug, then while he waited for the kettle to boil he went to find Seren.

She was sitting on the floor in the lounge, making a fuss of the dogs. John stayed quiet and watched her from the open doorway. Listening to her chattering inanely to her new best friends made him think this wasn't such a lame idea after all.

'Hey, trouble,' he eventually said. 'Wanna go upstairs and pick a bedroom?'

Seren looked up, grinning. She nodded her enthusiasm. As she did her ponytail bobbed up and down and Otis tried to get her face with his tongue. She rolled back onto a pink shag-pile rug and erupted into a fit of giggles, which made Otis even more eager to lick her. John laughed at both of them and glanced around the lounge. He saw his mother's passion for net curtains was as strong as ever. Masses of brilliant white lace, like the underskirt of a bride's dress, bedecked the lounge's bay window and matching white doilies gartered the bottoms of glazed ceramic pots on the sill. The couch was a chunky, corduroy affair with various chenille throws draped over it and a matching armchair sat in the alcove opposite the television. Seren was sprawled in front of an Adam-style gas fireplace, which at some point had replaced the old coke-fuelled Parkray. Lined along the mantel were framed photographs: his mother and Norman; his brother Chris with wife Laura and their two daughters; his brother Nick on graduation day; Norman's daughter with her partner and trio of tots; and a snapshot of Otis and Mindy lying together on a different couch. John was taken aback, hurt in fact, by his absence from the family line-up. It took a few moments for him to realise that his mother must have removed his photographic contribution on purpose, in preparation for him staying over. He could guess what the missing picture was: him and Amy with a baby Seren.

Tactfully done, Mother, he thought, shaking his head. *Tactfully done.*

On the way upstairs the dogs scurried past John and Seren as if partaking in a race. They snapped and yapped at each other on the landing, evidently excited at the prospect of having and entertaining guests. John showed Seren the bedroom he'd shared with his older brother Nick first. Two single beds had been replaced by a double, and the old grey and black striped walls had received the same magnolia treatment as those downstairs. Now devoid of teenage-boy angst the long room was bright and airy: a lilac bedspread along with his mother's trademark lace at the window and a set of pine drawers, with a few dust-gathering trinkets, made it a pleasant enough guest room.

'Can I have this room?' Seren asked, picking up a porcelain greyhound from on top of the drawers and tracing her finger along the line of its long snout.

'Don't you want to see the other two first?'

She shook her head, the display of decisiveness making her ponytail whip the sides of her face. John went to the window and looked out across the rain-glistening roofs of bungalows in the street to the rear of the house, each bit of tile and guttering surprisingly fitted together in his mind like the pieces of a well-used jigsaw puzzle. In the distance the rest of Horden was slouched in a grey funk as the weather busied itself besmirching summer and the resolute stone hulk of St Mary's glowered at him. Mocking. *Where have you been, John? I've missed you.*

John glowered back. *Fuck you.*

When Seren joined him by the window he put his hand on her shoulder and said, 'It's all yours, kidda.'

Next he showed her what used to be his eldest brother Chris's room. In the nineties it had been a taboo space full of black upholstery, semi-naked women staring brazenly from the walls, angry music, bad smells and a black ESP and amp that John was forbidden to touch. Now the room was all whites and pastels. Plain walls were offset with a pink dado rail that ran around the middle like gift-wrap ribbon. Beneath the window a desk was home to his mother's sewing machine, against the right wall was a pink futon, smothered in pastel scatter cushions, and against the left wall a bookshelf was filled with books, reels of ribbon and jars containing buttons and beads. The room was a far cry from the decadence that had once been Chris's private space.

John noted that the furniture would need to be shuffled around and the futon dismantled and laid out lengthways if he was to occupy this room, because in its current sofa position the futon wasn't long enough to accommodate his fully stretched six-foot-two. He wasn't altogether keen on disrupting his mother's feng shui, though. 'Sure you don't want this room instead?' he asked Seren.

'I want your old room,' she insisted.

'Alright. Looks like I'm left with Gran and Norman's room then.'

This seemed to amuse her, she giggled into her hand. 'I bet it's all pink and frilly.'

'You have to remember that Gran's rediscovering her feminine side after all those years being surrounded by testosterone.'

'What's that?'

'The stuff boys are made of.'

'Yack.'

'Indeed. That's why Gran likes pink.'

'But, still, poor Norman.'

'Hey, there's nothing wrong with pink.'

'Pink's for *girls*.'

'Gran *is* a girl. So are you.'

Seren's eyebrows lowered and she gave him stink eye. 'Did your old room used to be *blue?*'

'No,' he admitted. 'Black and grey. But teenagers are a whole different breed.'

She looked thoughtful for a moment. 'Can I have a black and grey bedroom back home?'

'Pretty premature for the goth years, kidda. Maybe in a few years. Now come on, let's see how pink my new room is.'

As expected his mother's bedroom was elaborately floral and too lacy. The smell of roses and talc was inherently stronger. Aside from the kitsch décor the room retained the best view from the house. Beyond the net-curtained window, past the railway lines, allotments and fields, the North Sea was right there, staring back at him. A stark band of pewter beneath leaden clouds. The rain was fairly coming down now, sheeting against the window and not looking like it would let up any time soon.

'Can we go over there?' Seren asked, pointing to the railway bridge.

'Yeah, course we can.'

'Did you fetch my wellies? I'll go and put them on.'

'You mean now? You want to go *now?*'

'Otis and Mindy need to go for a walk,' she reminded him.

John sighed, a long exhalation that marked his reluctance. 'Yeah, I suppose they do. But I thought you didn't like the rain?'

Tapping her fingertips on the window sill, an unrhythmic tune, she shrugged nonchalantly. 'I don't mind it now, Petey Moon says people don't get lost in the sky and that rain's just rain. He says people do sometimes get trapped, but if that happens they mostly stay where they were. So that means they couldn't get lost because they'd be where they were in the first place and they'd know where that was, isn't that right?'

John breathed in slowly and looked down at her in wonderment. 'Er, yeah, I suppose so.'

'So can we go out in the rain? *Please.* '

'Oh alright,' he said, smiling, despite his lack of enthusiasm to go out and get wet again. 'Go find your wellies and raincoat amongst the stuff in the hall, I'll be down in a tick to see if I can find some dog leads.'

Seren scampered off and John rested his forehead against the lace fabric that covered the cold window pane. He listened to her feet beating an excited dance on the stairs and wondered at the possibility that things might finally be looking up. Seren actually seemed to be enjoying herself. And him? He could deal with this. Surely it was no coincidence he'd come full circle. In fact it could prove to be the therapy he needed. He jogged downstairs and whistled with a chirpiness that was founded on genuine optimism, and when he realised he was doing it he whistled all the more loudly. This was the start of something new.

What he didn't realise, however, was that something within the house was stirring, awakening to the sound of him being there.

Something dormant that had never forgotten.

Something profoundly evil.

8

The care assistant with the overweight midsection and jiggling breasts looked at Sissy Dawson's plate of untouched food. Mince and dumplings had congealed. A mound of mud-brown gravy with a film of greying white fat resting on top was accompanied by pasty dumplings, which looked spongy and undercooked. Piled to one side were boiled carrots and potatoes, slimy in their watery residue, and next to those a spoonful of boiled white cabbage. The cabbage was the smallest portion of Eden Vale's Saturday evening meal choice, but the smell of it dominated above all else. It infiltrated every nook and cranny of the care home, tainting fabric and upholstery and lingering like a stale fart in every under-ventilated sleeping quarter and enclosed corridor. The stink would take a day or two to shift, by which point something equally as unpleasant would no doubt take its place. Human decay or vegetable soup, it didn't much matter. It was all horrible. And bad smells were par for the course at Eden Vale, where people waited to die.

'Aw now come on, Mrs Dawson,' the care assistant said, 'you've got to start eating your dinners.'

Sissy, her face drawn and withered, collapsing into a dentureless mouth, clucked her tongue and said, 'When they make me something nice, Kevin, I will.'

Kevin was a big lad in his early thirties. He had a likeable face, much younger than his years, and his skin looked impossibly soft, perhaps because there was no evidence of a beard or moustache. His thick, fair hair was a kick in the arse off ginger, and his pale blue eyes were patient pools of empathy. He was a six-foot man-child who Sissy preferred to all the other care assistants at Eden Vale. There was nothing outrageous or deviant about him. Sensitive to others' needs, often putting them before his own, Kevin was a genuine caring man who'd probably been mollycoddled too much by his mother as a boy. He carried too much weight, particularly around his stomach, chest and neck, and Sissy wondered if it was this or the fact he was shy that hampered his efforts to find a wife. He interacted well with all the old biddies at Eden Vale, being a bit of a mother hen himself, but Sissy could imagine he'd be awkward around women his own age.

'What's wrong with mince and dumplings?' he asked, fussing with the propped pillow behind Sissy.

'Nothing, when they're done right.'

Kevin shook his head and smiled despairingly. 'You'll waste away to nothing if you don't start eating properly.'

'Good.'

'Oh don't say that.'

'It's true. I wish God would hurry up and decide what He wants to do with me, Kevin. I'm tired. Can't be bothered no more.'

'Now don't be like that, Mrs Dawson.' Kevin's broad forehead creased. He stepped back and regarded her, then his eyes sparked with something of an idea. 'Listen, it's Kitchen Lynn's birthday today and there's some chocolate cake on the go downstairs. Do you fancy a slice? You can have mine if you like.'

Although it was a very kind offer, Sissy didn't hear. Her full attention was now on the open doorway to her room. There was a distant, compelling noise drawing closer. Like brooms sweeping dead leaves into piles on a crisp autumn morning. She listened, her intrigue quickly turning to dread.

Something bad had arrived at Eden Vale.

The air had altered. There was a sharpness to it as though someone had opened a window nearby, which couldn't be the case, she knew, because none of the first floor windows could be opened. Eden Vale's safety regulations saw to it that the clientele were as trapped as the stagnant smells from dinner. Fear chilled Sissy's veins and the hairs on her arms stood on end. She sensed wrongness, and not the day-to-day wrongness of the staff. Something much, much worse.

'Mrs Dawson?' Kevin stroked the back of her blue-veined, arthritic hand. 'Is everything okay? Would you like me to fetch you a piece of...'

'Shhh.' Sissy looked at him. Her sunken eyes, the indiscernible colour of puddle water, were wide and fearful. 'Can you hear that?'

'Hear what?'

'All that...*whispering.*'

'Whispering? I'm not sure I know what you mean.' Kevin cocked his head to one side and listened hard. He heard nothing more than the usual comings and goings of the care home. 'There is no whispering.'

Sissy's bottom lip began to tremble. She clutched the care assistant's fleshy wrist with one shaky hand and reached up to her hollow mouth with the other. 'There is. *There is.* Make it go away, Kevin. Please make it go away.'

The *whish-a-whish-a-whish* of dead leaves had changed. The imagined autumnal debris was now a chorus of muted voices. Their exact words went unheard, but she knew they spoke of death. They ascended the wide staircase and, step by dreaded step, moved along the dowdy corridor closer to Sissy's room. Growing louder and louder. Numerous voices spoke at the same time, but none of the speakers listened to each other.

'Mrs Dawson? Are you feeling alright?' Kevin stooped so that his face was in line with hers. His eyes showed alarmed concern. 'Would you like me to call for Dr

Chatterjee?'

'They're coming for me,' she whimpered. 'What should I do?'

The television in the corner of the room burst to life with a crackle of white snow and a high-pitched whine. Kevin lurched backwards, clutching a hand to his chest, and Sissy gripped his beefy arm. 'Oo yer bugger,' he said, laughing nervously while looking at the television. 'Scared the life out of me that did. Has it done that before? I'll get Gerard to come and take a look at it.'

Sissy didn't answer: the television was the least of her concerns. The voices were now right outside her door, the noise of eternal unrest surging into the room with a tumultuous roar like a gale force wind ripping through the lattice tower of a pylon. She held fast to Kevin's arm, watching in horror as strange figures began to file into the room. An army of anthropomorphised swirling dust motes that moved towards her. The television's whine stepped up in pitch and Kevin tried to pull free from her so that he could clamp his hands over his ears. But she wouldn't let go.

'No,' Sissy shrieked. 'Don't. I can't...no. *Go away!* Make them go away, Kevin.' Her fingernails dug into the softness of his skin and Kevin carefully, but firmly, tried to prise her hand off again. He didn't seem to notice the figures at all. The figures whose grainy white faces were surreal masks of incensed pain. Their words were clearer now and, even above the squeal of the television, Sissy caught snatches of the ghostly cacophony: '*Sissy, Sissy, Sissy...You know, you did...The end of all...Now.*'

Instinctively she knew who the phantoms were, but didn't know what they wanted or why they'd come. Her heart was beating too fast for someone of eighty-five and she wondered if this was it, if this was her time of reckoning. Had God sent them to take her away? Was

He answering her prayers at last? And if so, would they escort her up or down?

Up. Please, Lord, let it be up.

Or could it be that they'd been sent to taunt her? A last test of endurance, a final debt to be paid.

Whatever the reason for their being there, they began to gather around the foot of the bed. Hideous deathbed angels. Sissy could feel the portentous nature of their turmoil sizzling in the air all around her like static electricity. It made her skin prickle with overwhelming fear. She resisted looking at them directly, but in the end couldn't help herself. She saw that most of the apparitions had defining human qualities, adult ones, whereas a select few looked more alien. Six foot foetuses. And it was the sight of these ones, with their scrunched faces, underdeveloped blind eyes and domed heads, that made Sissy's bladder open. Warmth spread beneath her, soaking into the sheets.

'It's the children,' she mewled, trying but failing to sit up. 'They're all grown up. Look! Just look at them all, Kevin.' She pushed herself backwards, wanting to distance herself from their accusatory faces.

'Mrs Dawson what are you talking about? What children?' Kevin sounded anxious. He finally freed his arm from her grip and placed a firm hand on her skeletal shoulder to stop her from scrabbling about on the bed. 'You're really starting to worry me, I'm going to call for the doctor. Now just try and calm down, okay? I'll be back in a tick.'

Sissy watched his bulky body, in Eden Vale's signature blue polyester, pass straight through the spectral gathering at the foot of her bed, unhindered. She begged for him not to leave her alone; a plea that came out as an unintelligible whimper.

Before he left the room, Kevin went to the television and jabbed its standby button repeatedly. When it refused to switch off he held his finger down for an indeterminable amount of time, tapping his foot, his face wracked with bemusement. When still nothing happened he bent and pulled the plug from the wall. Black and white fuzz continued to bluster about on the screen and the ear-ringing whistle hurt his head for a short while before the snow eventually condensed into a small white blip and the maddening sound ceased. Kevin's shoulders sagged with relief and he gave Sissy the thumbs up. As he passed through the ghostly crowd once again to get to the door, he rubbed his freckled arms and said, 'I'll see Gerard about having your radiator switched on as well, Mrs Dawson, it's gone a bit chilly in here, hasn't it? And don't worry, I'm sure he'll get the telly sorted in time for Family Fortunes. Now hold tight, I'll go and give the doctor a tinkle, see if she can pop round to see you.'

After he'd gone Sissy sobbed freely, tearing at the mattress with her misshapen fingers in an attempt to move her useless body away from the phantom mass, which had now filtered down both sides of the bed. This close their faces looked more substantial than mere dust motes, as though the peak of Sissy's fear was somehow negating their transparency. Had she not known better, they could well have been real flesh. Their sunken eyes and downturned mouths, which looked to have never known joy, were like Hallowe'en masks in a grisly parade. They all watched her watching them, and they seemed to gloat and revel in her state of helplessness. When their hands reached out to touch her, the transparent dry ice of their skin burnt hers. She closed her eyes and sank back into the pillow as far as she could, swatting their intangible hands away and rubbing her arms to shake off the piercing cold. She repeated the Lord's Prayer three times, the words memorised and precise on her lipless mouth, but still the spirits remained, their voices an unrelenting raucous chatter inside her head: '*You know, you did...With Her...We are...Sissy, Sissy, Sissy...You know, you did...End it.*'

There was a new smell now, permeating the air with such rancidness that it thwarted the cabbagey fustiness and made Sissy gag.

'Please, God, please, God, please, God,' she chanted, over and over. 'Please forgive me. Please do. You *must* know I didn't mean to do it. You must know that I never *meant* to...I didn't *want* to...you must know I never...you *MUST!*'

The black television screen exploded with a loud pop. Glass shrapnel sprayed as far across the room as the bed, tiny pellets lodging in Sissy's face and neck. She shrank back and squeezed her eyes shut. The room was plunged into a thick, eerie silence. She whimpered, a pathetic sound lost to the quiet, and lay clutching the sheets, too afraid to move, too afraid to open her eyes. Her heart filled her ears with the sound of trying to pump blood too quickly from her core, and her bladder twinged, threatening to give out again.

Are they still there? Still watching me?

It was silent. Hard to tell.

Perhaps the mass visitation had been nothing more than a sleep-deprived, hunger-induced hallucination. Or manifestations of guilt summoned by her own death-wish.

No, the stink of decay was still there, clinging to the back of her nose. Death-flesh festering in a world it no longer belonged to. Ripe badness, a terrible smell she couldn't ignore. The spirits had been as real as real could be. There was no denying them.

But had God answered her prayer? Had He made them go away?

'Oh please be gone. Please be gone,' she moaned, her breaths ragged with terror.

When still there was no sound and the complete

quietude made her ears pound with the remembered noise of the exploding television and her nigh-on exploding heart, Sissy took a deep breath and opened her eyes.

Immediately she wished she hadn't.

They were still there. All of them. Surrounding her bed. Watching. And worst of all, a naked woman was hunched on the bed before her. Straggly grey hair fell over her face and there was a feral quality to her demeanour as though she was a wild animal regarding its prey. The scream that formed in Sissy's throat came out as no more than a strangulated whine, and she thought for a moment she might choke on her own tongue.

The phantom woman inched closer to Sissy, her insubstantial hands and knees making impossible indents on the bed, validating her presence. Sissy felt light-headed, but still her consciousness held tight.

Please, God, please, God, please, God.

Behind ratty strands of long old-woman's hair, Sissy could see that the spectre's eyes were like inkwells, black in their entirety. Her wrinkled corpse-face was unfamiliar and yet strangely familiar.

I don't know all of your names. And I'm sorry that I don't. But you...don't I know you?

The old woman raked hair away from her face with gnarled, clawed fingers, as if to cure Sissy's curiosity by revealing herself more clearly.

Sissy immediately gasped, the absolute recognition winding her.

'*Eleanor?*' The name cracked from Sissy's throat like dry wood, sending splinters to lodge in her heart.

The phantom woman, a formidable younger version of Sissy herself, opened the black gash that was her mouth and grinned. Then bringing forth the smell of rotting flesh and sixty-four years' worth of corruption, she crooned, 'Yes, Mother.'

9

Several times John awoke disorientated, all too aware that he wasn't in his own bed. An orange glow crept around the edges of drawn floral curtains, lingering as intractably as his own consciousness and lending enough light for him to see the smiling faces of his mother and Norman on the bedside table next to him. Turning onto his back he studied the light shade suspended from the ceiling. It looked like a dead jellyfish, greyscale and lacklustre, floating beneath artex ripples. It was one of those fabric dome structures with tassels around its circumference, which he remembered were popular in the eighties and nineties. He wondered if it was the same fixture that had been there when his dad had lived in the house, though surely not.

His thoughts stayed with his dad. He hadn't spoken to Billy Gimmerick, not properly, since Seren was a toddler, just after Amy had passed away. Not because John held a grudge about what his dad had done to the family all those years ago, but because they were both lousy at staying in touch. John promised himself he'd make an effort to pay the old man a visit while he and Seren were in the vicinity. That is, if he could catch him while he wasn't at the pub. His dad's preferred pastime was drinking, alcohol being his remedial anaesthesia to matters of yesteryear. The irony of which didn't surpass John.

Like father, like son.

Somewhere off in the distance he could hear a dog shouting and a house alarm wailing a repetitive plea to an uncaring night. Neither sound was loud enough to have roused him from sleep, but both were persistent

enough to deter him from dropping back off. He tossed
and turned. Turned and tossed. Water pipes somewhere
above, in the loft, rattled a cooling noise of discord; a
tick-tack-clang that heightened his awareness, again, of
not being in his own bed.

John closed his eyes and concentrated on blotting out
all sounds and emptying his mind of all thoughts, which
proved to be an exercise in immediate defeat because the
more he concentrated on concentrating on nothing at all
the more he focussed on one sound over another. The
wooo-ooo-wooo-ooo of the alarm and *ruh-ruh-ruh* of the
dog. And when the water pipes stopped groaning a
different sound took their place. *Bzzzzzzzp. Bzzzz. Bzzz-
bzzz-bzzzzzzp.* A fly must have found its way into the
bedroom at some point and was trapped between white
net and impenetrable windowpane. It had chosen now of
all times to make a useless bid for freedom.

Bzzzzz. Bzzz. Bzzzp.

John gripped the duvet and tugged it up to his chin,
mindful now of a growing chill – a chill characteristic of
November, not July. He rolled onto his side, wrapping
himself tightly and bringing his knees up to his chest,
foetal position, then submerged the lower part of his face
beneath the duvet. Exhaling deeply through his mouth he
tried to heat the space within the cotton cocoon he'd
created, but after ten minutes of breathing heavily and
listening to the fly's kazooing, he was still tense with
coldness and more awake than ever. Sleep wasn't
revisiting any time soon.

Fuck's sake!

John cast the sheets aside and sat up, his bare skin
tightening uncomfortably with exposure to the room's
unseasonal cold, a rash of gooseflesh pricking up all
over his body. Shuddering, he snatched his robe from the
bedpost and flung it around himself.

Bzzzzz. Bzzzzp. Bzzp. Bzzzzzzz.

Frigging fly.

He marched over to the window and dragged the flowery curtains along the curtain pole before sweeping aside the lacy netting behind. A plump black speck skittered across the white sill. It skimmed over his fingers, tickling and offending him with its unwelcome touch. John flung the window open and chased the fly out into the night with the back of his hand. Its departure was an instant relief. He stood unmoving for a moment, looking out at the garden below, expecting a greater chilliness to slap him in the face. But there was a stillness to the orange darkness of the front street, a warmth which contradicted the morgue-like cold of his mother's bedroom.

The insistence of the barking dog and faraway house alarm could be heard with defined precision now the window was open, both sounds lending a sinister undertone to the night because, evidently, all was not well on someone else's doorstep. Just left of his mother's house, where the railway bridge began and the streetlights ended, everything was doused in thick shadow. Clouds blocked the moon's natural light, creating an eerie landscape of unknowableness. Residential area and wilderness had become two separate entities. Off in the distance, somewhere, the sea was black, camouflaged against darkest sky. There was no knowing where one ended and the other began. It was at that moment, while gazing into the night's umbra, that a sobering thought occurred to John: *Anything could be lurking out there.*

The barking dog already knew it.

Overcome with an unshakeable, discomfiting sense that someone he couldn't see was looking right back at him from the blackness down by the bridge, or somewhere along the railway embankment, John shivered. Unease, similar to what he'd felt when he'd returned to Horden the previous day, was charged with such negativity that his scalp began to tingle and he felt short of breath. The threat of something unseen, something unknown, overwhelmed him to the point of irrational fear; a silent, stealthy predator stalking him in the dark, or a childhood bogeyman hiding beneath the bridge, waiting, watching, breathing. Whatever it was that caused him to feel this way, primal instinct was now grabbing him by the throat and screaming at him, telling him he was in danger. Warning him that unseen eyes were mocking and taunting, waiting for the right time, the right moment…

To do what?

He didn't know.

Ghost fingers crawled a spidery trail up his spine, making him shudder. He clapped the window shut and stepped backwards, swishing the curtains closed against the night. Running a cold hand over his face, he gasped for air.

Jesus, get a grip.

Exhaling heavily, he leant against the wall, listened to his heart whumping and shivered against the cold.

Go put the heating on and get yourself a drink. Then have a bloody word with yourself.

Out on the landing a smell redolent of household rubbish and bad meat caught John off guard. A dirty blow to the gut that knocked him sick as soon as he stepped out of the bedroom. The smell wasn't the worst of it either. A long grey shape swayed about in front of him, making him recoil in abject terror. Two hind legs and a tail that stretched down from a slender torso immediately identified the suspended entity as being the body of his mother's dog Otis. The lurcher's neck was crooked, bent at an awkward angle, his leather lead had been wrapped around his neck several times and was attached to the brass bolt of the loft hatch. He'd been hanged. And gutted. The lower half of the dog's body was festooned with its own glistening entrails, and a steady *blop, blop, blop* filled John's head as blood dripped down onto a saturated dark spot on the carpet.

Clamping one hand over his mouth to stifle a cry, John scrabbled around the wall with the other to find the light switch. When his fingers found it and stark light filled the landing, he was both relieved and appalled by what he saw. There was nothing but empty landing space. His mother's dog wasn't hanging from the loft hatch. Nor was there a pool of blood spoiling the beige carpet.

The taste of bile soured his mouth and John thought he might be sick. The grisly image of Otis with gaping intestinal tract, broken neck and lifeless eyes remained distinct in his head. Every single bit of it. Ingrained there forever. In fact the vision, or hallucination, had been so graphic and clear he felt shocked beyond comprehension that it *wasn't* real. And the smell. The bad smell was still there. Lingering. That part was indisputable. But after looking about the landing there was no obvious clue as to what might be causing it. Flicking the light off, in case it disturbed Seren, he stood in the dark and massaged his forehead.

Keep it together, mate. Just keep it together.

Downstairs the severity of the fluorescent strip light in the kitchen prompted Mindy to look at John and groan. The whipplington was lying on a large bone-printed beanbag next to the dining table. At first John was alarmed to see that Otis wasn't lying with her, but then he saw the grey lurcher over by the back door, sitting on the doormat. Alive and unbloodied.

'You need to be out, fella?' he said, feeling the need to speak aloud just to inject a smidgen of normality into the room with the sound of his own voice.

Otis whined.

John opened the back door and both dogs shot outside.

He watched their light forms mooching about on the driveway till they moved round to the lawn at the front of the house, then he stepped outside and followed them, walking down the path till he got to the gate. He stood looking seaward, directly into the black, challenging himself not to be intimidated by whatever unseen threat he'd imagined before.

See, nothing there.

Earlier he'd taken Seren over the bridge, past the allotments and onto the field beyond. The dogs had had a good blast in the long grass while he and Seren had walked to the edge of the beach banks to look at the yellow sand and pebbles down below. The beach was cleaner than he'd ever known it to be; miles of shale with no hint of black coal. Seren had wanted to climb down the banks, but the rain had drenched the tops of her jeans so he'd insisted they go back to the house. On the return walk they'd stopped to look at some New Hampshire Reds that were strutting and bawking beneath a corrugated iron shelter in someone's allotment. And strangely, now, looking down across the bridge, John found himself thinking about those chickens.

It was hard to imagine that all the allotments were full of unassuming things such as the chickens. Leafy veg, brightly coloured water vats, other livestock and delicate flowers. Or, indeed, that the field behind was luscious green. Night had stolen all the charm away from this place of grandfathers' favourite pastimes, making the allotments an eerie place where the chickens probably slept warily in their coops, waiting for morning, and where yellow chrysanthemums didn't even exist, John thought. Because if something can't be seen then it ceases to exist. At night-time there were only grey chrysanthemums.

A lone star low in the sky, or a ship at sea, shone like a

beacon for lost souls. It caught John's eye and winked. Apart from this tiny light on the horizon, everything to the east dwelt in shadow. And it was this substantial blackness that gave John cause to reconsider the idea that anything *could* be lurking out there. But standing out in the open he didn't have the same feeling of foreboding that he'd had in his mother's bedroom. He felt calm. Alert, but calm.

The sound of an engine and muffled late-night radio made him turn his head. A car had turned into the street, its headlights reaching as far as the stretch of pavement outside his mother's garden. A white taxi cab pulled in some way down the road and the front passenger door swung open. John could hear a woman talking loudly over the top of Phil Collins begging for one more night. He watched disinterestedly as a figure with long black hair and a dress that could be any colour stepped from the car. She staggered sideways, steadying herself on the side of the car. Then tottering back to the open door, she leaned down and said to the driver, 'Aye, I'll be alright, Mick. It's these bloody shoes, man. Murder.' She said something else which John didn't catch, then slammed the door shut. Before passing through a gate a few doors down she looked up the street, her eyes faltering on John. He continued to watch openly as she walked the length of the garden path, her murderous heels scraping concrete. Less than a minute later a house door banged shut.

A drive belt screeched and commanded John to watch as the taxi reversed from the street. The sound of Phil Collins had been replaced by a couple of radio hosts whose voices were nothing more than a low murmur of unintelligible conversation, which, for whatever reason, made John think of dead people mumbling; smothered voices coming through on death-plane radio waves, having found their way into the periphery of reachability to convey messages to the living through the chasms of non-space only to get caught up in the magnitude of non-belief and misinterpretation.

Yep. Keep trying. I can't hear you.

A gust of wind whistled through the laurel hedge at the far side of the garden, whipping up rose bushes and ruffling the lawn. It hit John, surprising him with a sharpness that cut straight through the fleecy fabric of his robe. He hugged himself and looked round. Both dogs were waiting by the back door, their tails between their legs. Happy to oblige their request to be let in, John jogged back up the garden path.

Inside he fiddled with the thermostat on the kitchen wall and it wasn't long before the boiler hummed to life and the nearby radiator clunked and then churned with the sound of water and air heating. He chugged Southern Comfort straight from the bottle then switched out the light. On his way back to bed, he stopped halfway up the stairs. The malodorous smell from earlier remained. Like stagnant water, nauseating in its persistence. And there was a sound now too. Gripping the balustrade to steady himself in the darkness, John tilted his head and listened. There was a low voice, incomprehensible but rapid – urgent, almost – coming from upstairs. He imagined Seren sitting up in bed, make-believe conversing with Petey Moon.

Inching up the stairs, careful to avoid the ones with loose boards, he continued to listen to his daughter's whispering. By the time he got to the landing she had fallen quiet. Must have heard him coming. He paused outside her room, his ear to the door. All he could hear was his own pronounced breathing above the weighty silence that ensued. Slowly, softly, he twisted the handle and pushed the door inwards. And instantly he knew there was something wrong.

The smell from the landing was stronger and much

more putrid in here, testing the strength of his gag reflex and souring the whiskey liqueur in his belly. An icy surge of wintry cold air enveloped him, and he exhaled swirling grey vapours from his mouth with a low moan.

'Seren?' His voice came out as a hoarse whisper, as though his usual timbre couldn't quite cut through the spoiled, freezing air. 'Are you awake?'

The question was met by silence. Not even the sound of his daughter's breathing could be heard. He went over to the bed and found his little girl sprawled on top of the sheets, her eyes closed.

'Seren?'

When she still didn't react to his voice, he leaned over and touched her cheek with the backs of his fingers. Astonishingly she was warm. He waited a moment, expecting to see the smallest of smiles crease the sides of her mouth. Or her eyelids to quiver as she peeked at him from beneath her lashes. But her expression remained neutral and her chest rose and fell, keeping the same deep, regulated pattern. Covering her with the duvet, he went to the window. Despite the coldness, he was keen to rid the room of its awful stink. He cracked the window open and breathed in deeply.

Turning back to face the room, the glossy shine of the white radiator caught his eye. When he ran a hand over its bevelled surface it felt like a sheet of crimped ice against his palm. He turned the temperature valve clockwise as far as it would go then winced as the radiator rattled to life with all the brashness of loose change chinking into the metal tray of a slot machine. Gritting his teeth together, he looked over at Seren. She didn't stir.

Leaving her door slightly ajar, John went back to his own bed. Beyond exhausted, yet wide awake. Beneath the duvet he lay listening to the house shift and sigh in response to the central heating, while his thoughts ran amok. Unwelcome images of Otis hanging from the loft hatch kept popping into his head. *Blop, blop, blop* all over his mother's carpet. Who would do such a thing? The *bzzzz bzzzzp bzzz* of a fly that was no longer there. And radio hosts whispering till his eyes grew heavy: *Do you remember when...? The shame of...How could you? Don't blame...You didn't really...I need you...She needs you...Always...Cold...Don't...What about me...? You mustn't...Stop...Remembering. Love.*

At some point sleep fully took him and when he awoke the next morning he couldn't remember what his dreams had entailed, but he had a feeling of deep unease and unsatisfied rest. His optimism from the previous day now seemed misplaced. Before going downstairs he decided to check in on Seren. Her bed was empty, except for Geller, and the room smelt fresh, a motherly bouquet of roses and talc. The curtains were open and weak sunshine sifted inside, greeting John like a headache. The daylight also showed a mark on the ceiling directly above the bed. A patch of what looked to be mould about the size of a football with tiny individual spore circlets clustered around it. Rubbing his chin, John cast his mind back to the previous day. Had it been there then? He didn't think so, but he couldn't remember for certain.

Downstairs he found Seren in the lounge. She'd worked out how to use the television and was watching a documentary about meerkats.

'Why didn't you wake me, kidda?' He looked at the carriage clock on the mantel, shocked to see it was almost ten.

Seren, still in her pyjamas, hardly acknowledged him. She shrugged her shoulders.

'Was your room okay last night?' he asked.

'Mmm.'

'Notice any strange smells at all?'

She shook her head.

'You sleep okay though, yeah?'

'Uh-huh.'

'And were you warm enough?'

This time she turned round to face him. '*Dad,* I'm trying to watch how they build their bloody homes!'

'Alright, alright.' John held up his hands and backed out of the room. 'Keep your bloody hair on.' He went through to the kitchen and filled the kettle and while he waited for it to boil rummaged in the cupboards, looking for detergent with which to clean the bedroom ceiling. It was while he was on his hands and knees in front of the sink unit that someone knocked at the back door.

He found a woman in her mid- to late-fifties on the doorstep, her skin American-tan, hair fake-black, and eyes peridot-green. She was wearing too much eye makeup for that time in the morning, he thought, and her chiffon shirt, leather-look skinny jeans and stilettos combination was hardly regular getup for a Sunday morning. She looked nothing but trouble, but on first impressions he found her appealing on some taboo sexual level.

'Oh hi,' she said. The huskiness of her voice implied she was, or once had been, a heavy smoker. 'Are you Jude's son? John?' She looked him up and down, slowly.

'Er, yeah.' John pulled the robe's belt tighter at his waist. 'And you are?'

'Pam,' she said, arranging her thick, nylon-shine hair about her shoulders. 'Pamela Tanner. Five doors up.'

'Ah. The one with the Jack Russell.'

'Sorry?'

'Doesn't matter. Can I help with something? I mean, was there anything...'

'No, no. It's just your mam said you'd be staying here so I thought I'd better introduce myself, especially after seeing you last night…'

'Oh. That was you?'

Pam nodded and her heavily-kohled cat's eyes blinked rapidly for half a dozen beats. 'I'd been to a mate's birthday do, see.'

'Okay. Great. Well, er, thanks for the intro…'

'Hey, why don't you stick the kettle on? We can have a cuppa, get properly acquainted.' She stepped up onto the second step and pointed to the kitchen behind him.

'Er, now's not a good time actually,' he said, sidestepping to block her entry, somewhat taken aback by her forwardness.

'Oh. Right.' She studied his face for a moment, her eyes intense, unyielding.

After a stretch of awkwardness where neither of them spoke, Pamela Tanner eventually stepped back onto the driveway and said, 'Another time though, yeah?'

'Yeah. Uh, whatever.'

'Great.' She nodded then, blinking with the same quick-fire sequence as before, said, 'Oh and now you know who I am and where to find me, don't be shy. If you need anything, *anything at all*, just give me a knock.' She threw him a wink and smiled, her teeth so immaculately white they had to be bleached or porcelain veneers. 'I'll see you right. Day or night. Doesn't matter to me.'

John smiled thinly. *I'll bet, you dirty bitch.*

'So you'll be staying for four weeks then?' she asked. Her eyes lingered on the exposed part of John's chest before moving up to the fullness of his mouth. They eventually settled on the turquoise seriousness of his eyes.

'Er, yeah, that's the plan,' he said.

'Good, it's always nice to have a new face in the street.'

'I'm sure.'

'Hey, you should drop by mine one night. We can have a drink. It's no fun living alone, I know.'

John's eyes narrowed, but he managed a wan smile. *Sure, I'll pop round. If nothing else we can say we have alcohol and loneliness in common, then after some pointless conversation where we bore the pants off each other, I'll let you suck my dick.* He shook his head and thumbed over his shoulder. 'Sorry, I'll have to pass. Got my six-year-old with me. She's always in bed by eight.'

Pamela Tanner's lips curved into a satisfied smile and she did that thing with her eyes again where she blinked too fast. 'Excellent. In that case I'll swing round here with a bottle of red one night around nine-ish. Merlot or shiraz?'

Fuck!

10

Natasha Graham sat with her chin resting against her fist, elbow propped on the counter, watching rain outside the window. It was a miserable day, to match her mood, and the sky was the colour of old bruises. There'd been a constant trail of customers coming and going all morning, it was the first weekend of the school break and things were only likely to get busier from here on in. During summer Whitby was always awash with tourists, British and foreign alike, and the fickle weather front made her shop a good base for shelter on days like today, perhaps spurring more impulse buys than she'd care to admit.

One Hundred & Ninety-Nine owed its name to the Whitby steps nearby, the very ones renowned for featuring in Bram Stoker's *Dracula.* The shop specialised in knickknacks and gifts that were compliant with day-trippers' and holiday-makers' desire for homemade and exclusive souvenirs that stood apart from the usual tat. Natasha had been running the shop for close to twelve years. When her dad had passed away, a heart attack on his way home from the pub, she'd moved to Whitby, using her inheritance to set up the business and to get onto the property ladder. Not once had she looked back. She endeavoured to source quirky and individual wares, anything not redolent of the souvenir shop of bygone years. No one wanted things like ashtrays, fridge magnets and thimbles anymore, well, not ones with Whitby emblazoned across them in gaudy primary colours. *One Hundred & Ninety-Nine* was boutique chic, decked out with a whole array of specialised goods, including stationery, fashion accessories, homewares and tasteful retro paraphernalia. Metal plaques with pictures and inscriptions that referred to anything from wine and beer to friendship and home life were a particularly popular choice. People, it seemed, liked to inject small doses of wit and wisdom into their homes these days. *One Hundred & Ninety-Nine*'s walls were adorned with such plaques, Natasha's personal favourite being: WHEN LIFE GIVES YOU LEMONS, MAKE LEMONADE. And yet here she was now, nibbling on the broken, inflamed skin of her fingers.

Tonight was meant to be date night with Lee. He'd called the previous evening to say he'd booked a table at the Italian restaurant on Church Street and that afterwards he was taking her for drinks around town. But she couldn't say she was looking forward to it with any sense of joy. She was in no mood to be gallivanting around town in her fineries. Sometimes Lee failed to understand what it was she needed, even when she told him outright. And right now what she needed was time and space. Alone.

Fiddling with her mobile phone, she deliberated, indecision unsettling her to the point of frustration till, finally, she keyed in Lee's number. She listened to the dialling tone. It rang about a dozen times before his voice mail kicked in: 'Lee Riddell. Sorry, can't take your call right now. Leave your name and number and I'll get back to you.' After the beep she said, 'Hi, just me. Listen, I'm not feeling too good, can you cancel tonight's reservation? You should go for a few beers with Tris at The Granby instead. You've been meaning to catch up for a while, haven't you? Anyway, I'll speak to you later. Bye.'

It was around five-thirty when she pulled the shop's shutters down and headed home, a spate of blustery northerlies prompting her to speed-walk. As soon she got into the warmth of her apartment she poured a large glass of chardonnay and tried Lee's number again. Her Siamese cat, Maverick, slinked around her legs while she listened to the answerphone kick in.

'Lee, call me when you get this please.'

She took her wine through to the lounge and flopped down in front of the television, reclining the sofa to its furthest stretch. Two hours passed by in a marathon of pointless gameshows and talkshows before the doorbell chimed. Her heart lurched.

Oh please don't let that be you Lee.

It was.

He was standing outside her door, clean shaven and wearing a fitted white shirt that emphasised his trim body and made his tanned skin look healthy and appealing. His dirty-blonde hair had been trimmed since the last time she'd seen him and his designer aftershave suggested he was going somewhere nice. In one hand he was holding a bouquet of pink roses and in the other a silver bottle bag with ribbons around its handles.

'Oh.' Natasha winced. 'Didn't you get my messages?'

'Yeah.' He brushed past her, stepping into the apartment. 'I knew you'd argue about me coming round insisting that you come out, so I came anyway.'

Smiling weakly, she took the flowers from him. 'So kind of you, but I'm *really* not in the mood. How about frozen pizza? I can put the oven on. There's a Mark Wahlberg film about to start…'

Lee shook his head and put his free hand on her waist. Pulling her close, he said, 'Come on, Tasha, you'll feel much better once we're out. Promise. I want to cheer you up, so let me.'

She fiddled with one of the buttons on his shirt, deflecting her own attention away from his persuasive eyes, and shook her head. 'No.'

'Why not?'

'Because.'

'But *why?*'

'For a start, look at the state of me.' Her hair was tied up in a messy ponytail and the make-up she'd put on earlier that day was stale, any illuminating effects now completely lacklustre.

'So?' Lee shrugged. 'It'll take you what? An hour to get dressed, if that? I'll wait.'

'No, seriously, I don't want to go out,' she insisted, her tone firm. 'But you're more than welcome to stay.'

His smile dissipated and his grey eyes dimmed a little, but he leaned forward and kissed her on the forehead. 'Okay, if that's what you really want.'

'Yes. It is.' She led him through to the kitchen and took a second wine glass from the cupboard. 'White or red?'

Dipping his hand into the gift bag he'd brought, he pulled out a bottle of champagne. 'Actually, I brought this for us.'

Natasha stared at the bottle, her eyes narrowing. 'Am I missing something? Are we supposed to be celebrating?'

'Hopefully.' He fiddled in his trouser pocket and produced a small burgundy box. Popping the velveteen lid open with his thumb, he revealed a diamond solitaire propped on a bed of black satin.

Natasha's mouth opened but no words formed. For a while she couldn't blink or swallow. 'I, er…what is this? I don't know what to say…'

'Well, *yes* would be good.' Lee's face brightened with a smile of bravado.

'Yes? But…are you asking me…I mean, is it…?'

'Yes, Tasha, I'm asking you to marry me. After everything we've been through these past two weeks I thought it might cheer you up.'

'Cheer me up?' Natasha was incredulous, her reaction critical, not exactly friendly. 'Do you have any idea what's going on inside my head right now? Why would you think *this* would cheer me up?'

'I dunno.' Lee shrugged, his smile instantly diminished. 'You said before you'd like to get married.'

'Yes, but not like this. And besides, you were pretty clear that you didn't want to. Why the change of heart?'

'This whole thing has given me reason to think, to look to the future and realise what we could be, what we could *have.'*

'What we could have? No. Oh no.' Natasha waved her hands out in front of her and sat down at the breakfast bar. Her face was ashen. 'What happened was an accident…'

'Yes, but there's nothing to say we can't do it again. For real. It's made me realise what I want.'

'And what's that, Lee? You've got my head in bits here. For years you were dead set against the idea of marriage and kids, but now suddenly you're laying it on thick and telling me that actually you *want* the whole shebang.'

'What I want is for us to be together properly. Enough of this seeing each other a few times a week bullshit. It's like we're teenagers or something. I want to wake up next to you every morning. I want us to *be* together.' He walked around the breakfast bar and pulled up a stool next to her. Sitting down, he took hold of her hand. 'And I want us to have a family.'

'Whoa, I've been suggesting we buy a house for two years now…'

'I know, I know. I'm sorry.'

'And kids? You hate kids.'

Lee's eyes dulled and he looked genuinely hurt. 'No I don't, I just never wanted any of my own. Till now. I've changed my mind.'

'Well, I haven't. You're with the wrong woman if that's what you want.'

'Ah come on, Tasha, we'd make great parents.'

'No we wouldn't.'

'Yes we would.'

'*No.*'

'Why not?'

'I'm too old.'

'You've just gone thirty-seven for goodness sake, don't be ridiculous.' He grasped the sides of her stool and swivelled it round so that she was directly facing him. 'Plenty of women start having kids when they're well into their forties these days.'

'No they don't.'

'Yes they do.'

'Not this one.'

'But why?'

'*Because.*'

'For crying out loud, you need to let it go, Tasha. It was over before it'd begun. It's a common occurrence, happens to lots of women. Most of the time they don't even realise it. We can try again. It won't happen next time, I promise.'

'Damn right it won't because there won't be a next time.'

Lee's shoulders sagged, he looked crestfallen.

'Look,' she said, miserably, twirling her glass stalk round in her fingers. 'I don't expect you to understand, but the answer's definitely no. In fact, I've already made an appointment to see the doctor next week about getting the injection.'

'*Seriously?* But…can't we even talk about this? Give it some time at least?'

'No, I've made up my mind. And I think it's probably best if you leave, I can't do this right now.'

11

The day was overcast and the wind had a spiteful nip that was more mid-autumn than early summer. John and Seren wore thin fleeces over t-shirts. They walked down the beach road, John holding Otis's lead and Seren Mindy's. Birds chirruped above them, flittering unseen between the line of sycamore trees to their right, and cabbage white butterflies beat lazy trails along the sweeping grass verge. Eventually the tarmac road sloped down into a rubbled car parking area. Beyond that a narrow footpath led onto the beach. Grassy banks rose to the left of the path and the entrance to the beach was marginally obstructed by a row of four large, graffitied stone cubes.

'What are those?' Seren asked, pointing.

'Tank blocks.' John stopped walking to take in the vista. Being there was like stepping back in time, back to the eighties when the beach had been his playground. 'They were put there during the Second World War to make sure that if any German tanks invaded the beach they couldn't get past. Not easily anyway.'

'You mean so they wouldn't be able to get close enough to blow the village up?'

'Er, yeah, I suppose.'

'And they're the actual ones?' Seren's voice had risen in pitch. To her the Second World War was an impossibly long time ago.

'Yep.'

She ran her hand along the rough concrete side of the nearest block as they passed; she'd always felt the strong urge to touch historically interesting things whenever the chance arose, as though she might absorb the past into her fingertips and channel it into her mind like some form of psychic replay, to see what it had seen. And she loved the idea of contributing to an object's historic footprint, of becoming a part of it in turn.

'See up there?' John pointed to the end section of cliff to their left. 'Used to be a machine gun turret from the Second World War up there too. Might still be.'

Her eyes widened. 'Can we go up and see?'

'On the way back. Let's go down to the sea first.'

The North Sea was only a short stroll away, directly ahead. John had never found it a thing of obvious beauty, and still didn't. Its appeal, to him, was that it was there, always there, and the landscape it commanded was captivating, subtly changing hues with the seasons. The sea itself ran the gamut from plain grey to white-tipped-grey, blue-grey to ink-grey; he wasn't sure if it knew how to be cyan or turquoise. But then, Horden wasn't some Mediterranean jewel, it was a village of mostly dismal weather fronts and had been founded upon the harsh industry of fossil fuel mining. The North Sea complemented Horden well. Horden wouldn't be Horden without it.

He slipped the dogs' leads and they all walked on. To the north of them the banks of Easington jutted out, and to the south lay Blackhall, and Boulby much further in the distance. The beach was a stretch of rugged wilderness in both directions, Horden's section having had a good twenty-eight years, after the pit had closed, in which to recover and transform from coal-mine dumping ground to natural terrain. These days it was a hardened landscape, a likely setting for some edgy dystopian film. Stones like giant pieces of cinder toffee were strewn along the top section and John remembered thinking, when he was a kid, that they were the blast-out from some prehistoric volcanic eruption. The orangey-yellowness of their mineral content gave them a certain singed quality and there was always a faint smell of sulphur in the air.

John led Seren and the dogs further down the beach, leaving the orange rocks behind, till they got to the water's edge, where the air became tangy with seaweed and salt. He marvelled at a six-foot shelf they found themselves standing on. It seemed the sea had dramatically changed the topography of the shoreline in his absence, washing away parts of the beach and managing, over time, to create a vertical embankment of grit and shale. Spotting a sloping section where they could easily get down to the pebbled grey sand, still wet from the receding tide, John clambered down.

'So is this where you used to play when you were little?' Seren asked.

'Yeah.' He turned and reached up to take her hand. 'Do you like it?'

Dismissing his offer of help, she scuttled down the shale ramp and stood next to him. 'Sand's a bit shit for making sandcastles, but yeah it's pretty cool.'

John raised an eyebrow, but she didn't notice.

He picked up a pebble from the foamy tideline and skimmed it across the shallows. It bounced across the water's gunmetal surface three times before disappearing beneath. 'Are you glad we came to stay at Gran's house for the summer?'

'Uh-huh. It's nice having you about.' Seren bent and took hold of a small stone. Imitating John, she then threw it towards the sea. It made one resounding splash.

'What're you on about, silly? I'm always about.'

She took her eyes off the spot where her stone had sunk and looked at him squarely. 'Back home you *never* want to do stuff like this. You're always working.'

There, she'd said it. Concreted his recent mounting fear that for the past three years he'd been a lousy dad. The confirmation winded him like a punch to the stomach. So he'd made a botched job of parenthood because he'd failed to be there for his daughter when it mattered most. And the worst thing was, he'd been totally oblivious. Sure, he'd always made sure she was properly clothed and fed, but aside from the basics he'd been so wrapped up in himself, so self-absorbed, that he'd neglected the emotional and developmental needs of his little girl. His eyes stung blurry against the directness of the wind, and, moreover, the truth. He looked away, to the horizon, and blinked rapidly.

'If that's the way you feel, I'll have to see about changing things won't I?' he said at last, his voice tight as he stooped to grab another flat stone. He showed it to her. 'Here, like this.' Twisting his torso to the left and arcing his arm behind him, he kept the stone's length horizontal in his hand. When he pivoted his body back round, he uncurled his arm and released the stone towards the sea with a fluent sweep. This time he counted five skims before it sank.

Seren watched in awe. 'How'd you do that?'

John smiled. He could fix this. He could change. He could. He'd become a better dad. He searched the ground for another stone and showed her again, only this time slower. When she tried, she managed no better than another dull *plonk!*

They stayed there in that spot for a while, till Seren had managed three skims of her own, then headed south towards Blackhall Rocks. They passed a pond that apparently, at one time, had been a popular dumping place for dead dogs. Its surface was concealed by a mass of long, spear-headed reeds and John doubted there were any bloated, furry bodies floating in there now, but when Seren expressed an interest to go and take a closer look he insisted they didn't, distracting her, instead, by pointing out a piece of driftwood that looked like a crocodile: its gnarled body long and a knot in the woodgrain its eye. Next to it was a matted nest of dried brown seaweed, entwined with lengths of fishing wire, bejewelled with colourful flies and metal sinkers. The heap of beach treasure reminded John of the tangled mess he'd seen at the bottom of his mother's costume jewellery box back in the eighties.

Crows watched their progress from the banks sides, their sorrowful caws offset by the frequent *bock-bocking* of an unseen pheasant. It took John, Seren and the dogs ten minutes to get to the rock pools of Blackhall Rocks, where scores of parp sea anemones, the colour of raw liver, glistened underwater, their domed bodies like canker sores growing from the rock itself. Seren delighted in how bizarre and squidgy they looked and it wasn't long before John had to tell her off for poking one with a stick. They found an abundance of barnacles and dismembered crabs' pincers too, and a starfish that looked calcified. Otis found a semi-decomposed gull on the beach and started rolling on it before John could stop him, which Seren thought was hilarious till John told her she'd be the one to bath him when they got home.

By two o'clock the sky was the same wishy-washy shade of off-white-grey that it had been when they'd set out earlier, and the breeze just as fresh. All the walking had warmed them up, though, so when their stomachs declared lunchtime they found an unsheltered rock to sit on and John unzipped his fleece. He took off his backpack and rummaged inside, pulling out a Tupperware lunchbox.

'Ham without butter.' He handed Seren a cellophane package.

'Did we bring some for Otis and Mindy?'

'No.'

'Why not?'

'Dogs don't eat sandwiches.'

'I bet they do.'

'I bet they don't.'

'I'll save them my crusts.'

'Nice try, kidda. Get them eaten.'

Seren huffed and the pair of them ate in silence for a while, watching as an angler approached from Blackhall. The man was wearing an army camouflage coat and blue jeans tucked into green wellies. In one hand he carried a fishing rod and in the other a tackle box. When he passed by he tipped his head at John and said, 'Alright, mate?'

John tipped his own head in acknowledgement. 'Alright.'

When the man was out of earshot, Seren turned to John and said, 'Did you know him?'

'No.'

'Why'd he call you mate?'

'He was being friendly. That's what people say.'

'But why did he ask if you're alright if you don't know him?'

John laughed. 'He wasn't initiating a rundown of how I'm feeling, you daft bugger. It's just another way of saying hello.'

'I don't get it.'

'You overthink things, kidda.' He blew steam from the tea in the lid of his Thermos flask and took a sip.

Seren sucked on the straw of her cartoned orange juice and looked back the way they'd come, towards the tall reeds of Dead Dog Pond. She was quiet and contemplative for a while, her light blonde hair wispy around her face where the wind had freed it from her ponytail. Digging the toes of her white trainers into the dirty sand, eventually she turned to John, her blue eyes serious, and said, 'Petey Moon's gone.'

This revelation was a pleasant surprise to John, but he tried to keep his hopefulness hidden under a display of nonchalant chin rubbing. 'Gone where?'

'I dunno. He was there last night when I went to bed, but I've not seen him today.' She pulled on her bottom lip, worriedly.

'Maybe he's gone home.'

She considered this for a moment then, despite looking unconvinced, said, 'Maybe. He didn't like it at Gran's house.'

'Oh?' This surprised John in a not-so-good way; his eyes narrowed. 'Why not?'

'Dunno.'

'Do *you* like it at Gran's house?'

'Yeah.'

'Good.'

'But what about Petey Moon?'

'I'm sure that wherever he is he'll be fine.' John smiled in quiet celebration. Now that he was behaving like a proper dad it stood to reason that his daughter would no longer need an imaginary friend. For this to have happened so quickly, though, was a huge leap forward, for both of them.

'Dad?' Seren was looking at him again, all serious.

'Uh-huh?'

'Have you seen the woman in Gran's house?'

This question caught him off guard. He regarded her curiously. 'What woman?'

'The woman with black hair.'

'*Inside* Gran's house?'

'Uh-huh.'

'No, I can't say that I have.'

'Oh.' She sucked the remaining dregs from her orange drink, which created a loud gurgling noise, then fell silent.

'So what woman are you talking about?' John persisted.

Poking her finger through the cellophane parcel of crusts in her hand and keeping her eyes downcast, Seren was quiet for a few moments then said, 'I dunno. Last night there was a strange woman in my room.'

12

The wind swiped in from the North Sea, thrashing Natasha's loose hair into knots and stinging her eyes so they watered. She dabbed at her lower lids with the backs of her fingers, leaving smudgy tracks of mascara on her knuckles. Pulling the blue cardigan she wore tight around her body, as though the thin cotton might shield her from the wind's probing, nipping fingers, she stepped onto the grass, beneath which might or might not be the boundaries of someone's grave. Her toes curled at the thought and she trod softly, just in case.

A few other people were strolling through the churchyard, mostly sticking to the stone path, their chatter diminished by the wind's incessant voice. Natasha imagined most of them were probably tourists on their way to or from the ruins of the abbey at the top of the cliff. A group of young goths mooched melodramatically around the entrance to the church, and a man with white-blonde hair and a sense of high fashion made eye contact with Natasha on his way past. He was holding hands with a woman and he listened while she talked. There was a slight swing to their hand-holding arms that proclaimed them happy and carefree. He smiled. Natasha returned the pleasantry, but her smile was forced. It wasn't too long ago that she and Lee had enjoyed a happy relationship. Now everything she'd thought they were as a couple was under question.

She had come to the cliffside after work, not wanting to go straight home. Her apartment, she knew, would be filled with quiet hostility; the remnants of last night's proposal and subsequent argument lingering and causing an aloneness that not even Maverick could vanquish. All because her adamancy on a matter close to heart had been offset by Lee's refusal to accept what she wanted. They'd said things they probably hadn't meant to say, but things they considered true nonetheless. Natasha's heated emotion had been pitted against his angry words and their newfound differences had placed them at odds with all they'd ever been and all they'd ever agreed upon, thus making a mockery of all they'd hoped to be. The rift between them this time was huge, quite possibly unfixable. But neither of them could be wrong for wanting what they wanted. Even though she was confounded and confused by Lee's change of heart, she accepted that everyone has a right to change their mind.

He wanted kids now.

She still didn't.

Her chest ached with a growing emptiness for the relationship she'd thought they had.

How had it all gone so terribly wrong? Got so misconstrued?

The graveyard offered a neutral environment in which to reflect, its sloping banks of grave-marked grass a pinnacle upon which Natasha could retreat into herself and feel distanced enough from the hustle and bustle of the harbour village down below. Up here she felt temporarily detached from real-life, standing in the presence of the dead. A thought which greatly comforted her. Up here she felt calm.

Weathered names and brief biographies on elaborate gravestones provided her with some measure of thought-provoking solitude, as well as familiarity. These had all been real people at one time, with their own sets of problems. She'd often visualise their lives, imagining how each serif-fonted person might have looked based on the strength and sound of their capitalised names, and what tragedies might have surrounded their deaths. The epitaphs even helped to put her own life into context;

many of the departed had been extremely young men and women. Some of them children. Some babies.

Picking her way through grassy aisles, with no particular destination in mind, Natasha wondered what her own graveside inscription might someday be, imagining something along the lines of: *Natasha Graham; lonely spinster known locally as 'Cat Lady'.*

She sighed.

She hadn't heard from Lee all day. She needed time to think and expected he did too. Had things turned out differently, had she not miscarried the blastocyst before it had had time to make itself properly at home in her womb, she would have explored the idea of becoming Mrs Riddell. For the past couple of years she'd often visualised herself in a cream wedding gown: slim-fitting with a fishtail back and sweetheart neckline, nothing too fancy. Her hair set in gentle waves with understated jewels clipped here and there. No bouquet. No bridesmaids or page boys either. Minimal fuss. Just a simple registry office affair with a cluster of immediate family from Lee's side and some very close friends in attendance to witness the happy day. Lee had always been opposed to the idea, declaring it a waste of time and money, but last night he'd shocked her with his new set of ideals: marriage *and* kids.

How could a person flip his objectives on their head overnight? Just like that.

This was why she couldn't marry him. Not now. She couldn't live with that kind of changeable mentality. Above all else, Natasha *needed* stability.

For Lee, at the moment, there was a happy family life just ahead of them, a gauzy romanticism that she could fully appreciate because she'd dreamt that same alluring dream a long time ago. But how long till he got bored? How long till he outgrew the fad and had another overnight change of heart? Would he stick around?

She'd rather not find out the hard way. Perhaps if he knew her entire backstory he'd understand her reluctance to start a family.

Was it too late to tell him now?

Yes, she thought so.

He might be annoyed that she'd not been completely open from the start. Well, no, that wasn't fair. It wasn't that she'd not been open, she just hadn't told him every minute detail about her life. She'd never needed to. That aspect of their lives, not having children, had been something they'd always agreed upon. Until last night. Besides, he didn't need to know. It wouldn't change the way she felt even if he did.

Eventually she dawdled home, deflated and sombre. Gravely saddened by how much things had changed within the space of a few weeks. Excited talk of a winter trip to Chicago had been replaced by an unexpected pregnancy and subsequent miscarriage. She wished she could go back to cosy nights on the couch planning shopping expeditions on North Michigan Avenue and strolls along Navy Pier. Instead she sat on the couch alone, half watching television while Maverick, bizarrely, kept his own company in another room of the house, until she fell asleep.

...

She arranged baby-pink carnations in a crystal-cut vase and when she turned around her mother was watching, eyes vacant.

'Mam?'

Diane Graham didn't respond. She was propped in bed by four white pillows. Her once long hair was now cropped short and laden with grey. Natasha could see it hadn't yet been brushed. Sickly brown crescents lay on their backs beneath her sunken eyes, denoting the gradual ebbing of her health. Diane Graham's mind was caught up in a receding tide, withdrawing to some faraway place forever because in her world the moon only waned, no matter how much medication she was given.

Natasha went to the bedside and sat down in a draylon armchair which smelt of charity shops. Leaning forward she smoothed the covers at the side of her mother's veined hand, not because they needed smoothing but because it gave her something to do. At the same time her mother's fingers began to move rhythmically, tip-tapping across the turned-down white cotton as though she was playing on a piano.

'Mam?'

Diane tilted her head to the sound of Natasha's voice but didn't reply, seemingly lost to whatever finger symphony was going on inside her head. A fly began to bang repeatedly against the window. *Bzzz bzzzp bzzz.* The noise, a validation of its frenzied thoughts on being imprisoned, filled the quiet monotony of the room with all the ruckus of a chainsaw. Natasha frowned. She took hold of her mother's hand, stilling the silent piano-playing, and squeezed gently.

'I've come to see how you're doing,' she said, her words more pronounced, more forceful. 'I brought you some flowers.' She pointed to the carnations over by the window.

Diane looked to the pink-filled vase. Her watery blue eyes showed pleasant surprise. 'Oh that's lovely, pet. My favourites.'

Natasha swept her mother's unkempt fringe to one side, away from her eyes. 'I know, that's why I brought them.'

'Smashing.'

'Dad sends his love.'

'Hmmm.'

Natasha edged further forward. 'Listen, I've got some news for you, Mam.'

'*My* dad sends his love, you say?' Diane's empty eyes suddenly sparked with fine fettle. 'That's nice. I'll bet he's lost without me? And Gina? I hope she's not been getting into all kinds of mischief.'

Natasha closed her eyes and ground her teeth together; Granddad had been dead for the past eight years and Aunty Gina had grown up sensibly and got married long before that. Natasha had learned not to say as much, though, the old news about Granddad was always new news to her mother. To go on correcting her would be an act of cruelty. It was just unfortunate that each time Natasha referred to her own dad, Peter Graham, her mother never seemed to remember that she had a husband. As a consequence Natasha's dad had stopped visiting a long time ago, the experience much too upsetting, but he still sent his love. A lot of the time Diane didn't remember who Natasha was either, which caused resentment to fester. A large, angry mass of debilitating hopelessness that Natasha had to fight to suppress. None of this was fair.

'Gina stopped by earlier,' her mother said. 'For my shoes. The navy courts with the white bows. I said she could lend them.'

'That's nice.'

'Hmmm. Brought me some flowers too. She's a good lass, our Gina.' Diane leaned forward, the ridge of her clavicle bone sharp above the v-neck flannelette nightdress she was wearing. 'They don't last long in here though. See?' She pointed to the carnations. 'They're dying.'

Natasha breathed deeply. 'No, Mam. I just brought those flowers for you, not Aunt Gina. They're fresh.'

'They are?' Diane looked at Natasha as though seeing her for the first time.

'Yes.'

'Who are you again?'

'Natasha.'

'Oh.' Her mother's eyes glazed over. 'That's a pretty name. Do I know you?'

'Yes.'

Diane seemed to ponder this for a while, becoming silent and retreating back to whatever thoughts her broken subconscious plied her with. Her fingers started tapping out a tune on the bedsheet again. Natasha's eyes felt hot. She listened to the fly. Bzzzzz. *Bzzz. Bzzzzzp.* Found that on some level she could relate to it.

'I've got a daughter, you know,' Diane announced quite suddenly, spreading her hands flat over her stomach.

'I know.'

'You do?'

'Yes.'

'Ah.' She smiled a faraway smile, her eyes distant, unreachable.

Natasha's lip trembled. She leaned across and stroked the back of her mother's hand.

'Would you do me a favour?' Diane asked, looking down at the unfamiliar hand on her own.

'Of course.'

'My little girl, can you give her a message?'

'Yes.'

'She has long brown hair, just like yours, and the biggest, golden brown eyes you'll ever see. You'll know her when you see her.'

'I'm sure.'

'You are?'

'Yes.'

'Good, as long as you are.'

'Absolutely. What's the message?'

'When you see her…'

'Yes?'

'Tell her I love her.'

...

Natasha awoke on the couch, tears soaking her cheeks and dampening the cushion beneath her head. The living room was now dark save for the glow from the television, which lit up the furniture with intermittent flashes.

Oh Mam.

Wiping the heel of her hand across her cheeks, Natasha sat up. As she did her stomach spasmed, a searing hot agony that made her yelp. Sucking in air through clenched teeth, she rocked forward and swung her feet to the floor.

'Ow, ow, ow...*OW!*'

Maverick, who had made the back of the couch his own snoozing zone at some point, flew past her head and landed on the floor. He pelted towards the open doorway, as though he was chasing something unseen, then his ghostly form came to a stop once he'd reached the door. He turned back to Natasha and hissed, his needle teeth glistening under the high-drama of someone being murdered on BBC1, then darted out into the blackness of the hallway beyond. Natasha clutched her stomach and cried out again, this time in fright. Her hands met with a swollen, tender mound beneath her pyjama shirt which seemed to have a heartbeat all of its own. Tightly stretched skin pulsated strongly against her palms. She sprang to her feet. The painful cramping had begun to lessen in intensity but her head pounded as though her heart was pumping all of its blood there. In the throbbing darkness her eyes glittered with the threat of passing out, but she cradled her enlarged abdomen and staggered across the living room towards the light switch.

Before she got there another crippling contraction rendered her immobile. She dropped to her knees.

Oh God, I know this pain.

Her breaths came in short, sharp bursts and she hitched her shirt up to look at her stomach. In the low glow of the television the white flesh of her abnormally convex belly was as tight as the skin of a drum and covered in bulging, black varicose veins that moved like earthworms beneath the surface. Natasha's mouth filled with saliva, an automatic reaction to her revulsion. She rocked backwards and retched hot wetness into her lap. Tears blurred her eyes and vomit burnt the back of her nose.

This can't be real. It can't be.

When this latest contraction began to subside she scrabbled to her feet and lurched for the light switch. Clean, white light filled the room, hurting her eyes. She blinked rapidly and looked down at her exposed stomach and found there was nothing there to see. Nothing but her usual flat and unblemished belly.

The glitter behind her eyes stormed to a blizzard and she fell forwards.

13

'Were you having a bad dream?' John's hair was blowing about in the wind, dark strands sweeping across his eyes so that he had to keep brushing it upwards with his fingers. The blustery gusts cutting in from the sea seemed suddenly colder. He wondered if it was his imagination.

Seren shook her head and continued to poke holes in the cellophane bundle of uneaten sandwich crusts. 'No.'

John's neck prickled. He turned the collar of his fleece up. 'So what are you saying, kidda?'

'I *already* said. There was a strange woman in my bedroom last night. She had long black hair and was talking to me.'

'What did she say?'

Kicking the backs of her shoes against the large rock they were sitting on, Seren looked towards the sea and shrugged. 'I dunno.'

'You don't know?'

'She was talking really quiet. I couldn't hear.'

'I see.'

'No you don't.' She looked at him accusingly.

'You're right, I don't. I think you were dreaming.'

'It wasn't a dream, Dad.'

'Night terror then.' He knew how chilling and confusing they could be. Perhaps they were hereditary. There was no fun to be had from the fevered state of mind and brief paralysis that came with being caught between the gossamer layer of sleep and full awakening. It was a horrible place to find yourself, hallucinogenic and disturbing, and certainly a condition conducive for imagining a dark figure at the foot of the bed.

'It was *real,*' she insisted.

'You'd think a night terror was if you had one.'

'Only, I didn't.'

Even though his theory was more logical, a subtle feeling of dread began to creep over John. Why did the woman his daughter was telling him about give him internal chills that set his nerves on edge in a way that talk of Petey Moon never had?

'What did she look like?' he asked, wishing he hadn't as soon as the words were out; feeding his daughter's (and indeed his own) obscure, imaginative horror was hardly constructive.

'I dunno, it was dark. She was over near the door.'

John made a half-hearted snort of amusement, a short exhalation from his nose. 'It was probably Gran's dressing gown hanging on the back of the door, silly.'

'Since when do dressing gowns talk?' she huffed. 'Just because I'm six doesn't mean I'm stupid, you know. I know what I saw. It was a woman.'

'Well, it still sounds to me like you were having a bad dream. I've had that type before. The space between consciousness and unconsciousness is a funny place, kidda. Sometimes I've sworn something must have been real, but really it wasn't.' He turned away from her unwavering blue gaze and stuffed the clear Tupperware box back into his backpack, he didn't want her to see any element of doubt that might be showing on his face. He felt a renewed sense of foreboding about the previous night. About the strange sequence of occurrences he'd experienced himself. His mother's dog hanging by its lead on the landing, draped in its own wet intestines. The sound of its blood dripping. The dark stain on the carpet. The god-awful smell. The deathly chill. And then the mould patch on the ceiling. Since he'd got up that morning he felt that he couldn't ponder any of it for long because, even though on some instinctual level none of it felt right, he was meant to be the grown up here. He needed to keep his shit together and think rationally. He needed to be the level-headed one. Always. It was the excitement of the trip. It had to be. They were both experiencing some kind of combined emotional hysteria. That was all. 'Come on, let's get going,' he said, standing and swinging the backpack over his shoulder.

The afternoon had darkened without them having realised. Clouds the colour of baby gulls churned above them, moving fast; sky-surf riding on the back of the increasing wind. The angler who had passed by some time ago was nowhere to be seen, swallowed by the sea or having written the day off as a bad one and sloped home to watch the football. John didn't think the latter was a bad idea. He assumed a brisk pace and they made it back home just before the heavens opened.

There was no more talk of strange women in the house, not even when it was Seren's bedtime. John had casually suggested she might like to swap rooms, but she wouldn't have any of it.

'What're we doing tomorrow?' she asked, climbing into bed next to Geller.

'I dunno, trouble. I'll have a think.'

A faint smell of bleach tainted the room, killing Judith Gimmerick's floral blend with an unpleasant but inoffensive smell that stayed at the back of John's nose, reminding him of newly cleaned toilets and the school janitor's cupboard. He craned his neck and looked up at the ceiling. It was all white.

'Can we go out again, like today?'

'Maybe. If the weather behaves itself.'

Thunder grumbled in the distance like defiant back-chat and the wind spattered rain against the back of the house. Seren looked to the window and giggled nervously. Whatever the weather had in store for them the next day seemed irrelevant because right now it was creating the perfect conditions for bad dreams and ghosts.

Not good. Not good at all.

'Want the light leaving on?' he asked, taking Seren's glasses and putting them on the bedside table.

She raised her eyebrows and shook her head, determined to prove that she had no problem sleeping there and that neither strange woman nor storm could oust her.

'Goodnight then, kidda. Get some sleep and I'll think of something cool for us to do tomorrow.'

At the doorway John flicked the light off and kept his gaze on the blackened room, allowing his eyes to adjust. The chest of drawers and slimline wardrobe soon became visible as rectangular silhouettes against the lighter walls and the bed was a black wedge against the far wall. There were no shapes that might be mistaken for a woman and his groping hand confirmed that there wasn't a dressing gown or anything else hanging from the back of the door.

Shaking his head, he closed the door and went to his own room to collect his robe. His plan for the rest of the evening was to have a long soak in the bath, accompanied by a bottle of Norman's Rioja from the wine rack in the kitchen. Lightning flashed as he slung the robe over his shoulder, highlighting everything in his mother's bedroom in shades of grey. The subsequent roll of thunder was louder, much closer this time. He went to the window to see if he could catch any subsequent forked flashes of pink over the sea and found three dead flies on the sill. He pulled the curtains closed against their upturned bodies and headed downstairs. Thunder rolled, a deep resonant sound like stone grinding against stone, and he imagined the lid of a crypt being slid open somewhere beneath the house. The dead coming back to life. He stepped off the bottom stair and heard the unmistakable creak of the garden gate. He looked at his watch. Ten o'clock.

Here they come.

A quiet knock on the back door's windowpane suggested a caller who didn't want to disturb the entire household. But the fact the caller was at the back door and not the front suggested familiarity, someone who sought a late-night answer. Otis and Mindy beat John to the kitchen, their noses pressed to the tiny gap between the door and its frame, their bodies shivering with suspense. John ushered them out of the way and opened the door.

'You again?'

Pamela Tanner was standing on the doorstep beneath a red umbrella, a bottle of Echo Falls in her hand. There was an inebriated playfulness about her which implied she'd already been drinking. She smiled that porcelain veneer smile of hers and said, 'Hey handsome, wondered if you could do with a bit of company? I saw the bedroom light go off, presumed the little 'un must be in bed.'

John stared, unsure how to respond. Was it by chance she'd seen Seren's light blink out or had she been actively watching and waiting? The latter was almost too creepy to consider.

'So, are you gonna invite me in out of this rain or what?' Pam said, stepping forward.

John moved back so she didn't brush against him as she forced her way inside. She shook the excess water from her brolly outside then shut the door behind her, sealing them in together so that John felt both trapped and imposed upon. His throat constricted.

'Filthy isn't it?' she said, kicking her crystal-embellished pumps off and walking barefooted to the counter with her bottle of wine.

'What is?' John saw how her feet made sweaty prints

on the floor tiles, or maybe it was rain water residue, and how black tattoo ink swirled around both feet in complex symmetrical designs contrasting with toenails painted prohibition-red to match her lips.

'The weather.' She put a hand on her hip and stood in a way that invited him to look at her.

John shrugged as if the weather was none of his business. He noticed that she smelt of rain, fresh air and perfume, and that her shop-bought smell was a grown up, no-messing fragrance. Strong and bold. There was nothing floral-light or fruity-sweet about Pamela Tanner. She wore a black Lycra tube dress that came down to her knees, clinging to her everywhere it touched and emphasising her confidence. She was trim but ample, he saw. Shapely in all the right places but with subtle lumps and bumps above her knicker-line and below where her bra sat. Her outfit would make most women half her age feel self-conscious, but she was simply owning that dress. Pamela Tanner exhibited a cool fierceness, a fierceness of which John was automatically wary. She was way more trouble than he needed. Way too old for him too. He ran his hands down his face and took a deep breath.

Oh man, how will I get out of this alive?

'You seem like the quiet sort,' Pam said, turning her back to him while she unscrewed the top off the wine bottle. Without being prompted she reached into the cupboard where Judith Gimmerick kept her wine glasses and took two out. 'As you can tell, I'm not shy so I thought I'd make the first move.'

John surrendered any of the half-formed comebacks that came into his head before they could reach his mouth. He was completely out of touch with the ritual of blatant flirting, especially when he had no desire to join in and play the game. This was no fun at all. And something about the way she looked at him so brazenly, like she was undressing him with her eyes, made him feel awkwardly juvenile. He hated this.

She laughed at his obvious discomfort, the sound a warming purr. 'Hey chill out, fella. Just having a bit of friendly banter, that's all. I hate thunder, gives me the heebie-jeebies. I've come round for a drink and chat. No harm in that is there?'

'Not at all. Make yourself at home,' John said, finding his voice at last and injecting it with a detectable amount of sarcasm that he was pleased with. He watched as she poured the wine, unfazed. Otis and Mindy were still fussing around her legs, evidently a damn sight happier about her being there than he was.

'Here.' She reached out and offered John a glass of red, demanding eye contact as she did. Her fingers deliberately touched his when he accepted. She smiled, her eyes holding his without reprieve. John was the first to look away, taking a generous mouthful of wine while thinking he'd need a lot more, and fast, to get through the next few hours. Although not a pushover, he couldn't think how he might tell Pamela Tanner to get lost without causing some neighbourly rift that his mother wouldn't thank him for. This was just awful.

Pam took a sip from her glass then led John through to the lounge, which made him even more concerned about how the evening might pan out.

Just go with the flow. Drink more wine and go with the flow.

She sat down at one end of the couch so he took the armchair, the furthest seat away. This seemed to amuse her. Her eyes sparkled. She positioned herself straight-backed on the edge of the couch's cushion as though she was the epitome of elegance, but really it was the best posture for her to keep, John thought, to avoid unflattering midriff folds.

'I told Jude I'd look after the house,' she said.

'Hmmm.' John could understand why his mother had declined the offer.

'I'm pleased it turned out this way, though.' She took another drink of wine, her tongue lingering on the edge of her glass.

'Which way's that?'

'This way, dopey. *You* being here.'

'You are?'

'Yeah, you and me, we'll get along like a house on fire during the next few weeks.' She knocked her shoulders back and sucked her stomach in by about half an inch.

'Hmmm.' John's eyes wandered to the photographic line-up of his family on the mantel, his body language deliberately as unenthusiastic as his verbal response. He didn't dare ask what she had in mind.

'You'll see.' She winked her assurance before unashamedly checking him over, head to toe.

John lifted his glass and took a swig.

'Fancy a game of poker?' Leaning forward, she dipped a hand into her handbag. Thick silver bangles on her arm banged together, their metallic jangle somehow exotic. She pulled out a pack of cards and John instantly looked worried. Noticing, she laughed; a gravelly, throaty sound that might have been sexy if not for the smoker's catarrh at the end of it. 'Don't look so scared, we can keep it clean.'

'Keep what clean?'

'Poker.'

'I don't know how to play.'

'I'll teach you.' She was already slipping the cards from their case.

'Cards aren't really my thing.'

'Try it, you might like it.'

'Is it easy?'

'That's entirely down to you.'

Pamela Tanner shuffled like a pro and the next two

hours passed much more pleasantly than John had expected. They talked about everyday stuff while she slaughtered him at poker, and it turned out she was a good listener as well as a good talker. John had begun to relax after his second glass of wine. He went on to open two bottles of Norman's Rioja to share, then they started downing whiskey shots. It was during his fifth double whiskey that his eyelids became too heavy to keep open between blinks. One minute Pam was talking about her upcoming holiday to Playa de las Americas, her nimble hands working the deck of cards, her voice a lulling huskiness, and the next minute he was gone, travelling down a great black spiral of alcohol-induced oblivion which felt oh so good.

That night he slept like he hadn't slept in years.

14

When John awoke morning light was streaming in around the drawn curtains of the lounge. For a moment he didn't know who he was. His mouth tasted vile, dry and stale, and he had a pain in his shoulder from being slumped in the armchair too long. Rubbing his eyes with the heels of his hands he sat up and looked about. The movement hurt his head. Badly. Like blisters popping along his frontal lobe where he imagined his dehydrated brain had been rubbing against his skull. His eyeballs filled with a myriad of electric dots that burst with acid, searing his optic nerves. He felt he might die, his body poisoned. He saw a pair of socks, his socks, on the floor over by the couch and couldn't remember having taken them off. Then he remembered Pamela Tanner.

Oh God.

Then he saw a crumpled mound on the arm of the couch. His t-shirt.

Oh God.

He certainly couldn't remember having taken *that* off. Confused, he looked down at his bare chest and saw that the flies of his jeans were undone.

Oh God. No…just no.

A terrible sickliness rose up from the pit of his stomach, bringing with it the bitter taste of last night's whiskey and wine. He swallowed it back down and sat forward, nursing his head. What did any of this mean? Had he and Pamela Tanner…?

No.

He'd remember.

Wouldn't he?

Or had she taken advantage of him while he'd slept?

Inexcusably and unforgivably overstepping some boundary and letting her hands touch parts of him while he was unconscious?

Please God, no.

Movement upstairs made him bristle.

Seren.

He had to make sure Pamela Tanner wasn't still in the house, passed out in the kitchen or something, because that would be awful for his little girl to come downstairs to. He wasn't that kind of dad. Not that anything, as far as he was aware, had happened between him and Pamela Tanner. But still, if Seren were to come downstairs and find the pair of them nursing last night's hangovers she'd put two and two together, and whatever number she came up with wouldn't be at all a bad guess.

He lurched to his feet, ignoring as best he could the pounding insistence inside his skull. His fingers were shaking as he tackled each fly button into its relevant hole and he willed himself to remember having gone to the toilet in the middle of the night, because being so drunk he might not have bothered doing his jeans up afterwards. But he was rewarded no such memory. Hunched over, with his palm clutched to his forehead, he reached for his heavily creased t-shirt. As he did so something fluttered to the floor. A playing card that landed face up. A raven-haired monarch defined in ink. The Queen of Spades. He left her where she was, her illustrated green eyes staring after him as he struggled into the t-shirt and hobbled through to the kitchen.

'Pam?'

She wasn't there. Two clean wine glasses were overturned on the draining board and the back door key was lying on the doormat. She'd left without waking him. But when?

Does it even matter?

What mattered was his partial state of undress. Why

the hell had he awoken with no shirt on and his jeans undone? Yet again, at the thought, his fragile insides cramped and threatened to reject a bellyful of soured wine. He staggered to the sink, just in case.

You're blowing things way out of proportion. Calm down.

Pamela Tanner had more front than Fenwick's window display at Christmas, that much was true, but surely she wasn't demented enough to strip the clothes off a sleeping man. What would be the point?

Maybe he'd got his second wind and had played more poker, losing his socks and shirt to Pam's syrupy-voiced manipulation. A frightening thought, but one he could live with. He filled the kettle and took a mug from the cupboard. When he turned round Seren had crept into the kitchen and was sitting at the table.

'Morning, kidda.' His voice was especially low, gritty with the parched thickness of his throat. 'Want some toast?'

She regarded him for a moment, her face deadpan. 'Why are you wearing lipstick, Dad?'

His lungs deflated and the underside of his face flashed cold. *'I am?'*

'Uh-huh.'

He rubbed his mouth with his fingers and looked at them. They were coated with the faded red of Pamela Tanner's lips, a truer red ingraining the whorls of his fingerprints.

Shit, shit, shit.

Seren continued to watch him, waiting for whatever explanation there could possibly be, and his hangover stepped up to the extent he needed to sit down.

'Er, there's this lady who lives a few doors down.' His flustered spew of words marked some kind of guilt, guilt he didn't even know was warranted. 'She popped round to say hi and, well, er, I guess she's a bit too friendly.'

He wiped his mouth some more on the back of his hand.

'You're not a cross-dresser then?'

'*What?* No!'

'Good.'

'Why would…how do you even know what a…'

'Alfie Barnet's uncle's a cross-dresser. He gets beat up for it. Alfie Barnet, not his uncle. Although his uncle did once…'

'No, Seren, I'm not a sodding cross-dresser.'

She looked down, her fingers picking at the corners of the cork placemat in front of her. 'So, this lady a few doors down, did you snog her?'

'No! No I bloody didn't. As I said she's just a bit too friendly. Got me on the lips instead of the cheek.' He felt woozy, his hurting head awash with confusion. He didn't even know what the truth was himself. *Had* they kissed?

Fuck my life.

Seren shrugged like it didn't matter either way, so long as he wasn't cross-dressing. She looked out of the window. 'It's sunny.'

'It is.' John stood up again and put a teabag and some sugar into his mug before pouring hot water in. Usually he didn't take sugar, but this morning he needed two. 'So. Do you fancy going on an adventure?'

'Where to?'

'Let's see.' He managed to put two slices of bread into the toaster, his guts roiling at the thought of food, then turned to her. 'I'll take you down the dene, show you the cundy if you like.'

'What's that?'

'A tunnel that runs beneath the coast road.'

'Okay.' She didn't look overly enthused.

'Trolls live there.'

'Liar.'

'They might do.'

'Why would they?'

'Because it's pitch black inside, you can't see a thing till you come out the other end.' John pictured the cundy's entrance in his head. A dilated black pupil, endless and formidable, surrounded by lush greenery. It quickly turned into Pamela Tanner's eye. Watching him. Queen of Spades. He jabbed the teabag with a spoon and squeezed it against the side of the mug.

'Okay, that sounds cool,' Seren said. 'But why's it called the cundy?'

'Not sure, kidda. It's a water conduit. Maybe cundy's a shortened nickname for that.'

Seren shook her head. 'I don't get it.'

'Me neither.'

'What else is in the dene?'

John blew on his tea and sipped. 'All sorts, it's massive. Too big to do in one day, but we'll see the viaduct near the cundy.'

'What's that?'

'A really tall rail bridge that crosses a section of the dene.' He omitted to tell her it was also a suicide hotspot. 'Next week, if you like, I'll take you to see the Devil's Lapstone.'

'Is it really?'

'The Devil's? Legend says so. He offered to help build Durham Cathedral but on his way he dropped one of the stones that he planned to use on the foundations.'

'Why would he do that?'

'Drop it?'

'No, help build the cathedral. Him and God aren't friends.'

'But that's exactly it. It was a trick. He wanted to do a botched job so that when people went to the cathedral to pray the shoddily built foundations would crumble beneath their weight and the whole building would fall down on top of them.'

'Sounds a bit silly, God would have realised what he

was up to. Besides, if the Devil dropped the stone why didn't he just go back and pick it up?'

John grinned. 'Sounds to me like you're too scared to go and see it with me in case he comes back for it.'

Seren folded her arms and rested them on the table. 'No I'm not. I'm not scared of anything.'

'Really? Now that's a boast if ever I heard one.' The toaster popped and John set about buttering the toast. 'How about spiders?'

'I like them.'

'Heights?'

'Boring.'

'Tight spaces?'

'I'm only small.'

'Sandwich crusts?'

'Funny.'

'Pink?'

'Don't be a dick.'

John banged the plate of toast down in front of her, hurting his own head. '*Don't* call me that!'

A troubled silence ensued.

Keeping her eyes downcast, Seren ran a finger round the edge of the plate and, in a small voice, said, 'That woman came to my room again last night.'

John exhaled heavily, glaring at her with a tight-lipped scowl. He said nothing.

'I couldn't hear what she was saying at first. It was as though she was trying to tell me something really, really quietly in case someone else that she didn't want to might hear. You know, like a secret.' Seren looked up to gauge her dad's reaction, to see if he was listening. He was. 'But then she came closer and told me that she knows where Petey Moon is.'

John tensed, reluctant to be roped into this line of conversation again, especially at that moment in time, but curious enough to want to know where she was going with it. 'And where's that?'

'I'm not sure exactly. But she says he's with lots of others and they're all lost. Trapped. Same as her.'

'Jesus, Seren,' he chided, 'I already told you, she's just a dream.'

'No she's not.'

'Is.'

'Not.'

'Seren!'

'I can prove it.'

'How?'

Her eyes were wide, beseeching. 'I told her to give Geller to Petey Moon, till he finds his way back.'

'And?'

'Go and check my room. Geller's not there.'

'Great, so you've hidden Geller to prove that I'm wrong?'

This time Seren scowled. 'I'm not lying if that's what you mean.'

'I'm not suggesting you are, but you *are* mistaken. This woman isn't real.'

'Yes she is and I can describe her. She looks just like Aunty Emily.'

'Aunty Emily?'

'Yes, but I'm not going to tell you what else she said because you won't believe me.' She stood up, almost toppling the chair, and stormed from the kitchen.

John sat down, cradling his sore head in his hands, and listened to her feet thunder up the stairs. Moments later a door slammed shut.

Aunty Emily, eh?

He took his mobile from his jeans pocket and scrolled through his contacts till he found Emily. His half-sister.

It made total sense. Why hadn't *he* thought of it?

He pressed dial and squeezed his eyes shut against the sunlight that was pouring in through the window, trying to burn his retinas out. The phone rang eight times.

'John?'

'Em.'

'Hey, how you doing, bro?'

'Good. You?'

'Walking to work.'

'Ah. Listen, I was wondering if you'll be about in the next few weeks?'

'About where?'

'Peterlee.'

'Of course, I live here, stoopid.' She laughed; a sound that had been too long absent from his life, John realised.

'Great. How would you like to come and visit your favourite big brother?'

'Holy shit. Are you up north?'

'Certainly am.'

'Why didn't you tell me, knobhead?'

'I just did.'

'Where are you?'

'Staying at my mam's for a few weeks. Fancy coming round? Seren would love to see you. As would I.'

'At your mam's house?'

'Yeah. She and Norman are off cruising the Med.'

'But...wouldn't she mind me coming round?'

'She wouldn't know.'

'Hmmm. I'm not so sure. Maybe we could meet in the town centre for coffee instead?'

'The thing is, I was wondering if you'd like to stay over for a night or two. Maybe longer. I think Seren could really do with some female company at the moment.'

'But, your mam...'

'Don't worry about it. If it makes you feel better I'll talk to her when she gets back, just so we're not sneaking about behind her back. Old Jude isn't too unreasonable you know. She doesn't speak to Dad anymore, but she knows you're not to blame for what happened.'

'But Chris and Nick…'

'Are arseholes. What can I say? My mam's not the same as them.'

'Well…' Emily was quiet for a few moments, deliberating, and John could hear the noise of traffic zipping about in the background. 'Alright. But only if you're *absolutely* sure.'

'I absolutely am.'

She shrieked, a piercing shrillness that bored a hole through his skull and brain. 'I can't wait to see you both!'

John held the phone away from his ear, grimacing. 'Great. When are you coming?'

'After work? Four-ish?'

'Perfect.'

'Oh, which Barbie doesn't Seren have?'

'All of them.'

'Seriously?'

'She hates Barbie.'

'Since when?'

'Can't remember.'

'Why's that?'

'She's going through a phase. A long one.'

'Well what can I fetch?'

'You don't have to fetch anything.'

'I know, but I want to.'

'Anything dinosaur related, I guess. That's what she's into at the moment. Which is what I'm saying, she needs her Aunty Emily to bring out her feminine side a bit.'

'Hey shut up, doofus, there's nothing wrong with dinosaurs. They're as much for girls as they are for boys. Dolls suck. They're for *girls*.'

'Oh great, you sound just like her.'

They both laughed.

When John hung up he felt uplifted. Emily coming to stay was exactly what he and Seren needed. Seren could do with someone other than him to hang out with for a while, and he would certainly appreciate the adult company. Having Emily around might also save his vulnerable, sorry arse from any further advances made by Pamela Tanner, which could only be a good thing.

By the time he went to the bathroom to get showered, his wine-head had begun to dissipate. Another cup of tea, a couple of paracetamols and a reconciliatory chat with Seren had done the trick. But now, having kicked off his jeans, he stood in the middle of the bathroom staring down at his white Calvin Klein's suddenly too afraid to move. Too afraid to take them off. Because what if…? Supposing that…?

It was too dreadful a thought to think.

Oh God.

Closing his eyes, he peeled the stretchy fabric of the boxer shorts down past his hips and let them slip to the floor. Taking a deep breath through gritted teeth he stood there naked for what seemed like an age.

Please, please don't let it be so.

Please no.

God, no.

Just. No.

He opened his eyes and counted *one, two, three* then looked down.

Relief made his knees feel soft and all the air his lungs had withheld until that point came out of his mouth in a long rush. There were no incriminating marks on or around his dick to suggest that Pamela Tanner had been anywhere near it.

Amen!

He stepped into the hot shower, instantly embraced by steam. Even though the smudge of Pamela Tanner's lipstick was already gone from his mouth, he scrubbed at his lips till they prickled. Then he washed them some more. By the time he was done his already-full lips were swollen and sore, but he felt better. He stood under the shower-head for around fifteen minutes, lathering his body and letting the hot jets massage his scalp, hoping the soap and water might cleanse his conscience of all that might have happened the night before. When his fingers were as crinkled as raisins and his skin the colour of a skinned rabbit, he turned the shower off, dragged the curtain open and reached for a towel. He stopped mid-stretch when something caught his attention beyond the swirling veils of steam that shrouded the room.

A single word written on the mirror above the basin.

Its capitalised letters had become obscure as watery courses trailed down from each one, but the message was still readable and somewhat terrifying in its abruptness:

REMEMBER

15

Doctor Chatterjee had upped Sissy Dawson's medication. She found herself drifting between sleep and consciousness, not quite sure which was worse because the ghosts were there no matter what. In difficult dreams or painful reality, they congregated all around her and in her head. Eleanor. Elizabeth. William. Polly. Even the three babies who hadn't been named. Then there were all of the other little ones. An army of ageing, decaying ghouls there to torment her. And what was worse was that they hadn't come alone. *She* was close by.

Sissy could feel the familiar dark probing of her brain, a parasitic depravity too strong to fend off. Inside, her skin prickled with a chickenwire tangle of fever, scratching and poking sensitive nerve-endings like the onset of influenza. Her bones ached, a deep glacial chill that had burrowed into the marrow. She imagined a slight knock or change in temperature would shatter her baby-bird-skeleton, the fragments of which would then disintegrate and be absorbed into her bloodstream making her nothing more than a bag of offal with white hair.

All those years, when she believed she'd managed to evade evil, she'd been deluded, Sissy realised. A naivety that had brought respite, if that's what it could be called, but no sense of peace itself because She had never been too far away. Not truly. Faint and only just on the cusp of contact, but always there. Sissy acknowledged this now, with an understanding that that's why she could sense the corruption all around her at Eden Vale. Because She thrived on the wickedness of people and the carnal activities in which they partook. She had been using Sissy as a receiver to pick up signals of human badness, tuning in to see what smut She could find amongst the sordid frequencies of the morally debased. And boy were there plenty. Extreme examples of the deadly sins were Her channels of choice, lust being Her favourite because She revelled in sexual deviancy. And so it was that, tainted by association, Sissy's soul was bitumen-black.

It was this corrupt newsfeed, Sissy realised, that had kept Her ticking over. She knew Eden Vale's staff's dirtiest most dishonourable secrets, and somehow they kept Her alive. Even at Her weakest She had always been stronger than Sissy, but Her newfound strength was increasing at such an alarming rate that Sissy instinctively knew that something had changed. Something significant. But what? What was the source of this momentous new energy? And why was it happening now after so many years had passed?

The questions were met with no identifiable answers and Sissy quaked in her skin, willing her bones to crumble. She could feel the days of insanity coming back to her like a dutiful dog to its master. Panic swelled in her chest.

Please God, not again. Please show mercy on my demented soul.

But her request went unanswered. There was no mercy to be given today, just as there wasn't the day before or the one before that. The dead children all around the bed continued to regard her with soulless-black eyes that were absent of childhood and they continued to chant through mouths that were filled with adult teeth. Sissy couldn't make out what they were saying, their diatribe one continuous chain of words strung together, filling her head like dead leaves on a dead summer wind. She clamped her withered hands over her ears and began to sob.

'No more, no more. Please, no more.'

But on they went: *'The darkness...Cold...Here, we all are...She is...You...Awake...You must...Must not...We need...End of...End it...End us...Now... Before the...Stirring.'*

Tears seeped from beneath Sissy's scrunched eyelids. She clamped her palms together as if in prayer and screamed words of her own inside her head... *Onward, Christian soldiers, marching as to war, with the cross of Jesus la la la la la...* But the ghosts' chorus of nonsensical words made for a grim lullaby that couldn't be escaped or ignored. On and on and on it went: *'Tireless...In   the darkness...Feeding...Taking...Using...She is...She will be...You cannot...You must...Die...Soon...We shall.'*

Rolling onto her side, no longer caring about the pain that wracked her swollen joints, Sissy propped herself onto her elbow and shooed at the ghosts with lunatic grunts. If she could just get down onto the floor then she might be able to slither away from their verbal onslaught. Escape their incessant babble. But her thin arm could barely withstand the weight of her own flimsy body, it shuddered and buckled, threatening to collapse her back down onto the mattress. Worried she might fail her mission before she'd really tried, she heaved sideways and flung herself from the bed. Moss green carpet rose up and hit her face with a dull wallop, threatening concussion and promising a black eye. The cheap nylon also grazed the skin off her cheekbone with an undulating sting that wasn't nearly enough to distract her from the snapping sound her wrist made. Squawking in shock, she tried to gain leverage on the carpet using the clawed hand at the end of the severed bone to drag herself forward. The pain hadn't yet fully registered, and her feet were caught up in the sheets so she hung from the bed at an awkward angle. Kicking and struggling, she made shrill noises. The spectres looked on, gathering close to her heaped body. And their babbling took on a different tone, one of excitement. Or urgency, perhaps. The sheet that was tangled around Sissy's feet pulled even tighter as she battled with it, snaring her, holding her fast, and her sense of panic heightened because pain began to emanate from her broken wrist in fierce waves that suddenly made everything flash in intermittent shades of red. Cold sweat stabbed at her forehead. The intensity of the pain was enough to increase her efforts. She twisted, kicked and convulsed, shouted, screamed and swore, until eventually the sheet inched loose from where it was tucked beneath the mattress, becoming slack enough to release its hold. Sissy's legs clattered to the ground, her hip taking the brunt of the fall. Brittle bone fractured upon impact and immediately a new hurt, even worse than that from her wrist, blazed through her body. The internal inferno created a backdraft which reached all the way up to her shoulders. This time Sissy screamed and screamed till her throat was red raw. She didn't see that the ghosts trembled at the sound. And she was too preoccupied to notice when they diminished altogether.

16

As promised Emily arrived just after four. Her boyfriend dropped her off at the gate in his souped-up electric blue Citroën C2. John went outside to introduce himself, to see who his little sister was involved with and to determine any disapproval he might have on the matter. But as soon as he stepped onto the pavement Emily, still in her green and black Asda uniform, squealed excitedly and rushed at him. She threw her arms around his torso and squeezed tight. Her hair smelled faintly of the bakery and she seemed to have grown an inch or two taller. John returned her hug almost as forcefully.

'You've lost weight since last year,' she said, dropping her arms and stepping back. She looked him up and down with eyes that were the same blue and equally as judgmental as his own.

John raised his eyebrows, feigning surprise, but really her observation was no revelation. His thirty-four inch Levis were cinched by a leather belt that was on the fifth and final hole to keep them from falling down. He remembered a time they'd been too tight. 'You think?'

'Definitely. You need to get some pies down your neck, matey.'

'Alright, Mam. Did you fetch any?'

'No, but I will tomorrow. And jammy doughnuts.' She poked him in the belly. 'I've seen more meat on a whippet.'

Apart from being a little bit taller, Emily looked no different to the last time John had seen her. Fresh-faced and willowy with long dark hair that hung in glossy, texturised strands as though she'd been swimming in the sea and had let the waves and salt dry naturally in it.

Unlike John she had a tirelessly sunny disposition and an unfailing energy that would be well suited to working with children. Her infectious smile made him feel instantly happier.

'That's Cam by the way,' she said, pointing to a broad youth who'd stepped from the Citroën.

At the mention of his name Cam came over to shake John's hand. 'Alright, mate? You must be the big brother she keeps harping on about.'

John smiled, the corners of his eyes crinkling. 'Aye, must be.'

'Cameron Goodale.'

'Good ale? Nice one.'

Cam was slightly taller than John. He had shaggy fair hair that was more strawberry than yellow blonde and warm brown eyes that weren't afraid to maintain contact. His smile was sincere, and John thought he might well forgive him the ridiculous car because he'd had the decency to step out and introduce himself properly. That said a lot about a man. At least, to John it did.

Emily set about heaving a large holdall from the boot of the car, making John wonder if she was planning to stay the entire month. Cam hurried round and helped her to the gate with it, scoring himself extra brownie points. When they wrapped their arms around each other and kissed goodbye John turned away, faking interest in the neighbour's garden till they were done. Cam then got back in the car and did a U-turn. As he drove out of the street the Citroën's exhaust created a low, bassy growl that made John's internal organs hum. 'Seems like a canny lad, not sure about the car though. Here, give me that.' He reached down and took the holdall. 'So, how are you?'

'Fifty shades of awesome.'

'Good for you.'

'And you?' Again her blue eyes were scrutinising him

closely.

'Seven shades of, er, you know what.'

'Shit?'

'Hopefully not now you're here.' He put his arm across her shoulders and squeezed her to him. 'Anyway, Seren's dying to see you, let's get inside.'

John left the girls in the kitchen and took Emily's holdall upstairs, having already assigned her the futon in his mother's sewing room. As he climbed the stairs Seren's inane chattering and Emily's enthusiastic responses to whatever she was saying filled the house with a sound that reminded him of childhood. Of weekend mornings and family togetherness, when the house had been full and busy, lively with the sound of kids larking about and his mother vacuuming and pottering about the place. His dad complaining that he couldn't hear the television over the racket, but nobody taking any notice because it didn't matter anyway, it was only football replays. The smell of home-baked bread wafting from the kitchen and the promise of summer both comforting and enchanting. Back then there had been no responsibilities except for staying in touch with friends and the odd round of washing up. No worries either, apart from who could pull the best wheelie and whether the blonde girl who lived above the corner shop was going out with anyone. John hoped Seren might look back at her own childhood someday with the same sense of cosy nostalgia. From now on he had to help make lots of happy memories with her.

He opened the door to the sewing room and a loud bang startled him. Dropping the holdall, he turned. It sounded like something heavy had fallen over in Seren's room.

'Everything alright up there?' Emily called up the stairs.

Crossing the landing, John opened the door to his

daughter's bedroom. 'Yeah, fine,' he replied, scanning the room. There was nothing noticeably out of place in the predominantly lilac space. No fallen wardrobe or collapsed set of drawers. No misplaced ornaments or broken curtain rail. No faulty fixtures or fittings of any kind. Just the usual calm of an empty room.

Unsure why he thought of it, he looked up and expected to see that the ceiling was mouldy. It wasn't. But the cord tassels on the ceiling light were moving, invisible fingers teasing them in a clockwise circular direction. John presumed he'd caused a draught when he opened the door, but then the shade itself began to move. Backwards and forwards. Backwards and forwards. Swinging like a pendulum in a widening arc, continuing to build momentum as though someone was pushing it. Eventually the plastic cable it was suspended from began to buckle erratically, making the sateen dome structure crash against the ceiling. John stood watching, mouth agape, transfixed by the spectacle and hoping Emily and Seren didn't come upstairs to see what was going on, because he had no way of explaining.

The air around him felt supercharged. It touched his bare arms with a thickness like the static build-up on the surface of a CRT television screen and it caressed his neck with the weighty promise of any decent lover's breath. He rubbed at his skin, feeling increasingly paranoid that there was something else in the room. Something unseen that was toying with him and had enough substance to move the light shade. Something sentient. Something he didn't want touching him.

A harrowing moan drew his attention to the landing, making his innards flinch and his hair follicles react defensively.

Otis was standing at the top of the stairs. His wiry body was visibly shaking and his front legs were set in a combative stance. He didn't seem to notice John and was, instead, glaring beyond him into the bedroom, his eyes wide and snout curled into a toothy snarl. When he issued another strangulated growl to the empty room, John bent down and extended his hand. 'Hey, boy, you feel it too?'

And then everything fell flat.

The sound of his voice had broken through the tension, the atmosphere neutralising all around him as though the charge had been earthed by his words, thus banishing the unwanted, probing energy back to the circuitry aether from where it had come.

Otis whimpered and cowered low, his tail so far between his legs that it ran along the length of his underside. John tried to coax him with his hand again but the dog turned and fled down the stairs. For a long moment John was too afraid to move and listened till the sound of Otis's frightened paws had retreated to the kitchen. When he finally summoned courage enough to turn around John saw that the ceiling light in the bedroom was completely still.

With tentative steps he went to the centre of the room and stood beneath the tasselled shade. Eyeing it suspiciously, he watched for the faintest of movements. Anything to confirm that it had been moving back and forth so violently just moments before. Anything to suggest that he wasn't delusional and losing his grip on reality.

Nothing.

Not even a slight waver of the cord tassels.

Raising his arm, he prodded the shade with his index finger and watched it move in a lazy, pendulous arc. Then he hit it again, harder this time. Still it didn't move with the same ferocity. In fact he imagined he'd need to punch the damn thing to get it to bounce off the ceiling like it had. He couldn't comprehend what had just happened. Moreover, he wasn't sure he wanted to. The electric-crackle of the air had been the same as that which he'd experienced when he'd found Otis hanging from the loft hatch, entrails and all, so perhaps the episodes were psychosomatic. Maybe the sensory perception of having static all around him was some sort of forewarner to a hallucinogenic interlude about to happen. The very idea terrified him. He clutched his head and squeezed his eyes shut.

It could also be stress or depression presenting itself in a whole new way, he supposed. Something upsetting the balance of hormones in his brain, something that could be controlled with the right medication. Or maybe not. What if his brain was short-circuiting with the onset of some other mental condition that was untreatable?

No, don't even think it.

But no that couldn't be true. This latest episode *must* have happened because his mother's dog had shared the experience. Otis had been visibly spooked by something too.

Because he heard the loud bang, you idiot.

John went for a lie down on his mother's bed before he felt able to rejoin Emily and Seren downstairs. He tried not to dwell on the fact that he might be going crazy and hoped not to let the possibility affect his interaction with the girls. His kid sister had come to stay, this was meant to be fun for everyone. Besides, Emily looked up to him and didn't pity him like other family members did. He didn't want either of those things to change, so he forced himself to act cheerfully for the rest of the evening. He didn't think either of them suspected anything. By the time Seren had fallen asleep on the couch, her head in Emily's lap, it wasn't yet nine o'clock.

'Here, I'll take her up.' John rose from the armchair. His little girl was lightweight in his arms, all legs and elbows. He cradled her to his chest and she didn't object. Upstairs he nudged her bedroom door open with his hip and flicked the light switch down with his elbow, stealing a wary look at the light shade. This time it wasn't the light shade which gave cause for concern; the patch of mould had returned. Right above the bed. Only now it was denser than before, sticky black like old blood seeping through the plasterboard.

'Shit.'

'Hmmm?' Seren groaned, becoming rigid in his arms. She rubbed her eyes.

'Shhh it's alright. Go back to sleep.' John backed out of the room and switched the light off. 'You'll have to sleep in Gran's room tonight.'

'No.' Seren's eyes cracked open and the whine in her voice indicated an unwillingness to cooperate.

'There's something wrong with the ceiling in your room, kidda. I'll get it sorted tomorrow, then you can have it back.' His explanation seemed to mollify her, she went limp in his arms again and by the time he settled her down into his mother's bed she was snoring gently.

He crossed the room to shut the curtains and found half a dozen dead flies on the sill. By morning he figured there may well be a dozen more. He left them where they were and found a wind-up torch in the front pocket of his travel holdall, then out on the landing he used a wooden pole to slide a set of aluminium ladders down from the loft. The bang he'd heard earlier, the swinging light shade and the ceiling mould *had* to be connected, so for the sake of his mother's spare room he had to check the loft. And for the sake of ease (and his sanity), he hoped to find that something heavy had fallen over and leaked. The alternative was a burst pipe, something he wasn't qualified or equipped to deal with.

A chill rushed down with the ladders, one that made the hairs on his arms stand up and his breath look like dry ice. He shivered and settled the rubber-stoppered feet on the carpet, then began to climb. The rungs were like sweaty ice against his left hand, the warmth from the house having created an instant layer of condensation, and he held the torch aloft in his right hand, aiming its beam upwards. Soon an unfamiliar wood-panelled sloping wall came into view and, as his upper body passed through the rectangular hatch into the intensified coldness of the loft, he saw that his mother and Norman had at some point renovated the upper space of the house. A light switch to his right suggested electrics had been installed. When he pressed it a low light from an energy-saving bulb glowed with all the ambience of a lantern. Now with handsfree illumination, John turned off the torch and pulled himself through the hatch fully.

The loft was no longer a dingy chamber of bin-linered Christmas decorations, black soot and the exoskeletons of insects caught up in ancient spider webs. Now it was a carpeted practical space with things stored neatly on metal shelving units around its circumference. A header tank was supported on one of the shelves. John immediately checked it over for leaks or damaged casing but nothing seemed awry. There was a pile of boxes stacked next to the water tank, above Seren's bedroom, but there was nothing that could be directly linked to the incriminating mess on the ceiling.

Shit.

This meant the problem wouldn't be a quick fix, it was nothing as simple as a superficial spillage. Could the problem wait till the following day though? Yes, he thought so. He'd need to source some of Norman's tools so that he could take up the carpet and floorboards to see what he was dealing with. And besides, the stuff on the ceiling wasn't indicative of a serious leak, water wasn't exactly gushing out all over the place. It could definitely wait till morning.

He went back downstairs to warm up, the loft's cold having seeped into his epidermis to become one with him. Emily poured him a generous measure of Southern Comfort, which warmed his insides, and they chatted for another couple of hours before both declaring it bedtime. By that point John felt relatively relaxed, now convinced that it was a pipe in the loft that was leaking fluids and not his brain.

Upstairs he checked on Seren. She was lying in the same position he'd left her, Geller noticeably missing from her arms. He wondered where she might have hidden him and how long it would be till she got bored of the whole charade. The sound of the toilet flushing downstairs filled the house with ordinary familiarity, and a few moments later he bumped into Emily on the landing.

'What time should I be up in the morning?' she asked, barefooted in shorty pyjamas. Her dark hair was plaited long and thick down her back. She looked more girl than woman without any makeup on.

'Seren will let you know when's good for her, I'm sure,' John said, smiling. 'Otherwise, whenever you like.'

Her cheeks dimpled when she smiled back, her full-lipped mouth very similar to John's. 'Okay. Night night then.'

'Night night. Oh and, hey, I know you have work and Cam and probably loads of other stuff going on, but feel free to stay with us as long as you like. It's nice having you around. Seren thinks you're the bee's knees.'

Emily considered this for a moment and nodded. 'Thanks, I'd love to hang around with you guys for a while.' She clicked open the door to the sewing room and, before disappearing inside, said, 'Oh and I *am* the bee's knees.'

John stuck his tongue out then went to his old room. He'd considered sleeping on the couch but decided it was more of a proactive approach to sleep in the room below the suspected leak, in case the leak got considerably worse during the night and he could at least try to prevent a flood. He didn't bother switching on the light, telling himself there was no need. He stripped his clothes off and left them in a heap on the floor, then climbed into bed.

Lying on his back he looked around at the walls and ceiling, recalling certain details like the way the streetlights presented a rectangular strip above the curtain rail and how the crack in the coving above the door looked like the letter Y. The dark patch of mould above him wasn't familiar though, and he hated the way the light shade was watching him. He turned over onto his stomach and buried his face between two pillows. Stretching out, he slid his arms beneath each one. His right hand touched something cold and flat. He gripped it between his fingers and held it up to the street-lit glow of the window.

Queen of Spades.

How the hell did that get there?

Swiping the playing card to the floor he flopped back down onto the pillows, scrunching his eyes shut in frustration. With all that had been going on he'd managed to put Pamela Tanner to the back of his mind, yet now here she was right at the forefront again, as though she was still playing games with him. And suddenly he couldn't rebuff the strong thought of her mouth on his. Red. Hot. Wanting. Her tongue touching his. Teeth teasing his lips. No empty promises. He felt vulnerable and feverish, his mind not his own.

He saw black clouds seducing a wedding day sky.

Smother me with everything you have.

And Argus butterfly wings bound with titanium spider thread.

Till there's no way out.

Then storm waves conquering a castaway's beach.

Because I'd like you to destroy me.
Because you can.

The window was open but the room was sealed within a stifling vacuum that he hoped could be broken, because this crazy, wanton urgency to do things that might or might not disgust him was confounding, yet the intrigue that motivated it unstoppable. His face flashed hot and the excess heat spread rapidly down his body. To his neck, arms, chest and belly. Pamela Tanner's hands touching him all over. Wanting. Needing. Knowing. Right down to his groin. Where he was overcome by such a ferocious desire he felt aroused and horrified all at the same time.

Turning onto his back he reacquainted himself with the stain on the ceiling, until staring at it for too long made it look like the spade symbol.

No escape.

Pamela Tanner was inside his head and under his skin and all over his body.

He focussed on the ceiling light instead and thought about untacking carpets and lifting floorboards and repairing broken pipes. He thought about making sandwiches to take to the dene and cutting across the beach and picking out the right path and walking under trees' canopies and passing beneath the grand arches of the viaduct and arriving at the cundy. Only, once he got there he was at one end of the tunnel, Seren the other and Pamela Tanner was somewhere in the middle, waiting for him in the thick, endless black.

Sleep wasn't easy for John that night, but it did eventually come.

17

John slid the hot baking tray onto the middle shelf, looked at his wristwatch and set the oven's timer for forty-five minutes. He slung the checked tea towel over his shoulder and called, 'Coming, ready or not.'

Tiptoeing into the hallway, he listened. There were no creaking floorboards or door hinges. No creeping footsteps or muffled laughter. When a thorough search of each downstairs room and cupboard proved fruitless he went upstairs, checking first the sewing room. Emily's large holdall was lying on the floor, items of her worn clothing and underwear scattered about the carpet next to it. The spare duvet he'd found in his mother's airing cupboard was a messy heap on top of the futon. A perfect hiding place. He lifted it.

Seren wasn't there.

Next he went to his mother's room. 'I'm closing in on you, kidda.' His voice broke the brooding presence of the house which buzzed in his ears; a susurration of expectancy. He looked under the bed. She wasn't there. Inside the mirror-fronted wardrobe. Not there either. Creeping back out onto the landing he went to the final room, the room with the mould, the room of his childhood, and put his hand on the doorknob.

'I wonder where she can be.' He grinned, expecting to hear a stifled giggle.

None came.

He opened the door and was confronted by a brashness of black, grey and red. Barcoded wallpaper wrapped the room on all sides, an attack on the senses, and bedding on two single beds, as black and degenerate as the Devil's moustache, smelt of teenaged boys. His brother's red Tamiya Hotshot was sitting in the middle of the room, facing him. He remembered it well because he'd got one of the biggest poundings of his life for having broken it, back in the nineties. He'd taken it without permission and accidentally smashed it head-on into Stuey Griggs' Clod Buster. Stuey's monster truck had survived the collision but the shiny plastic casing of Nick's Hotshot had splintered and the front wheel alignment had been damaged beyond repair. Yet now here it was, good as new, purring beautifully as though talking to him on some animistic level.

What the fuck is wrong with me?

John gripped the door to steady himself and looked up. In place of the tasselled light shade there was a rectangular hole in the ceiling. A black opening into the nefarious oblivion of the loft, which had no business being in this room. The hole was wrong in its simplistic nature, it was too deliberate and square to be an accident. From this angle it was impossible for him to tell what horrors were living up there, or indeed what might come down to stay.

But that's okay because none of this is even happening.

He rubbed his temple, not taking his eyes off the hole for a second in case it should change or disappear or swallow him whole.

Just another episode. It'll pass.

The sound of scurrying overhead denoted small feet on wooden joists.

'Seren?'

A short burst of excited laughter announced she was still playing hide and seek.

'What the hell are you doing up there?' he demanded.

She didn't answer.

Clambering onto the bed, concern overruling any hesitancy he might have felt, John put his hands through the hole in the ceiling and gripped wooden boards at either side for leverage, managing to resist an almost insurmountable urge to pull away when grit and cobwebs settled around his fingers. He took a deep breath, bent his knees and sprung off the mattress, hoisting himself upwards. Old dust caught at the back of his throat, a layer of dry staleness that made him cough. Darkness greeted him wholly as he settled onto his hands and knees on unseen joists. All around him was a blackness that seemed to have substance, like the insidious dark inside the cundy. A blackness he thought might consume him if he stayed still for too long.

'Seren?' His voice came out an urgent whisper. He hoped it wasn't loud enough to make grim things in the dark stir. He held his breath and listened. Nothing stirred. His eyes tried to adjust, desperately wanting to see, and after a while he thought he could make out the blacker silhouettes of rafters above him. Then he decided he was probably wrong and that his brain was playing tricks as it was wont to do of late.

Then a light flickered on.

He blinked rapidly against its abruptness. A small orange flame that tinged everything round about with insipid colour and texture blinded and disorientated him all over again. Seren was crouched in the corner furthest away from him, her face a sullen mask of shadows above the large burning candle she held in her hands.

'What are you doing?' he asked, afraid to move away from the hole in the ceiling in case he got lost in the dark, dusty chamber that shouldn't even be there. The toe of his right shoe was hooked below the ledge, anchoring him to the ceiling of the black and grey striped bedroom below.

Seren didn't answer.

'Come on, kidda, let's go,' he urged, rubbing his face where silvery spider trails, imagined or not, tickled.

She made no attempt to move and held firm to the candle even though hot wax ran down the backs of her fingers.

'Our fairy cakes are almost ready.' He held out his hand to her. 'Come on, let's decorate them together.'

Her face tilted downwards so the flame chased away some of its shadows, and John saw her handicap: she wasn't wearing glasses. Groaning at the prospect of what he must do, he brought his right foot fully into the darkness and began to shuffle along the two parallel joists towards her. 'Stay there, sweetheart. I'm coming for you.'

'No. I have to stay here now.' Her voice was eerily monotone, almost as expressionless as her face.

'Stop playing games, it's not funny.'

'It's not supposed to be. I belong to *Her* now.'

John stopped crawling. It felt like an intrusion of insects was scattering beneath his skin, as though a stone in his mind had been disturbed, thus revealing their hiding place. He shivered. 'Who?'

'You know.'

'I don't.' He started inching forward again, his arms leaden, knees hurting and the wood rough against his hands.

'You should.'

'Pack it in, Seren, this really isn't...*aaargh!*' As John put his hand down something spiky pierced his skin and drove straight through the meaty flesh of his palm. For a moment he couldn't move. The sensation of metal scraping against his bone rendered him paralysed. Then adrenalin kicked in and he slowly, quickly, agonisingly prised his hand away from the protruding prong in the joist. Hotness welled in his eyes and white flashes of pain blotted out the dark. Losing his balance he fell sideways, clutching his wounded hand to his chest. Blood poured freely, coating him with sticky warmth and dripping into darkness, feeding unseen monsters. He thought he might crash through plasterboard and into the bedroom below, but thin wooden slats supported him as he landed on his side in the groove between the two joists. He sucked in air through clenched teeth and looked up.

Seren was still hunkered in the corner. She made no attempt to go to him and he watched in terror as she brought the candle up to her face and puckered her lips.

'No, Seren. *Don't.'*

She blew.

The candle's flame went out and John was surrendered again to a darkness that touched his soul with all the horror of loneliness. At almost the same time cold breath swiped his cheek in hoary swirls of rancid decay, and, as he retched at the smell, wet corpse lips brushed the outer rim of his ear. He thought he might die. Curling up tightly he willed the plasterboard beneath him to give out, wanting to see the noisy walls of the bedroom below because, even though they were wrong, he could deal with them better than he could deal with this. But the boards remained intact. He couldn't imagine that he'd ever make it back to the hole, not without the halitosis of death breathing on him again. And he didn't dare move in case witches' fingers snagged his hair and clothes to pull him even further into their domain. This time, because of the noise he'd created and the excitement he'd caused, monsters had definitely stirred. He could feel the presence of evil just as surely as he could feel his own heart exerting itself, offering his blood up freely to the unknown. Clenching his eyes shut, preferring the darkness inside his own head to the darkness surrounding him, he waited and listened. Not daring to move. Not even to swallow.

When nothing had breathed on him or touched him for a long while, finally he unfurled and opened his eyes.

'Seren?'

But she wasn't there. He could sense that now. Perhaps she never had been. He was all alone, with the scritchy-scratchy darkness that teased him with its swelling magnitude and threatened him with new horrors. He reached out and grabbed the joist his shoulder was wedged against, planning to use it to feel his way back to the hole. He *had* to get out. But as his hand gripped old, dry wood a crackle like that of a Geiger counter erupted, an animalistic growl that made his body shrink back and his skin bristle painfully. The throaty sound came from everywhere and nowhere, swooping down from somewhere amongst the rafters perhaps and bringing with it a strong smell of rot and decay. John found he could no longer breathe and was beyond all comprehension when a sickly, decrepit, old-woman voice croaked into his ear: 'She's mine.'

...

John awoke with a start, sweaty and disorientated and struggling with the duvet. Bland dawn soaked through the thin fabric of the curtains and he heard a gull *ha-ha*-ing outside. Holding his right hand up, he was relieved to see no blood. And the ceiling was a full stretch of white artex. Closing his eyes, he rolled onto his side and sighed.

He lay still for a while, contemplating whether to attempt more sleep or just get up. Then jolted upright, his stomach knotting.

The ceiling!

It wasn't right. It mocked him with too much unspoilt whiteness. And the walls. Vertical stripes imprisoned him on all sides.

Not again. Please not again.

He scrabbled from the bed and stood on shaky legs,

unsure what to do. Then came two short raps on the door. An uneasy silence followed. He hardly dared move. Maybe if he ignored…

Tap, tap, tap.

'Who is it?' His voice came out high and he hated that it betrayed him, hated the rising fear that crept up his throat like sour bile. He swallowed and waited for a response, then watched as the handle turned. The door nudged open slowly, stiffly, deliberately, prolonging his suspense. And the hinges creaked menacingly, as if in collaboration with whatever lay beyond. He felt sick with dread. What new terror was this?

Pamela Tanner.

She was standing outside his room, a large cardboard box held in her arms. 'Hey handsome,' she said, 'special delivery for you.'

John edged backwards, no less worried.

'What's the matter?' Her voice was golden syrup and her green eyes shone dark and luxuriant, an unnatural colour that shouldn't exist in the daybreak's lazy light. 'This is better than first class service, don't you want to see what I brought you?'

He shook his head.

She laughed and stepped forward, her tanned, bare feet exotic on the room's grey carpet. She was wearing the same tight black dress as before, but her black hair was now lacquered into a bouffant with a tiny golden crown resting on top.

'Take it,' she insisted.

When John made no attempt to comply, she came forward and thrust the box to his bare chest, leaving him no other option.

'What is it?' The parcel was light in John's arms, but he could detect slight movement inside.

'A surprise.'

'I don't like surprises.'

'You'll love this one.'

'What is it?'

'Open it, see for yourself.'

A muffled whimpering came from within. A soft, kitteny mewl. John eyed Pamela Tanner warily and laid the box on the floor. Hunkering over it he set to peeling multiple layers of parcel tape off with his nails, thinking to himself that whoever had wrapped the package hadn't intended him to have easy access, and instinctively knowing that whatever was inside needed to be set free as soon as possible. When the box's flaps were loose he flipped them open and peered inside. A bundle of white knitted blanket, aged and grey, had been thrown in like a substitute for bubble wrap or tissue paper, concealing whatever was at the bottom. John stared, not wanting to touch the tarnished wool because if it was symbolic of what lay beneath, he wasn't sure he wanted to see.

Pamela Tanner had sidled up behind him. She ran a cold hand down his bare back, prompting his flesh to prickle. 'Go on, take a look,' she urged, excitement lacing her voice.

Ignoring her hand, which had come to rest between his shoulder blades, he reached down and lifted folds of the ambiguous blanket between thumb and forefinger. He laid it on the carpet next to his feet then looked back into the box. A newborn baby, naked and pitiful, lay at the bottom on cold, uncushioned card.

'What the hell?' John spun round to face Pamela Tanner, furious and petrified at the same time. 'Whose baby is this?'

Pamela Tanner's whole demeanour was laughing. 'Why, she's yours, John.'

'No.'

'Yes. Don't you remember?'

'Remember?' *No!*

The baby's eyes blinked open and her face became

flushed with all the angsty prelude to a scream…

…

And John awoke for a second time. He sat up, exhausted. It was starting to get light and he saw that the room's decor was correct, but there was screaming. He could hear urgent screaming elsewhere in the house.

'*Seren?*'

He shot out of bed, pulled on his boxer shorts and ran to his mother's room. Seren was sitting upright in the double bed, eyes wide. A smell of something terrible greeted John at the door. Bad meat or old blood, something organic that had decayed over time. He wondered if this was really happening, or if it was round three of the crazies. Emily rushed out onto the landing and bundled into the back of him. 'What's going on?' she asked. 'And what the hell's that smell? Smells like something died in here.'

John went to the bed and sat down next to Seren. 'What's up, kidda?' He reached over and stroked her hair.

'She told me I have to leave.'

'Who did?'

'The woman.'

Emily rushed to other side of the bed. 'What woman?'

'The one who…'

'Alright, alright,' John said, holding his hands up, reluctant to let Seren draw Emily into her imaginary world. 'Why would you want to leave?'

'I don't.'

'So what are you talking about?'

'*The woman with the black hair*. She says that I have to go now.'

'Why?'

'Because the other woman is coming for me. The bad

one.'

Emily reached over and drew Seren into her arms. 'There's no bad woman coming for you, dafty.'

'How do you know?'

Pulling a mock-fierce comedy face, Emily said, 'Because she'd have to get through me and your dad first, and us Gimmericks are hard as nails.'

Seren looked less than encouraged, but managed a smile anyway.

'Look, why don't you let Aunty Emily sleep with you?' John suggested. 'The pair of you can have another couple of hours in bed.'

'Hey, I'm up for that,' Emily said, nodding. 'Early mornings are for losers.'

Seren frowned but wriggled back under the duvet.

John stood up, folding his arms over his chest. 'I'll leave you to it then, I'm gonna open some windows and find out what that bloody smell is.'

When he was at the door, Emily called to him, 'Hey, John.'

He turned and saw his sister was grinning mischievously, her head on the same pillow as Seren's. 'Yeah?'

'You'll never make a decent underwear model if you don't start getting some pies down your neck.'

'Cheeky cow.'

She laughed. 'Hey, you'd be lost without me.'

John extended his middle finger. 'Love you too.'

He left the room and was only halfway across the landing when he heard her calling for him again. Only, this time, there was an urgency to her tone that conveyed panic. He bolted back and found both girls sitting upright, looking up.

'What the *hell* is that?' Emily said without taking her eyes off the ceiling.

John followed her gaze and saw slivers of black mould

snaking across the white expanse. The furthest tips stretched as far across the ceiling as the area above the bed, as if reaching over to pluck his daughter into the dark space above them. Into a state of non-existence. He thought of Seren's candle-lit, sombre face, and how hot wax had encased her small fingers.

I belong to Her *now.*

Who?

You know.

But he didn't. He really, truly didn't.

18

That night Natasha saw her mother again. She was sitting in bed, her face made-up like it used to be in the days before she got ill: black mascara, tangerine blush and a heavy-handed approach to smoky eyes using a palette of mid- to dark-brown eyeshadow. Diane Graham was back to being a fashionista of the early nineties, the way Natasha liked to remember her. Her hair was dark and shiny, styled into a sleek bob, and she wore a floral silk blouse, its cerise lilies matching her lipstick with the chic coordination Natasha had actually grown to miss. From the waist down she was covered by over-starched white bedsheets, which otherwise ruined the image of normality and made Natasha wish they could have met in a park or at the beach. Out shopping or in a bar. Anywhere but here.

'Tash!' Diane leaned forward in anticipation. 'Are you alone?'

'Mmm hmmm.' Natasha tipped her head once, afraid to move or say too much. She didn't want to react too brashly in case she tipped the balance and awoke the imposter who lived inside her mother's head. The fraudster who had little idea of who Diane Graham was supposed to be, let alone Natasha.

'You're absolutely sure there's no one else?' Her mother's eyes narrowed with suspicion.

Natasha glanced over her shoulder at the closed door behind to substantiate her answer. 'Yes, Mam, there's just me. See?'

'Well don't dilly dally about over there.' Diane Graham's voice was a low hiss and she beckoned to Natasha with a hand richly decorated with yellow gold.

'Come here. Quick. I've got something to show you.'

'Something to show me?' The curious glint of mischief in her mother's eyes wasn't suggestive of the masquerading illness, so intrigue got the better of her. Natasha rushed over to the bedside, butterflies in her stomach. 'What sort of thing?'

Diane Graham scanned the room, as if expecting someone might yet be hiding behind the armchair or television stand or under the wardrobe. She lowered her voice even further and whispered, 'I've got to get out of here. I've got to leave. *Now.*'

'Why?' Natasha found herself matching her mother's tone so that she was whispering too. 'What's going on?'

'Look.' Her mother cast aside the bed sheet and brought into view a blanketed bundle.

Natasha's heart stammered and her mouth fell open. 'Is that a…?'

'Yes.' Within the crocheted blanket, Diane revealed a sleeping baby whose cheeks were pink and chubby. 'Precious, isn't she?'

Beyond the capability of coherent speech, Natasha simply stared at the newborn and nodded.

'You've got to help me get her out of here,' her mother said, flinging the sheets fully away from her legs, showing that she was all set to make her great escape in black leggings and leather ankle boots. 'You go ahead of me and tell me if the coast's clear. Once we get outside we run like we stole something, okay?'

Natasha, still transfixed by the baby, said, 'But, is that…I mean, is she…?'

'Yes. Yes she is. And I'll take good care of her, I promise. Now go.'

'But, why can't *I* have her?' Natasha's eyes had brimmed with tears.

'Oh sweetheart, you know why.'

'But…'

'I'll keep her safe, till you're ready.'

'I *am* ready.'

'No. No you're not. You've still got plenty of living left to do.'

'But I don't want...' The floorboards beneath them began to reverberate as though the building itself had developed a strong pulse. *Bah-dum, bah-dum, bah-dum.* The vase of pink carnations on the dresser rattled, the chipboard wardrobe vocalised its bareness with metal coat-hangers that clanked together and the fly at the window began a frantic new campaign to escape. Natasha gulped, her body rigid. 'What's that?'

'Oh no. No, no, no.' Diane's face paled and she scrabbled from the bed. 'We're too late. She's arrived. She's *here!*'

'Who is?'

Diane gripped the baby closer, covering the little one's head with trembling hands. Fear paralysed Natasha, she looked to the door as the booming grew louder, quicker, closer. *Bah-dum, bah-dum, bah-dum.* Up the stairs and across the landing. *Bah-dum, bah-dum, bah-dum.* Along the corridor. *Bah-dum, bah-dum, bah-dum.* Till whoever it was was right outside their door. *BAH-DUM.*

A terrible silence enveloped Natasha, Diane and the baby, a sickening prelude to something even more terrible that was about to happen. Natasha could feel the threat of whatever corruption lay beyond the unassuming hardboard veneer of the door, and it made her nerves jangle with dread. Even the fly at the window had ceased its busy-ness, finding a crevice in the sill in which to hide itself. The silence seemed to stretch on and on and, just when Natasha thought her nerves couldn't withstand much more, the baby whimpered. It was a soft sound but enough to shatter the uneasy quiet and prompt the door to burst inwards. The metal handle slammed against the partition wall, gouging wallpaper and puncturing plasterboard, and the whole room shook. Natasha reeled backwards.

Sweet Jesus Almighty.

Filling the doorway, preventing their escape, was a stout white-uniformed nurse who held a syringe aloft in latex-gloved fingers. But it wasn't the sight of the needle that made Natasha's guts feel liquefied, it was the nurse's face. *Oh dear God, her face.* Baby-smooth flesh covered a hairless head, upon which sat a nurse's hat, then translucent white skin, riddled with thick blue veins, puckered around a featureless face till it gave way to a hole where a nose should be. And this blowhole dilated with each intake of air then contracted with a loud snort.

'Mam?' Natasha's voice was small and weak in the aftermath of the violent outburst, and she appealed to her mother without taking her eyes off the thing at the door.

Diane was the first to move, she rushed around the bed and cried, 'The window, Tash. *Quick!*'

Natasha made to follow, but the nurse charged across the room and slammed her in the chest with a blow hard enough to break bones and cause internal bleeding. Natasha's feet left the ground and she flew backwards, wondering if she might spit out her lungs. She landed on the bed, the force of impact ramming it against the wall and bucking her back up into the air. Then she lay on her back, choking and struggling for air.

Get up or wake up. GET UP OR WAKE UP!

'Mrs Graham, give me the baby at once!' The nurse's blowhole flared like a large nostril as she spoke to Diane, her voice loaded with as much resonance as train brakes, metal screeching against metal. Natasha thought her eardrums might explode. Or even her entire head. She clamped her hands over her ears and wailed for the noise to stop.

'Never. *Never!*' Diane screamed back, her own voice

banshee-like. 'Here, Tash. Take her. Run!'

Stoked with adrenalin and a ferocious need to hold the baby, Natasha staggered to her feet, coughing and gasping and swallowing back the taste of blood, but when she tried to run she found that her boots were stuck to the carpet.

No!

Looking down she saw hordes of black tentacles reaching up from the floor, oozing tarry gunk all over the beige pile and wrapping themselves around her ankles. She tried to kick them away, along with her boots, but the carpet-borne appendages climbed higher and higher. They moved up round her calves and thighs then circled her hips, licking the bare skin beneath her shirt with the cold wetness of amphibian tongues. Natasha screamed and clutched the edge of the mattress, then tried to use the bed's weight to pull herself free. But it was no use, she was tethered to the spot, forced to watch as the faceless nurse tackled her mother to the ground, the baby crushed somewhere between them.

'No, get off! Leave them alone!' she cried, banging her fists on the bed.

Her mother fought and struggled beneath the nurse's bulk, but the nurse was quicker and stronger and easily thrust the syringe's needle into her neck. As soon as the milky white fluid had been injected, Diane looked at Natasha with defeated, dying eyes. 'I'm sorry, pet. You'll have to do it on your own now.'

'Do *what* on my own?'

'Get the baby out. Free her.'

'But how?' For a moment the slithering manacles eased on Natasha's legs, as if they'd detected a deadlock situation, but when Diane failed to respond and Natasha lurched forward to go to her, they gripped hard again, toppling her to the floor. Dazed and angry, scared and confused, Natasha kicked and writhed. But with every strain of resistance, her captors pulled tighter and tighter, cutting off the blood supply to her legs and making her feet numb.

The nurse rose to her feet, and despite her lack of eyes seemed to regard Natasha with a sneer. Then the black hole in her face became a terrifying split, from side to side, a horrific yawn which revealed sharks' teeth on a mandible that surely wasn't physically possible. She produced a croaking sound from the void in her face and snapped her jaws together in a display of victory, then looked down at the baby.

'No. Don't. Please don't,' Natasha sobbed. She tried to crawl forwards but her hands slipped in black slime and she ended up sprawled on her belly. Her arms were then held down by the snaking tentacles. 'Not again,' she begged. 'Please don't take her away from me!'

But the nurse stooped down, the blowhole in her face widening further, and Natasha watched helplessly as she swallowed the baby whole.

19

John felt as though he'd been up for several hours already. Really it was only two. After he'd left Seren and Emily in his mother's room, following the drama of the spreading mould, he'd got dressed, made breakfast, drunk two cups of black coffee, walked the dogs and had a root about in Norman's toolshed. Now, at eight a.m., armed with a toolbox full of equipment, he was sliding the loft ladders down and psyching himself up to deal with the problematic uppermost region of the house, where the strange damp seemed to be originating and the focus of last night's nightmare had been. The memory of the cackling in his ear and the leech-like lips brushing against his skin was enough to send shivers through him, which, strangely, made his hand throb. He checked again, just to be sure, and saw the skin where the spike had gone through was unbroken and unblemished.

It wasn't as though the loft played some fearsome part in his childhood. Nothing had ever happened up there to warrant this strange sense of foreboding which he felt mounting, and he'd never suffered nightmares about it before now. In fact he hadn't had many dealings with the loft at all, apart from to stand beneath the hatch and catch bundled up parcels thrown down by his dad every first of December and then to help put them all back up every first of January. He supposed the discovery of the mould and subsequent realisation that he would be forced into taking on a DIY project, which he hadn't factored into the four-week stay, must have inspired the nightmare. Hopefully, he thought, he'd be able to shake off the anxiety and stop thinking about the damn loft as soon as he'd dealt with the leak, or whatever it was that was causing the mould.

Let's do this thing!

John found the loft was just as cold as it had been the previous evening. Clapping his hands against his upper arms to stimulate blood flow, he also found that his merino wool jumper didn't offer much warmth. There was a staleness to the air, like the fermentation of body odour and flatulence in an under-ventilated, frowsty bedsit, which reminded him that he never had found out where the bad smell that kept forming downstairs was coming from. Now he supposed it might be linked with the damp. Bad water and a dead rat beneath the boards maybe.

Wonderful.

Unlike in his dream, the rafters above John were hidden behind wood panelling and the ceiling light Norman had installed was bright enough for him to be able see that nobody watched his every move, apart from Pamela Anderson. She looked at him from the far corner, an old poster of his brother Nick's resurrected by Norman, presumably. She wore a red bathing suit and beamed a white-toothed smile. A suggested wholesomeness about her was severely contradicted by the exaggerated leg line of the bathing suit and the plastic mounds of her chest. Ordinarily the sight of the poster would have amused John with the absurdity of it being there, instead he felt edgy.

The floor joists were covered by floorboards and a functional grey carpet. The carpet was rough beneath his feet and poked through the fabric of his socks like the bristly fibres of a doormat. He stood, curling and uncurling his toes, looking about. Stacks of cardboard boxes and plastic crates lined all four walls, most likely, he thought, filled with things that were of no earthly use to anyone, but things that for the sake of sentimentality would never be binned by his mother or Norman.

Getting down on his hands and knees John felt around the floor in sweeping arcs, to confirm the carpet was dry. It was. Still kneeling, he reached for the nearest tower of boxes that were piled above his old room and dragged the whole stack away from the wall in preparation for untacking the carpet. As he slid the boxes across the carpet he noticed the topmost one had a handwritten label affixed to it: PHOTOS ('70s). It looked like his mother's handwriting so he lifted the lid, curious to see snapshots of his parents together in happier days, but then the phone started ringing downstairs. He let the lid drop back down and waited a moment to see if the noise would rouse the girls, hoping one of them might answer it. No such luck. Cursing he stood up and scuttled down to the landing, fully expecting the shrill persistence of the phone to end before he got to it. It didn't. He picked the cordless receiver up in his mother's sewing room. 'Hello?'

'Oh, John. Hi, just me.' It was his mother. 'I thought for a moment you and Seren must have gone out.'

'Hey, Mam. Just busy that's all. Seren's still sleeping.' He didn't think to mention Emily, that could wait. He shut the door, in case the sound of his voice disturbed the girls, and went to sit on the futon. 'Everything okay?'

'Yeah, I was just checking in, making sure you're okay.'

'We're fine. How's the holiday?'

'Lovely, pet. We've met another couple, Terry and Aileen.'

'Great.'

'Terry's a retired police officer and Aileen used to work for the home office. She's all swanky with her Versace handbag and Jimmy Choos, but she's pleasant enough. Terry's a right hoot, puts me in mind of Tommy Cooper and he's got a laugh as wicked as Sid James'…'

John rolled his eyes, stifling a sigh. 'I'm sure he has, Mam, but how's the actual holiday going?'

'Wonderful. The food's great and the boat's lovely.'

'Ship.'

'What?'

'You're on a ship.'

'Same difference. Boat, ship, ferry, they all float on the water don't they?'

'So does a dinghy but you're not on one.'

'Oh stop being pedantic, John.' His mother huffed, and he imagined her scowling. 'But yeah, it's been really nice so far. We've got a decent sized room with an en suite bathroom. No bath, mind, just a shower. But that suits Norman better. Sometimes he gets stuck in the bath and can't get out on account of his arthritis. Oh and a maid comes and cleans the room every morning. She fetches clean towels and tops up the teabags and sugar sachets, which is a good job really because Norman drinks tea like nobody's business.'

'Great.' John leaned back and rested his head against the futon. He looked up at the white, unspoiled ceiling.

'Yeah, I just wish she'd come a little bit earlier while we're along having breakfast. Usually she calls later, just after Norman's used the bathroom. You'd think she'd have learnt her lesson by now.'

John closed his eyes and gently squeezed his thumb and forefinger into the corners. 'Yeah, you'd think she'd rejig her whole routine just to accommodate Norman's toilet habits, wouldn't you?'

'Well, I certainly would.'

John puffed his cheeks and exhaled slowly.

'We've got a little porthole in the room,' his mother went on, 'but it doesn't open so there's not much point really. Most times there's not much to see. Sky and sea, sea and sky. Terry and Aileen have a big balcony attached to their room. Nice for sitting out on to get a bit of sea air, you know? They're the money people though, I bet it cost them a fortune. I think me and Norman will invite ourselves round one evening, you know, for a bit of a neb.'

'I bet they'll really look forward to that.'

'Are you being sarcastic, John?'

'Me? Never. So where are you off to today?'

'Istanbul. I think we get eight hours to have a look about.'

'Sounds good.'

'Yeah, I hear there'll be lots of market stalls. Is there anything you want fetching back?'

'Er, off the top of my head I can't think of anything.'

'What about apple tea?'

'I'm good thanks.'

'Okay, as long as you're sure.'

'I'm sure.'

'How's Otis and Mindy? Are they missing me?'

'Yeah, I think so,' he lied; in truth the dogs hadn't pined at all. 'They're fine.'

'Aw that's good to hear, give them my love. And Seren. Tell her I'll fetch something nice back.'

'You don't have to, Mam.' He stood up and went to the window. Brushing the net curtains aside, he looked out at the slate grey sea and the sky which was only a few shades lighter. Movement below in the garden caught his attention. He was surprised to see Mindy scampering about on the lawn and Seren standing on the path in her pyjamas. He couldn't see Otis anywhere but, almost out of range, he could see the top of Emily's head.

'Don't be daft,' his mother admonished. 'She's my granddaughter. It's my prerogative to spoil her.'

'Well, whatever,' he said, straightening the nets and heading back to the door. 'I'm pleased to hear you're having a good time. You should probably go and get sorted for your day trip.'

'I think we're about ready to go to be honest. Camera's charged, Norman's got our money rolled up in his sock, and I've got water and sunscreen in my bag. Oh and a roll of toilet paper. Never can be too careful in these foreign countries, can you?'

'For chrissakes, Mother, I'm sure there'll be paper in the public toilets.'

'I don't really want to take that chance though, son. My bag's ample big enough, so I'd rather err on the side of caution.'

'A whole roll though?'

'Better safe than sorry.'

Out on the landing John saw that the door to his mother's room was closed, but the door to his old room was standing ajar. He peered inside, his eyes drawn to the ceiling. 'Hey Mam, have you experienced any problems with the back bedroom ceiling lately?'

'Problems? What do you mean?' Her tone instantly suggested she hadn't.

'I dunno, mould maybe?'

'*Mould?* Good grief no, how's that happened? Shall I go and get Norman? He's in the bathroom, would you like me to…'

'No, Mam, it's fine, I'm sure. Nothing to be concerned about at all. I'll check everything over and get it sorted, there's no need to worry. I shouldn't have mentioned it…'

'Whereabouts is…'

'Seriously, it's miniscule. Would hardly even notice it. In fact, maybe it was just a shadow or something,' he said, furiously backtracking. 'I'll go and have a better look when I get off the phone. I'm betting it's nothing at all actually.'

'Well, it can get quite dingy in that back room sometimes. That's why I chose the other one for my sewing...'

'Look, Mam, I'll not keep you, this is probably costing you a fortune. Go and have fun at the markets with Norman, okay? And make sure you haggle with those Turks.'

'Right-o. And I'll keep an eye out for anything you might like. Turkish slippers or some such.'

'Seriously, Mam, you don't have to. Just watch what you're doing and don't get into trouble.'

'Will do, love. Bye.'

'Er, yeah...bye.' John hung up and closed the door to his old room then went downstairs, expecting to find Seren and Emily. They weren't in the lounge or the kitchen, so he opened the back door and peered down the drive. He couldn't see them out there either.

'Seren? Em?'

When there was no reply he called the dogs' names and whistled. Neither Otis nor Mindy responded, causing a flash of concern to step his heartbeat up a notch. Where could all four of them be? The dogs' leads were hanging where he'd left them earlier, so they couldn't have all gone for a walk.

'Seren?' he called louder this time. *'Emily?'*

Movement upstairs made him rush to the foot of the stairs. Floorboards creaked, then his mother's bedroom door cracked open. Emily peered out, bleary eyed. 'Yo, what's up?' she asked, scratching her head.

'Is Seren up there with you? And the dogs?'

Emily looked back into the room behind her, confused. 'Um, no...'

'*No?* Well, where are they?'

John's anxious response made the sleepy look vanish from Emily's eyes in an instant. 'I...I dunno. What's going on?'

John spun round and raced to the back door. Maybe Seren was out in the garden at the front of the house and he'd missed her. Or playing games. Hide and seek, like in his dream. Had she snuck up into the loft?

Oh God.

But surely not with the dogs.

Pelting outside, John's stockinged feet beat hard against the concrete path. He turned the corner and leapt onto the square area of lawn at the front of the house. She wasn't there.

'*Seren!*'

Emily dashed out of the house behind him, her feet bare and the shorts of her pyjamas showing off most of her legs. 'John, what's going on?'

'Why did you leave her out here?' he demanded.

'What are you talking about? I didn't know she *was* out here…'

'Yes you did, I saw you both about five minutes ago.'

Emily fixed him with a look of concern and shook her head. 'I only woke up when you shouted. I didn't know Seren was…'

'You were *out here*,' he insisted, running his fingers through his hair as he tried to think straight, tried to work out what he should do. 'I saw you.'

'But you can't have, I was in bed the whole time.'

'No. I saw…I saw…'

'What? What did you see?'

'Your head. The top of your head.'

'*The top of my head?*'

'Yes. From the upstairs window.'

'So you saw someone with dark hair out here with Seren and presumed it was me?'

'Well, I…yes. Yes.'

'Fuck, John. Who was it then? Because I'm telling you it wasn't me.'

'I don't know.'

'And…' Emily looked around the garden. 'Where are the dogs? Why didn't they bark?'

John looked to the gate and saw that it was wide open.
'*Seren!*'

20

'On then, Christian soldiers, on to victorrry! Hell's foundations quiiiver...' Sissy Dawson stopped singing. The door to her room opened and for a fleeting moment the ghosts around her bed disappeared. Kevin was standing at the doorway, outlined by the sunshiny corridor behind him.

'Morning, Mrs Dawson,' he said, stepping into the room, his boyish face cheery. 'You sound like you're in a chirpy mood today.'

'Good grief no,' she croaked. 'I haven't felt chirpy since I was a young 'un.'

'Surely that can't be right.'

'God's honest truth.'

'But if someone's singing with as much gusto as you were just now, they've *got* to be feeling upbeat.' Kevin smiled down at her, his blue eyes radiating compassion. His unblemished face reminded Sissy of the skin on top of warm milk and she fancied that he smelt of gingersnaps.

'Now, how's them broken bones of yours doing?' he asked. 'You were very lucky not to have killed yourself pulling a stunt like that.'

'I'd say I was very unlucky in that case.'

'Aw I hate to see you down in the dumps, Mrs Dawson. Things will get better, though, you'll mend. You'll see.'

'And supposing I don't?'

'Course you will.'

'There's more to a person than skin and bones. All that stuff's superficial.'

'I'm not sure I follow, Mrs Dawson.'

'Do you believe in God?'

Kevin's neat mouth twisted in thought. 'Hmmm. I like to keep an open mind. I don't know that there is a God, but I don't know that there isn't.'

'*I* believe in Him.'

'I know you do, Mrs Dawson. And that's great.'

'Do you want to know how I know He's real?'

'Good old fashioned faith?'

'Partly. But I know of things that exist in this world that are bad. Terribly bad.' The expression in her eyes intensified to a warning glare. 'So that means He *must* exist.'

Kevin shifted his heavy bulk from one foot to the other, completely unaware of the gruesome gathering that stood all about him. 'Good versus evil you mean?'

'Yes, exactly that.'

'Sounds like you've got it all figured out then, Mrs Dawson. Now, is there anything I can do for you? Get you a cup of tea maybe?'

'Kevin!' She spat out his name as if it suddenly offended her tastebuds. 'I'm *not* a fool.'

Kevin looked genuinely taken aback. 'As if I'd even suggest such a thing…'

'These aren't the mad ramblings of a dying old woman, you know. I prepared myself long ago to meet my maker, but He doesn't want me. Not yet. So I've got to put things right before He'll accept me into His heavenly realm. I only hope that I can.'

'I can't pretend to know what you're talking about, Mrs Dawson,' Kevin said, clasping his hands together and tapping the tips of his thumbs. 'But whatever it is that you're feeling bad about, I'm sure none of it matters in the end.'

Sissy laughed, a humourless cackle that sounded to Kevin's ears like a quarrelling crow. 'Of course it matters,' she said, wafting her arm in the air to address her invisible tormentors. 'All of this matters. And it's all because I've seen *Her*. I've known Her. Felt Her in me corrupting my soul. She's conniving and filled with a wickedness you couldn't possibly know. And I pray that you never do, Kevin.'

'Oh you're not that bad, Mrs Dawson,' he said, laughing light-heartedly.

'Don't make jokes.' Sissy cautioned him with unyielding eyes. 'Not about this. *Never* about this.'

'Sorry, Mrs Dawson.'

'Alright. Well. Don't you want to know who She is?'

With an expression that was non-committal, he shrugged and said, 'Okay. Who is she?'

Sissy closed her eyes, perhaps so she didn't have to see any scepticism that might show on his face. 'A nameless, faceless evil. Old as time. A curse against humanity. Women and men are Her tools, children Her game. That is, She feeds on the depraved desires of adults and preys on the souls of the very young.'

'Yikes, sounds awfully sinister and a little too deep for me, Mrs Dawson.'

'You don't know the half of it.' Sissy opened her eyes again, unsure now as to why she was burdening him with all of this information. He was a genuine, caring man and he didn't deserve to be sullied with knowledge of Her existence. And yet still she couldn't help but tell him, 'She's coming back, Kevin, I can feel Her. I'm frightened. Truly, very afraid.'

Kevin stood for a while, bemusement silencing him. He was, evidently, uncertain what to make of all she'd said, or how to decide if, indeed, she was winding him up. When Sissy gave him no reason to think that she was, he could think of nothing better to say than, 'Would you like me to arrange a visit from Father Murray? Perhaps you could talk to him about all of this?'

'Ha!' Sissy scoffed before she could stop herself. 'If

God won't listen to me, what good would Father Murray be?'

'He could help put your mind at ease.'

'Don't make me laugh, I've never met him but already I know that Father Murray would be way out of his depth. No, what I need is to deal with Her myself, because if I don't I fear there'll be no amount of repentance that will persuade God to accept me into His loving arms. And what kind of purgatory would await me then?'

'I'm really not sure I know about these sorts things, Mrs Dawson. I'm just a carer.' Kevin rubbed his smooth chin, making it go red. 'So, if it's all the same with you, I'll give Father Murray a ring as soon as I've done my rounds.'

21

Emily rushed back into the house to put on some clothes. John ran out into the street, adrenalin and blood pumping around his body so fast his limbs felt numb, his legs not his own. Wind stung his cheeks and there was a sharpness to everything around him, an unfriendliness of colour and sound. The concrete beneath his feet was the same drab colour as the hospital entrance mat he could remember from all those years ago. And Doctor Murphy's trousers. Both things were defining elements, no matter how mundane, that served to form integral layers to the horrors he'd lived through. Stored away in his brain to remind him, not that he needed much reminding, that the most normal of days inclusive of the most normal of events had the occasional propensity to turn quickly and irrevocably bad. Life-changing days, the type that turned out for the worst, seldom started with an inkling that catastrophe would strike. They started out like any other day, and they happened to the most unsuspecting, normal of people. The sound of a nearby hedge trimmer was a nauseating burr of normality that reminded John of the insistence of the phone he'd heard ringing further down the corridor while he'd sat in Doctor Murphy's consultation room gripping Amy's hand in his. And earlier still, of babies crying in some other room, so close, yet so far away, while his world fell apart.

He looked right, to the end of the street. A car drove past. Then he looked left, over the bridge. There was no sign of his daughter.

'Seren? *Seren!*' So fraught with panic, in case devastation had found its way back into his life, John failed to see the old man who was regarding him from the drive next door, a spade in hand and a Clark's shoebox next to his feet.

'Everything alright, son?' the old man called.

'My daughter. Little blonde girl. She was in the garden.' John pointed to his mother's lawn, his gesturing frantic. 'Have you seen her?'

'Aye.' The old man leant the spade against the side of his house, seemingly unmoved by John's sense of urgency, and shuffled down the garden path, his checked-fabric slippers worn at the front where big toes threatened to poke through. He cut across his square patch of lawn and stood facing John, the wooden fence between them. Both hands were now stuffed into the large slouchy pockets of his beige knitted cardigan, but he took one out and extended his arm to John. 'Your ma's neighbour, Wilf.'

'My daughter.' John shook his head, too flustered to accept the handshake and not caring a damn at that point who the old man was. 'Where did you see her?'

'In your ma's garden.'

'Who with? Did you see?'

Wilf had a serious but friendly face, and up close his age was belied by skin that had harvested not too many wrinkles. A layer of silver filing whiskers on his jaw carried down to the base of his neck where it was met by a tangle of wire wool chest hair protruding from a burgundy polo shirt. He hacked up some phlegm and spat into the rose bushes, then said in a voice that was thick with age, 'Not when she was in the garden, no. I only just happened to glance out the window and saw her playin'. I was helpin' Ethel, that's the missus, clean the budgie's cage out. He died this mornin'. By the time we'd got sorted I looked outside again and saw your little 'un walkin' down across the bridge with some woman.'

Light-spots pricked the inside of John's eyes and he found it hard to focus on Wilf's face. He gripped his hand around a pointed fence post and asked, 'What woman?'

'Not sure, son. Sorry.' Wilf shrugged his broad shoulders. He took a crumpled cotton handkerchief from his pocket and dabbed around his nostrils, then explained, 'Eyesight's not too good these days, must admit. She had long dark hair. That's all I can tell you with any amount of certainty.'

Emily was now jogging towards them, the sound of her flip-flops slapping the concrete made both men turn. 'Any news?' she asked, her face sombre. 'I searched the rest of the house, even up the loft, but they're definitely not in there.'

'Go back inside. Call the police,' John said, not really hearing what she'd said. 'Tell them the neighbour saw her walking off with a woman with dark hair…'

'*What?*' Emily's complexion turned seasick-white.

'Just do as I said. Now! And stay here in case she comes back. I've got my mobile. Ring me.'

John didn't wait for a response, he left her and Wilf gawping after him as he turned and fled towards the bridge, his mind a whir of conflicting thoughts. Who had walked off so easily with his little girl? And where had she taken her?

Sharp stones underfoot were quick to remind him he wasn't wearing shoes. Acute pain along his instep made him gasp and wince with every footfall. But he kept on going, driven by blind fear and a certain amount of rising anger. Surely bad luck wasn't so closely partnered with him that tragedy was about to befall him again? How much pain was he meant to endure?

Once over the cobbled bridge and onto the dirt track and grassy verges down by the allotments, running became much easier and he picked up speed, running faster than he could ever remember having run in his life. By the time he got to the field at the top of the beach banks his side ached with a wicked stabbing sensation and his lungs felt as though they were filled with battery acid. His windpipe burned with every mouthful of air he sucked in. He bent over double, hands on thighs, and cried out to the grey morning till his throat was sore.

'Seren!'

In the wake of his plea he heard nothing but his own ragged breathing. Wind buffeted his ears, blocking any response that might have been. And he realised his own cry had probably gone unheard, lost to the same wind.

Way off to the left, across the field, a white dog scurried up from the bank's side. A small terrier that set to weaving in and out of tall grass. It sent a partridge up into the air, and John thought he could hear the faintest of yaps. Perhaps someone might have heard his own cries after all. He scoured the horizon looking for an owner, someone who could help, someone who might have seen a woman walking off with his daughter, but there was no one. Just the dog.

He started jogging, straight ahead, ignoring the knot in his right side that worked itself tight again. He would cross the field and then work his way along the cliff path, heading anticlockwise towards the dog and, hopefully, its owner. And then…And then he didn't know. What if the owner couldn't help? Was he to climb down to the beach? Or go back and do a search of the allotments? Seren could be anywhere. In the thick of the dene, or somewhere else in County Durham by now if the woman had lured her to a waiting car on the beach road. He was confounded that his daughter had willingly gone off with a stranger, that she hadn't shouted to alert him, but mostly he felt anger towards whoever had led her away. He tried to funnel that anger into his body, to spur himself on. Because the alternative would be to ponder devastating possibilities, and then he'd lose it altogether and be no good to anyone.

His socks were quickly made sodden by the dewy grass and a few times he almost slipped. If he hit a pothole in the tall grass he knew he could break an ankle, or obtain a sprain at the very least, but the risk wasn't enough to make him let up. He kept on, picking up speed and running through the pain that his lungs served him with. He was alert, eyes scanning the banks and surrounding green. Searching. But there was no one else about. Not even the small white dog. When he was about twenty metres from the edge of the cliff, he slowed to a trot and brought his thumb and forefinger up to his mouth. Placing both beneath his tongue he whistled, a loud piercing sound that penetrated the wind and lasted a good five seconds. He looked about expectantly. A gull glided above him, its wings fully outstretched, but nothing else moved apart from the windblown grass all around him.

'Otis!' he cried, before whistling again. 'Mindy!' By now he was standing at the top of the beach banks, looking down across the beach, way below, to the frothy shore of the low tide. The morning coast had a hazy quality and sea fret haunted the shoreline with a vignette of dankness. Off in the distance the banks of Boulby stretched out into the North Sea like a fallen, jagged monolith in a ghostly dreamscape. John whistled again and searched the rugged foreshore for movement. There was nothing. He started moving again, off to the left to begin tracing the cliff path, but stopped when he heard something in the opposite direction. A sharp rustling of something moving through grass, too heavy to be wind. Spinning round, he searched the field but saw nothing. Then movement drew his attention down the grassy decline of the bank to the right. *Otis!* The wiry lurcher was bounding towards him, tail wagging.

John stooped and clapped his hands together. 'Here, boy!'

Otis nuzzled into the palm of John's hand and licked, nudging his body against John's legs at the same time.

'Where's Seren?' John looked in the direction the dog had come from. 'Is she down there?' He pointed.

Otis whined.

'Show me.' The wind chill was now cutting through John's jumper, making him shiver. After the exertion of running across the field, he was rapidly cooling down now that he was still. He beckoned with both hands, urging the dog to take the lead. 'Show me where she is, lad.'

Otis took off, leaping sure-footed over grassy mounds and loose earth, clambering down the bank at a steady angle. John followed, not as easily on soaked, stockinged feet, but not slowing to caution. His hair whipped about, blinding him, and he warred with the frontmost strands, trying to keep them out of his face. Soon he was climbing sideways rather than descending further. He stumbled and staggered as fast as he could, hoping the dog wasn't leading him on some false trail of hope. The cold was now bone-deep and John clenched his jaw to stop his teeth from chattering. Every now and then Otis would wait for him to catch up, his tail wagging as if they were playing a game, then he'd launch off again. John watched as he vaulted up and over a large mound of earth that sprouted long tufts of beach grass, before disappearing out of view. Using the grass for leverage John pulled himself up onto the mound, the thin green blades harsh in his cold hands. Once at the top he fell to his knees, his legs giving out beneath him. Some ten metres down, sitting in the sand pit he'd shown her a few days ago, was Seren, and Mindy lying next to her. Relief consumed John. He was rendered immobile for a moment, and he didn't know whether to call out, sob or be angry.

Cupping his hands around his mouth, he at last yelled, 'Seren! I'm coming to get you. Stay there.' Using his feet, hands and backside, he scrambled down to the pit: an ungraceful effort which left yellow sand clinging to his wet socks and the hems and seat of his jeans. When he reached her Seren regarded him with wide eyes and he saw that she was trembling.

'What's going on?' he panted, managing to sound much calmer than he'd expected.

When she didn't answer he reached down and gripped his hands around her underarms, hauling her up into the air. Then he held her close in a fierce hug and looked around them. 'Who brought you here?'

She hugged him back, her skinny arms locking around his neck, but didn't reply.

'Seren.' His voice became stern with concern. 'Who?'

A few moments lapsed before she whispered into his ear, 'Megan.'

'Megan?' He twirled around, in case he'd missed someone skulking behind beach grass or mounded earth. 'Who's Megan?'

'The woman I've been telling you about.'

'Which woman...?'

'The one who visits my room.'

John closed his eyes. Cold, exhausted and on the verge of surrender, he felt as though the rest of the world was spinning around fast and he was the only one standing still. 'Please, don't start...'

'But it's true,' she said. 'Megan says if I don't leave Gran's house the bad woman will take me away. Forever.'

'*What* bad woman?' John spun around again to emphasise the fact that there was no one else there.

'The one that took Megan away. The one that stole

Petey Moon.'

John bit his lip and began to trudge upwards. He felt that if he spoke he might cry. So he didn't. The dogs followed close behind. It wasn't until they were all standing at the top of the bank that he'd composed himself and said wearily, 'I don't know who Megan is, kidda, but, truth be told, I'm starting to miss Petey Moon.'

22

With still over an hour before closing time, Natasha's nerves were getting the better of her. Agitated and restless, she found it difficult to sit still for more than ten minutes at a time. She felt as though she'd been throwing back taurine drinks all day and was now dealing with the edgy after effects. She'd taken to reorganising shelves that were perfectly tidy, stacking business cards that were already stacked and scrupulous clock-watching. She willed the minute hand on the vintage wall clock to move as quickly as the second hand. If anything, though, it seemed to have got stuck.

At home a summery maxi dress was laid out on her bed. Lee had arranged to call round later and, no matter what transpired between them, she wanted to look nice. Different scenarios for the evening had played out in her mind all day, her imagination covering every possible eventuality. If things turned out badly and the pair of them ended up going their separate ways, she thought she could deal with it so long as they reached the decision mutually and amicably. No toing and froing or bickering through weeks of uncertainty. Amidst these thoughts of arguments and the possibility of a broken heart, flashbacks of recent nightmares troubled her as well. She had a purpling egg on her forehead as a result of having fallen over while sleepwalking. That's what she put it down to anyway. She remembered the onset of labour pains and the freakish way her stomach had looked before she'd passed out on the living room floor, but none of it could have been real. It was a consequence of stress, nothing more, the past few weeks disturbing her in ways she never could have imagined.

The bell above the door rang and a thick-set woman with bleached hair walked in. She wore a brash combination of sage green and cobalt blue and was followed by a man who favoured beige.

'Afternoon,' Natasha called from her stool behind the counter.

'And so I had the wild mushroom risotto,' the woman said to the man, heading straight to a display case of handcrafted jewellery without so much as a glance in Natasha's direction. The man raised his eyebrows in silent greeting, or apology. Maybe even disdain. Natasha couldn't tell. She pulled a face at their turned backs, startling when the landline on the counter rang as though catching her out in some act of childishness.

'One Hundred & Ninety-Nine, how may I help?' she said into the receiver.

'Tasha. It's me.'

Lee.

'Hi. Everything okay?' Her stomach flipped, something about his tone suggested it wasn't.

'Yeah. It's just, I'm not gonna to be able to make it tonight.'

'Ah. I see.' She didn't. But she waited for him to explain.

'Something else has come up. I'll call later.'

'Er…okay.'

'Right. See you.'

'Yeah. Bye,' she said to the empty line. She stared at the receiver for a while before putting it back in its cradle. Lee had been upbeat when he'd called the previous evening, but now he sounded irked, detached. Had he had second thoughts about wanting to see her? If something unexpected had happened at work or if there was a family crisis he needed to deal with then he would have said as much, surely?

Realising now that nothing was going to be resolved

that night, Natasha sighed. All of her nervous energy plateaued and she suspected it wouldn't take too long for it to plummet to the depths of melancholy instead.

Had Lee done this deliberately? Was he making her stew for having rejected his marriage proposal? Could she even blame him if he was? Maybe she *had* reacted too touchily, melodramatically even, to his romantic gesture.

Romantic? Please!

There was nothing romantic in the slightest about asking someone to marry you just because you thought that's what they wanted to hear. Or, indeed, to cheer them up. The whole situation was such a mess.

When the phone started ringing again she whipped it up, her heart accelerating. She dared to hope he might have changed his mind, so they could resolve their disputes sooner rather than later. 'One Hundred & Ninety-Nine.'

'Is that Natasha?' It was a child.

Natasha's shoulders sagged. 'Er, yes. Yes it is. How can I help?'

'Hello, I'm Seren.'

'Hello, Seren, what can I do for you?'

'I need to talk.'

'What about?'

'It's a bit weird to be honest.'

'Go on then.' Natasha started fiddling with the phone's spiral cord, a curious smile finding its way to her lips. 'I've heard plenty of weird things in my time.'

'Okay. A new friend of mine needs your help. She's in trouble.'

Natasha's eyes narrowed and her smile disappeared. 'Er, do I know you at all?'

'No.'

'How did you get my number?'

'Online. I looked you up on my dad's tablet.'

'Ah, so you visited my website?'

'Uh-huh.'

'So who's this friend of yours?'

'Megan. She told me to contact you.'

Natasha stopped twining the plastic cord around her index finger. 'And who's Megan exactly?'

'Someone who knows you.'

Natasha looked around the shop, and then outside at the dove-grey sky. 'I'm sorry, Seren, I don't know anyone called Megan.'

'Yes you do.'

'No, I really don't.'

'Yes you *do*,' the little girl insisted.

Natasha closed her eyes and massaged her left temple. 'Look, is this some sort of prank call?'

'No, you have to listen to me.'

'I *am* listening to you.'

'Alright, the bad woman's coming back.'

Natasha sat up straight, opening her eyes. 'What bad woman?'

'The one who took Megan and Petey Moon away. And now she wants me. Can you help us?'

'Whoa, whoa, whoa.' Natasha splayed her hand on the table. 'The bad woman who took Megan away?'

'Yes. So you *do* remember Megan?'

'No. But…where is she?'

'Someplace in the dark. I don't know. She's trapped and can't get out and she's scared. So am I.'

'Look, kid, I really don't appreciate this right now…'

'I know, I'm sorry. I'm sorry about your sad news.'

'What sad news?'

'Megan told me what happened, and she wanted me to let you know that the bad woman had nothing to do with it this time. This time it was just awful bad luck.'

Natasha's jaw began to ache with building emotion. 'What do you mean? What do you think happened to me?'

'You lost your baby. '

Any verbal response Natasha might have had caught fast in her throat.

23

Wilf was making a big task of filling a small rectangular hole in his garden when John, Seren and the two dogs trundled up from the railway bridge. John managed to deflect conversation with a look of *not now* when the old man opened his mouth to speak. Emily came to the gate, her eyes puffy, cheeks pink and dewy. She bundled Seren into her arms and hurried into the house.

Once inside, John didn't feel like doing much of anything. He changed into dry clothes and apologised to Emily, telling her he'd understand if she didn't want to come back after her afternoon shift at Asda. Who needed such drama? In response she gave him a stony look and told him not to be *stoopid*, that if anything it made more sense for her to be around. She went then to change into her uniform and when she came back downstairs John was in the kitchen making a cup of tea.

'Will you be alright while I'm out?' She watched him pouring milk into his mug, concerned by how withdrawn he seemed. Ill, even. His shoulders were slumped, his stance haggard, made all the more so by his thinness. He looked like a man whose nerves had been pushed to the frayed edges of existence. His spectral blue eyes were haunted; components of anguish and defeat, desperation and sadness dulling his spirits with an unmovable despondency. And his face was fraught with a seriousness that emphasised sunken cheeks. He looked the most vulnerable she'd ever seen him.

'Course I will,' he muttered, not bothering to look up.

'Are you keeping her in for the rest of the day?' Since arriving home Seren had lain on the couch under a blanket watching television. She'd hardly spoken a word.

'Yeah.'

'And what about the loft? Are you still going up there to sort the burst pipe?'

John shook his head and sipped at his hot tea without blowing on it. 'I'll take a look later, when you get back. I don't want to go wandering off up there leaving her alone. Besides, there's no water or dampness coming through any of the ceilings, I checked while I was up there just now. And, believe it or not, the ceiling in my mam's bedroom is totally clear.'

'No way.' Emily's eyebrows dipped low in confusion. 'How can that be?'

'No idea.'

'Wow. That was some weird shit right there this morning.'

'Which bit?' John glanced sideways, his tone caustic.

Emily moved around the table to stand next to him. Dropping her voice to barely above a whisper, she said, 'Has Seren told you what happened? Why she ran off like that?'

Sighing, John rested his backside against the counter, as though the question loaded him with physical weight. Fidgeting with the striped mug in his hands, he ran his thumbs over its glossy surface to dispel some anxious energy. He felt fragile, as though he was standing alone against the world. His role as a father was testing him to the absolute limit. Most days it seemed like he was taking part in an amateur training session that wasn't delivering proper results. And, if that wasn't daunting enough, his sense of self was no longer reliable. Parts of his own consciousness were turning against him in a stealthy takedown that might be slow and gradual, or rapid and fierce. Dark roots of depression had begun to sprout like persistent weeds in the blackened, sun-starved patches of his mind. Thorny bramble stems soon to coil around his brain, puncturing and anchoring, then starving him of any optimism, making it impossible for him to think straight beyond the tangle of organic, barbed hopelessness.

'Back home she's got an imaginary friend,' he said after some consideration. 'Petey Moon.' His mouth pulled to the side in a show of disdain. Talking about Petey Moon made him feel like he was revealing some dirty secret. It was a name he always thought best kept from other ears in case it was an admission that his daughter, like himself, was not wired up properly. 'Anyway, sounds as though she's got one here as well.'

'An imaginary friend?' Emily shrugged, looking mildly perplexed. 'What's that got to do with the price of cheese?'

'She reckons this new imaginary friend told her to leave,' he huffed. 'She's adamant about it.'

'Ah, you mean the woman she was going on about this morning?'

'Yeah. Megan.'

Emily looked thoughtful, thrumming her fingers on the worktop. 'So, you're definitely sure she's making this Megan woman up?'

John regarded her with wide disbelieving eyes. 'Of course she is! Have *you* seen a bloody woman in the bedroom?'

'Well no, but…'

'She's obsessed with this idea that some bad woman is coming to take her away.'

'What do you think that's about?'

John shrugged and breathed in deeply. 'Your guess is as good as mine. Attention seeking? The upheaval of moving away from home stressing her out? Her age? Or maybe she's been thinking about Amy and is worried that the same thing might happen to her? I have no idea what goes on inside kids' heads, least of all my own daughter's. I still wonder if she just needs to spend some time with people other than me. She seems to have based this Megan woman on you.'

'Hmmm, maybe you're right to an extent,' Emily said. 'But that still fails to answer one pretty important question.'

'And what's that?'

'Who was the person you saw in the garden? You thought it was me.'

John ran a hand through his hair, anxiety forcing the action rather than the need to coax the long strands away from his eyes. 'I dunno, Em, I'm beginning to wonder if I saw anyone at all.' He thought about Otis hanging from the loft hatch, the dog's mutilated body with innards exposed. And he thought about the lampshade in his old room dancing about of its own accord. At the time he'd have sworn those things were real too. He had no desire to tell Emily about these mental hiccups of his though. Nobody needed to know.

'What about Wilf?' Emily persisted. 'He saw someone out there too.'

'But there *wasn't* anyone with her,' John said, exasperatedly. 'I was out there looking, there was no one else about. I checked. I scoured the whole area.'

'Just because *you* didn't see anyone doesn't mean you should discredit what Wilf said he saw. Maybe whoever took her got scared and scarpered. I think we should ask the police to pursue the matter…'

'Based on what evidence? I *thought* I saw someone? The old bloke next door said he saw someone but couldn't give a description. Even Seren denies there was anyone with her, apart from Megan. But, no, you're right, let's get the police to pursue the matter. And best of luck to them trying to arrest an invisible person, I'll let you give the description.'

'God, no need to be so sarky.'

'What do you expect?'

'Well, maybe this Megan woman's an effing *ghost*,' Emily hissed. 'Did you think of that?'

John's fingers tensed around the mug, the veins on the back of his hand becoming more pronounced. He glared at her and his voice became low. 'Don't. Just don't.'

'Hey, just because you don't believe doesn't mean it can't be true. How do you even know Petey Moon's made up?'

'Don't even go there.' John's blue eyes blazed. 'There's nothing spooky going on, it's all logical stuff.'

'Logical? Really? Did I miss something?'

'It's simple. Seren created an imaginary friend just like you because she loves spending time with you. It stands to reason. As for me, I imagined I saw you in the garden with her because I *expected* you to be there. Shit, Em, I'm really fucking tired, I barely sleep most nights. And the old bloke next door, he probably saw you out there yesterday and got confused with what day of the week it is. He's getting on a bit isn't he? And, besides, he was upset because his budgie just died.' John's jaw was tense and he worried his eyes lacked the conviction of his words. Emily didn't look at all convinced either, in fact she was looking at him with the type of pity he'd grown to despise over the years.

Laying a hand on his upper arm, she sighed and said, 'Hey, you know best, I'm sure there's nothing to worry about.'

John squirmed, anxious that the whole situation was out of his control, and uncomfortable that he was so desperately vulnerable because of it. 'Yeah, well, I hope so. Sometimes I feel like I'm really fucking this whole dad thing up.'

'Shut up, doofus.' Emily gripped some of the hair on his forearm and pulled. 'I live in a house full of shitty boys and, believe me, they get up to a whole lot worse.

Seren's an absolute angel in comparison. You're doing a great job.'

'A house full?' John raised his eyebrows, feeling suddenly ignorant about his kid sister's home life. 'How many's your mam got now?'

'Too many. And not one damn father figure in sight.' Emily shook her head, a clear indication that she wasn't willing to discuss the matter in finer detail. She grabbed her handbag from the back of the chair and said, 'Right, I'd better be off else I'll be late.'

...

When a mud-caked Arnold Schwarzenegger made it onto the helicopter in one piece and the end credits of the film began to roll, Seren looked at John. 'Can I go back in your old room tonight?'

Draining the last dregs of wine from his glass, John licked his purpled teeth and said, 'No, kidda, I didn't get chance to sort the ceiling.' In truth he'd had ample chance, just no motivation. His energy levels had depleted to the point where he couldn't be bothered to get out of the armchair after lunch. His muscles were tight and his head ached. Even his skin hurt. When Emily had got in from work she'd happily looked after everyone: cooking dinner, feeding the dogs, bathing Seren and topping John's wine up. She'd suggested he didn't drink, since he wasn't feeling well, but he'd insisted the alcohol would help.

'Want me to sleep with you?' Emily asked Seren, twirling her niece's ponytail round her fingers.

'Yeah.' Seren nodded, her eyes immediately brightening.

Easing herself onto her feet, Emily held her hand out. 'You ready to hit the sack now?'

'But it's only nine,' John pointed out, watching as

Seren sat forward and put her slippers on.

'I'm fairly whacked,' Emily said. 'It's been a busy day. I wouldn't mind turning in now if that's okay with you?'

'Of course it is, but it's…yeah, of course.'

Emily ushered Seren to the lounge door and paused. She waited till the little girl's footsteps had receded up the stairs and said, 'Maybe it wouldn't harm for you to have an early night as well, you know. You don't look too good. In fact you look bloody awful.'

'Cheers.' John was slouched in the armchair, socks off, twirling his empty glass around in his hand. The dark bits beneath his eyes contrasted against the whiteness of his skin and the lightness of his blue-green irises lent him a look of some Hollywood portrayal of the undead.

'I'm being serious.' Emily's face was grave. 'All you need is to backcomb your flipping hair, mate, and you'd make a good vampire.'

John cocked an eyebrow, smiling weakly at her analogy – he'd thought the same thing around a week ago. 'Is that a bad thing?'

'Yes, because you're not exactly a sparkly Edward.'

'How about a Lost Boy?'

'Try Nosferatu, doofus.'

'But Nosferatu didn't have hair.'

'I bet he did at some stage. Before he started drinking too much and not sleeping enough and not paying enough attention to what he was eating.'

'Alright, alright, for frig's sake.' John hauled himself out of the armchair. 'I'll go to bed already.'

...

Upstairs John lay studying dark patches that had crept back to the bedroom ceiling, pareidolia making faces and human features in mouldy residue. A woman's face, sad and bereft of colour, looked back at him; her eyes sunken, hair long and black, slit-mouth downturned. A ghoulish, cloaked figure in the east corner was stooped over a child. Or someone sitting down. Or a child on the back of a dog. He couldn't quite make his mind up. An open hand was outstretched in the opposite corner. Awaiting payment. The fingers were bony threads of grey and knuckles thick clusters of early decay on the white artex. Straight above him was the silhouette of a horned ram. Then the more he stared at it the more it became the face of a demon. Eventually it became a uterus. Barren and devoid of life. He found the sad woman again and saw she was now grinning. Her slit-mouth creased up at the sides. And on her head was a crown.

Turning onto his stomach, away from the ceiling's grisly storyboard, John searched for sleep while listening to the distant hum of traffic from the open window. The word REMEMBER popped into his mind. But for the life of him he couldn't remember that there was anything he might have forgotten.

...

When he opened his eyes dark swirls moved overhead. Thunderous clouds of badness that had gathered, increasing in volume and speed to create a spinning whorl on the ceiling. John was right in the eye of whatever storm was about to take place. All around him the air was thick with corruption and decay. A heavy smell of damp and rot clung to the back of his nose. He thought of Dead Dog Pond, imagining that's where he might be, his dead eyes seeing the murky surface above after someone had dumped his body there.

He watched as a hole, black as sin, opened above him. A yawning, dirty mouth that might swallow him whole.

Suck him up into an empty void. Or a nightmarish chasm filled with cobwebs and silence and things that might brush against his naked skin, unseen. Corpse tongues and croaked words. Or maybe it was something else altogether. The entrance to the cundy.

He shuddered, his back sticking to the sheet beneath him, a feverish sweat covering his skin. From somewhere high above, or somewhere deep within, he heard a voice. The cracked, aged sound of an old woman's throat. He strained to hear what she was saying, but her words were indecipherable, a handful of syllables like those from a cat's love song. As the hole in the ceiling grew wider, pulsing and dilating, her words became clearer, till he could make out, 'Here for the baby,' over and over like it should mean something to him. And perhaps it did. He felt that it should. But he couldn't think what.

'Here for the baby. Here for the baby. Here for the baby...' The voice scraped on and on, scratching the nerves beneath his skin, itching his fever. His hair was plastered to his forehead, his body glued to the bed. He scrunched his eyes shut till he saw searing white. Then using every bit of strength he could muster he lurched forward, sitting upright, and pressed his hands to his ears. Sucking in a great lungful of air he cried, '*Nooo!*'

Everything fell quiet. Almost too quiet. The crone's voice went along with the hole as the ceiling flashed white. John waited for something to happen, listening for something beyond the thundering of his own body.

Then there was a knock at the door. A succession of three sturdy raps.

Panting and shivering with fever, he whispered, 'Who's there?'

The handle moved down and the door inched inwards, the bottom scraping over carpet with a rush of noise that filled John's head with distant surf and a deep feeling of expectancy. Inaugural light stole through the curtains, enough for him to see everything in varying shades of grey, including the familiar figure that stood in the open doorway.

'Hey handsome,' she said in that low throatiness of hers.

Pamela Tanner's eyes were heavily kohled and her face was pulled taut because her hair was scraped back severely. A thick gold gem-encrusted collar bejewelled her slender neck, below which she wore nothing at all.

John remained upright, watching her, while needle-pains spread from his spine, communicating with every other nerve-ending in his body. His eyeballs ached. His skin was breathing fire. And he felt a keen, localised throbbing in his lower regions.

'Are you afraid of me, John?' Pamela Tanner asked. She stalked towards him, bare feet silent on the carpet.

John shook his head and lowered himself back onto his elbows.

'You should be.' She came to stand by the side of the bed, her darker-than-usual eyes not leaving his.

John looked away, her stare too intense, especially now she was so close. He lowered his eyes, submissively, and saw a small black tattoo on her hip: an upside-down heart skewered onto a drawing pin. The spades symbol. She saw that he saw it and took his hand, pressing it to the tattoo. Her skin was warm and smooth. He tried to pull away, but she held on, pressing his fingers together till they hurt, till the bones of his knuckles ground together.

'I know you,' she said.

It was a haughty assertion that made John defensive. 'No you don't,' he barked, trying to will away the presumptuous hardness inside his shorts.

'Oh yes. Better than you know yourself.' She looked down his body and smiled. 'I can easily rule you. I did once before. Remember?'

Remember? 'No!'

'Yes. And you'll know me again till you can think of nothing else.' She leapt onto the bed, a show of great agility and finesse, and straddled his legs. He tried to resist, but her legs clamped him tight and she shook her head. 'I *will* rule you again.' Maintaining eye contact she dipped her head and ran her tongue from his navel to his chest, then took his nipple between her teeth.

Feeling the wet warmth of her tongue, and anticipating the promises it foretold, John closed his eyes, ashamed. When she bit down hard on the sensitive skin, the sharp sensation distributed evenly around the rest of his body. And then she sucked. He groaned in pained pleasure, breathing her in. This close Pamela Tanner smelt of sea spray and turned earth, of ancient relics and dusty, unused rooms. There was nothing sensual about the smell at all, it was natural and base, of a dormant age and life that was reawakening, but somehow it raised further excitement in him. The excitement of him surrendering to the pull of what he'd been denying himself. Even the very thought.

She moved her face to his, her erect nipples brushing against the hair on his chest, skimming his skin, the tantalising movement making him a slave to his own desire, in thrall to her impulse. When their lips touched he didn't resist, readily accepting her tongue with his. Their fingers slotted together and he allowed her to pin his hands to the bed with a strength that might well have outdone his own had he tried to resist. Fresh air blew in through the open window but it didn't cool him, he was smothered by her. In fact he thought he might burn alive with the heat of his own blood.

When Pamela Tanner sat upright again, her lips fuller and redder, she released her hair so that black tresses fell loose around her shoulders, down past her breasts. Then she stroked John's sweat-slicked torso with teasing fingers. He lay with his hands above his head, where she'd left them, unmoving, delirious with the feverishness that thrashed his body and senses. She put her fingers beneath the elastic of his boxer shorts and pulled downwards with a quick tug. Paralysed with nervousness and anticipation, but eager with a heightened sense of yearning, John then watched as Pamela Tanner stooped and took him into her mouth. He melted further into the mattress, closing his eyes. Nothing mattered, not anymore. Nothing but her mouth and the firm grip she kept at the base of his shaft. He lay still for a while, rapturous, then when he could no longer abstain he began to buck up and down, his fingers tightly gripping the edge of the mattress because he didn't dare touch her with his hands. To do so would be an admittance of his hunger for her.

When, eventually, he came into her mouth, clouds of red burst behind his closed eyes like broken blood vessels dousing his vision. A wave of heated fulfilment surged through his whole body, making it shudder. But his gratification was short-lived. When he opened his eyes again Pamela Tanner was no longer there. A faceless female form straddled his legs. Lustrous black hair had diminished to an aged bald pate, and Pamela Tanner's tanned curves had been replaced with all the bloated blueness of a drowned body. The faceless woman's breasts hung down either side of an ample stomach mound, each down-pointed nipple the colour of rancid liver. Worst of all was the wide gruesome slash that hung loose in the woman's otherwise featureless face, and in this hole there were multiple rows of barbed teeth.

John made a choking noise and his hands became clawed as he clutched at the mattress, trying to move beneath her bulk, trying to drag himself away, because even more than her deliberate deadweight on his legs, he was aware of the fact that she was still holding onto him. He hardly dared to look, but couldn't help himself, and when he did he saw how her gnarled fingers were clutching the most intimate, rapidly shrinking, part of him with a firmness that both repulsed and frightened him. Again he tried to struggle free, desperately wanting her not to be touching him anywhere, least of all there. And she responded by opening her hideous jagged mouth wider to reveal even more teeth. Then a crackling noise emerged from her throat. A sound he'd heard before in dreams. She snapped her teeth tauntingly at his flaccid penis and as she did this John's fever broke and he felt suddenly cold, like all life was leaving him. And then he wished it would do so more quickly because she bent and took his cock into the serrated abyss of her head. He closed his eyes and screamed and screamed and screamed.

...

He awoke sweating and shivering, and his hand was quick beneath the sheet to clutch his crotch. All was intact.

Thank God.

But there was a fetid stench that filled the room and flies buzzed around the open window behind the curtain, a whole swarm of them by the sound of it. And now footsteps, out on the landing, followed by Emily's voice. 'Seren? *Seren!*'

Not again. Please not again.

John dived out of bed and threw his jeans on, then bolted from the bedroom. Out on the landing he saw the door to his mother's room was wide open and he could hear Emily's thundering footsteps at the bottom of the stairs now.

'What's going on?' he shouted, racing down after her. 'Where is she?'

'I don't know.' Emily flung the bathroom door open and poked her head inside to look around. 'I woke up and she was gone.'

John rushed through to the lounge, then the kitchen. Seren was in neither, but the back door was standing ajar.

'*Seren?*'

He fled outside, bare feet slapping on the concrete drive, and Emily followed close behind. This time he found Otis and Mindy snuffling about on the lawn and his daughter huddled on the garden bench below the lounge window. Her knees were drawn up to her chest and she looked at him with a sense of terror that resounded his own nightmare.

'What the hell are you doing out here?' he cried, not even noticing the damp chill against his bare torso.

'I'm not going back in there,' she whimpered. 'Megan says the bad woman's coming for me. She says she's nearly strong enough now and that…'

'Enough!' John pointed to the house, his expression furious. 'Get inside. Now.'

Emily, who was standing next to him, held out her hand and said, 'Come on, darl, let's talk inside where it's warmer.'

Seren shook her head and gripped her knees even tighter to her chest.

Seeing that her niece wasn't about to change her mind, Emily went to the bench and sat down next to her. 'Who's Megan? Want to tell me about her?'

'No.' Seren buried her face in her knees.

This time John went to the bench. Crouching before both girls, he said, 'Listen, this is what's gonna happen, I'm gonna check the loft over and then we're gonna pack our stuff up and head back home to Leeds, okay?'

Seren looked up, hopeful. 'Really?'

'Really. But there's one condition.'

'What?'

'That in the morning when we leave, Megan stays here.'

'But I want to go home *now*.' Seren's mouth downturned.

John groaned. His head was still fuzzy with wine and the bout of cold he seemed to be fending off felt like it was worsening if anything. 'We can't.'

'Why?'

'Because we can't just leave Gran's house the way it is. Imagine how she and Norman would feel if they got back home to discover their bedroom ceilings are all mouldy. I don't think they'd be very happy, do you?'

'But I don't want to go back upstairs.'

'What about if I sleep with you?'

'No. I'm not going up there.'

'What about the couch? You can sleep downstairs.'

She looked at him uncertainly, but this time didn't refuse.

'I'll stay with you, we'll camp out in the lounge,' he offered. 'Then tomorrow afternoon we hit the road and head home.'

Her small shoulders sagged in defeat and she nodded her consent, allowing him to take her back inside. John, straight away, went to gather some bedding. When he was half way up the stairs he heard the phone ringing. He ran the rest of the way up but by the time he got to the landing the ringing had stopped and he could hear the muffled sound of Emily's voice downstairs. When he returned to the lounge, arms laden with blankets and pillows, she was replacing the phone in its cradle and Seren was lying on the sofa, looking marginally calmer.

'Who was that?' he asked, tipping his head towards the phone.

Emily shrugged. 'Cold caller.'

John looked at the golden carriage clock on the mantelpiece. It was just after half ten. 'At this time of night?'

'I know, ridiculous.'

'Well, I hope you told them where to go.'

Emily smiled wanly. 'You know me.'

John covered Seren with a duvet then went through to the kitchen to triple check that the back door was locked. He put the key on top of the refrigerator, where she wouldn't be able to reach it, then started when he turned round and saw Emily standing next to him.

'Hey,' she whispered. 'I know it's none of my business and all, but I don't think you should be running about like that, not where Seren is.'

Regarding her with vagueness, he said, 'Running about like what?'

'With no shirt on.'

'Why the hell not?'

Emily raised her eyebrows. 'Forgot about something, have you?'

'*Excuse me?*'

'Duh.' Emily huffed and jabbed him in the chest. 'That bloody big love bite, dipshit.'

John looked down, horrified. Circling his left nipple, where Pamela Tanner had bitten him in his dream, was an undeniable set of teeth marks amidst angry purple bruising.

24

A deep sense of loss filled Natasha's heart with a hurt that lacked the sharp intensity of freshness but ached with all the deep-rooted insistence of healed broken bones in winter months. She felt restless and unsettled, Seren playing heavily on her mind. After she'd hung up, Natasha had dialled 1571 and jotted down the little girl's number on a yellow Post-it note. She'd then muddled on until home time in an unpleasant autopilot fugue. Now she was lying in tepid bath water, the bubbles of which had been reduced to a film of soapy residue on the surface gathering thickest and white around her protruding thighs.

Why me out of all the random strangers on the internet? Why not someone else?

Natasha chewed on her fingers. Gut instinct told her the little girl's phone call was in some way connected with her own bad dreams and experiences of late. She knew the idea wasn't some irrational conclusion borne from a hormonal imbalance post-miscarriage. She could sense something other-worldly scratching about beyond the boundaries of her normal perception with spidery, dead fingers which she imagined only the bereaved might feel.

Shivering, she sat forward, her skin taught with gooseflesh. The lukewarm water and comfortable temperature of the bathroom did nothing towards easing her chill. Beyond the sound of the bathroom's extractor fan the house was silent. All the unlit rooms at the other end of the hallway, although familiar spaces filled with her stuff, as they had been for well over a decade, now felt uninviting with the malignancy of some unseen threat. Natasha looked nervously at the bathroom's open doorway, regretting having not, at least, left the lounge's light on. She knew that once she left the spotlit sanctuary of the bathroom shadows elsewhere in the house would look darker than usual, they would be home to solid breathing hulks with blank faces and closed mouths, and inside those insidious mouths would be expandable jaws with hundreds of spiky teeth. Like the faceless woman from her dream.

Something was close. Something intangible. She could feel it. Premonition teased her skin with butterfly kisses; a creepy, crawly sensation that made her hair follicles pucker and scalp tingle. She shuddered and looked over at Maverick who was sitting on the closed toilet lid watching her intensely with his china-blue eyes.

'What is it, mister? Do you know?'

He purred piteously in answer, and seemed fully intent on letting her take charge of the situation.

Natasha reached across and pulled the plug out. When she stepped out of the bath, water slopped down the side of the bath panel and pooled on the floor tiles and a chill settled on her wet skin. After hastily drying herself she wrapped the towel around her chest, tucked the fold beneath her arm and scurried down the hallway, leaving a trail of damp footprints behind, pursued by a Siamese cat. When she slapped the lounge light on shadows retreated into other rooms, and she stood for a moment eyeing the living space, relieved to see that nothing more substantial lingered in their place. Nothing with a blowhole instead of a nose. Nothing with sharks' teeth. She thought tonight she might leave every light in the apartment on.

Picking up the cordless phone from the coffee table, she frowned when she saw its digital display: 22:33.

Shit, later than I thought.

Would it be terribly intrusive to call a stranger up at

that time in the evening? She thrummed her fingertips against her lips. Probably. But then, she wouldn't get any sleep unless she did. Retrieving the little girl's number from her handbag on the floor, Natasha held the yellow Post-it note close to her chest and closed her eyes, listening to the internal monologue that began to list and repeat excuses as to why she shouldn't pursue this madness.

'Oh just do it!'

Her thumb hovered over the phone's keypad and she looked down at her own handwritten scrawl on the paper, noticing something she hadn't noticed before. The dialling code was for Tyne and Wear, inclusive of Peterlee: her own hometown. It could mean something or it could mean nothing at all, but somehow she felt it was relevant and this spurred her on. She dialled the number and waited. It rang just three times before someone answered. 'Hello?'

'Oh, er, hi.' Natasha fumbled with the bath towel and started to pace in front of the couch. 'Sorry to bother you so late, it's just, well...a little girl from this number called me earlier. Seren?'

There was brief silence in which Natasha heard three of her own heartbeats, then the woman on the other end of the line said, 'Oh really? I hadn't realised. Can I ask who's calling?'

'Yes. Yes, of course. I'm Natasha Graham. Owner of One Hundred & Ninety Nine. A boutique gift shop in Whitby. That's where Seren called. At my shop. Are you her mother?'

'No.'

'Oh. Are you Megan?' Natasha brought her index finger up to her mouth and began to nibble on the inflamed skin to the side of her nail.

'Er, no. I'm Emily.'

'Oh right. You wouldn't happen to know who Megan

is? It's just, apparently, she was the one who suggested that Seren call me.'

Again there was a slight delay, then Emily said, 'No, sorry, I've no idea who that is.'

'Okay. Well, never mind.' Natasha sat down on the edge of the couch, a feeling of disappointment settling over her, making her legs feel leaden. All of her questions, it seemed, would remain unanswered and the conversation she'd had with the little girl now seemed more obscure than ever. Foolish even. 'Would you be able to let Seren's parents know about this then please? It's just, I'd hate to think the little tinker was running up a massive phone bill and them not know anything about it.'

'Oh yeah, absolutely,' Emily said. 'I'm fairly certain John won't know anything about this. Thanks for letting us know.'

'No problem. Oh and sorry again for disturbing you so late.' Natasha hung up and sank back into the cushions. She had hoped that after the call she would feel more relaxed, but she didn't. Dead knuckles still rapped at the edge of her sensory grasp. She felt scared not knowing who they belonged to, but even more scared that she might not be receptive to whatever message they might try to relay.

What if..?

No. Don't do this to yourself.

What the little girl had said was nothing more than coincidence, like a phoney clairvoyant who strikes it lucky by correctly guessing a name or favourite catchword or item of clothing once used by a now-dead relative. Chance, that was all it was.

But Natasha couldn't settle.

The bad woman's coming back.

What bad woman?

The one who took Megan away.

Where to?

Someplace in the dark.

She looked down at the scribbled phone number again. Something beyond the dialling code spoke of familiarity and tugged at some defunct part of her brain. But Natasha didn't know anybody called Emily. And just who was Emily to Seren? The other woman hadn't said. Natasha's thoughts were a jumble of confusion. What did it all mean? What was the answer to this seemingly impossible conundrum that gnawed at the edge of her understanding?

Then something Emily had said hit her with all the emotional impact of a high-speed head-on collision.

I'm fairly certain John won't know anything about this.

John?

John.

Natasha sprang forward and clamped a hand over her mouth, her eyes wide.

No. It can't be.

She looked at the phone number one more time and her blood ran cold with stark recognition. The truth had finally uncovered itself. Another dormant grenade from the past to blow up in her face.

Oh. My. God.

Realising all at once that her sense of foreboding hadn't been misplaced after all, great waves of confusion and anger, hurt and jealousy surged through Natasha. She would have preferred to have been plunged into a blanket of darkness that was filled with gaping mouths and sharks' teeth than find out this terrible truth.

Damn you all the way to hell and back, John Gimmerick. You contemptible, evil bastard.

25

John was in the loft again. He checked the header tank once more, just to be certain there were no cracks in the casing. When he was certain there weren't he moved all of the storage boxes to one side of the room to clear a large space, then went about untacking the carpet. He peeled the carpet and a thick layer of underlay back and lifted four boards up, enough to access the two copper pipes that fed into the tank. He checked each pipe joint for leakages but found none. Then checked again twice over. There was no hint of condensation either, the whole area bone dry. Frustrated and flummoxed by the whole business, he swore and set to putting everything back into place. He wasn't sure what else he could do. How could he fix a problem that didn't seem to exist? There wasn't even an explanation for the bad smells that frequented the first floor. He'd done about as much as he could do and he could cope with no more.

With the floorboards fitted and carpet laid again he started moving boxes back to where they'd come from, eager to get finished because each time he bent, stretched or swivelled the bruised bite on his chest rubbed against the cotton of his t-shirt, reminding him of the dream he kept trying to forget. The dream that had somehow seeped into reality. The quicker he and Seren left Horden and Pamela Tanner behind, he thought, the better it would be for them both.

After shifting three weighty boxes into a brand new pile John reached for a fourth, a large Quaker Oats box that sat on the floor. But when he tilted it backwards to get a firm grip beneath, he could feel that the cardboard was soggy against his fingers. Heaving it into his arms, he was then dismayed to see that there was a damp patch on the carpet where it had been standing for the past hour or so. He took the box downstairs to the kitchen and put it on the draining board, ready to investigate. Emily and Seren were sitting at the dining table, doodling on pieces of copier paper. Emily glanced up, 'Found something?'

'Maybe.' He started unsticking tape from the box's sealed flaps, curious about what on earth he'd find inside. 'This box is wet for some reason. It's the only damn thing up there that seems to be.'

'Let's hope all your report cards and swimming certificates aren't ruined then.'

'Huh?'

Emily pointed to the side of the box where he'd missed the words: JOHN'S STUFF.

John's brow furrowed and he sighed. 'Why doesn't that surprise me?' He pulled off the remaining tape, his negative sense of curiosity heightening further, and peered inside. One of his old sketch books lay at the very top. He picked it up and sifted through the pages, then handed it to Seren. 'Here, kidda, want to see some of your dad's old drawings?'

Seren took the book without much enthusiasm, but began to look through it nonetheless. She'd been in a strange mood all day, becoming more and more sullen as the hours passed. John knew she was keen to get going and expected that the longer he stalled the sulkier she'd get, which he understood because he felt the same pressing urgency to leave. Even the dogs didn't wander far from the back door, as though they were keen on the imminent escape plan too. Otis hadn't been upstairs since the episode with the swinging light shade and Mindy, strangely, wouldn't even go within ten feet of the stairs. They both seemed skittish and restless anywhere apart from the kitchen.

'Not much longer now,' John said. 'Just got to put a few things back into place after I've sorted this box, then we can get going.'

Seren didn't look up from the book or respond.

Emily stood up and joined John by the draining board. 'So, what else you got in there?' she asked, prodding the box's squishy side.

'God knows.'

'Bust lava lamp?'

'Maybe.'

'What's that?' She pointed to a black leather-bound book at the top of the pile.

John picked it out. 'Probably more drawings.'

'I had no idea you were an artist.'

'I wouldn't go that far, they're just scribbles.'

'Gimme a look.' She took the book from his hands and opened it. A graphite portrait of a female still-life model on the first page had faded with time but was highly detailed and impressive. It was a study of curves and symmetry, elegantly done. 'Doesn't look like a bloody scribble to me.'

John shrugged. 'It's nothing special.'

'It's certainly rude.'

'It's art.'

'Seems more and more like you could be the black sheep of the family, bro.'

John pulled a handful of CD cases out of the box, browsing their spines for anything interesting, and shook his head. 'You think I could take that title away from Dad?'

'Definitely.' Emily poked him in the chest where she knew it would hurt. 'You've been sneaking about the place like some ninja Lothario as well by the looks of things.'

'*Lothario?*' He laughed, despite himself. 'I hardly think so.'

'So how else might you explain that thing on your chest?'

John scowled, motioning towards Seren with a sideways glance. 'Not now, eh?'

'Okay, but you'll have to tell me later. Inquiring minds need to know.'

'I don't have to tell my kid sister *anything*.'

'Jesus, I'm not asking for gory details,' she chided. 'I just want to know who.'

'No one.'

'Yeah right.'

'Seriously. No one.'

'Shut up, you can't expect me to...hey, who's this?' Emily pulled a photograph from the pages of the sketch book. It showed a pretty brunette with kind brown eyes beaming at the camera, a can of lemonade in her hand.

John looked at the picture, but didn't reply. His demeanour instantly stiffened.

'Well?' Emily prompted.

'No one.'

'Wow, you know a lot of no ones.' She cocked an eyebrow.

'It's just an old girlfriend, alright!'

'Bloody hell, alright,' Emily said, taken aback by his defensiveness. 'Here, do you want it?' She held the picture out to him.

'Put it back where you found it.'

Nobody spoke for a while, the hum of the fridge filling in the silence for them. John glanced through a pile of old college papers, his thoughts hardly on them, and Emily continued to flick through his sketchbook.

Seren was the first to break the air of awkwardness. 'Dad, are you nearly done?'

'Not yet.'

'Can I go and watch telly till you are?'

'Yeah, course you can.' He watched as she got up and

pushed her chair beneath the table before leaving the room. Turning to Emily, he said, 'Hey, sorry, didn't mean to bite your head off just now. It's just…there's stuff going on round here that I don't understand. I'm feeling pretty tense.'

'No worries.' Emily offered a reconciliatory smile and pointed towards the lounge. 'I'll go through and keep her company. Here.' She closed the sketch book and passed it to him. Something fell out of the pages as he took it. A small square that fluttered to the floor. Emily bent to pick it up, her face clouding with puzzlement as soon as she looked at it. 'What's this?' She held a small black and white picture up for him to see.

A surge of emotion jolted John's very core. He took the picture from her, not realising that he'd stopped breathing.

'John?' Emily's face was now serious with concern. 'Whose is it?'

He brushed his finger over the glossy surface of the baby scan, his voice monotone. 'Mine.'

'Seren?'

'No.'

'Then who?'

'She died.'

'Shit, John. I'm sorry.' Emily stood transfixed for a moment, staring at the back of the scan. But then her shock quickly turned to dejection. 'How come I never knew about this?'

'It's not something I talk about.'

'But, I can't believe I didn't at least know. Am I the *only* person in the family, apart from Seren, presumably, who didn't?'

'Probably.' He took his eyes off the scan and looked her in the eye. 'Yeah.'

She folded her arms across her chest, hurt evident in her expression. 'That's okay though because I'm not really part of the family am I?'

'Don't, Em,' he warned. 'This happened before your time. This is not about you, so don't try to make it.'

She looked down to the floor. 'Sorry. It's just, I can't believe I didn't know.'

'It's nothing personal, Em. I *would* have told you, but it's not exactly something I'd easily, or willingly, drop into conversation.'

She nodded, her mouth downturned. 'What was she called?'

'She didn't have a name.'

'And who was the mother?'

'The girl in the photo.'

Emily took the scan from him and looked at it more closely. The outline of the baby was clear and she could easily make out a head and nose, arms and legs. She felt a great sadness to think that she should have been an aunt to a niece who was older than she was. But the baby hadn't lived. Hadn't even been given a name. Then something on the scan caught her eye, something that made her heart beat erratically. At the very top, above the embryonic image, was a line of informational text, part of which showed the mother's name: GRAHAM, NATASHA.

'Your old girlfriend,' she said, looking up at John, her face draining of most of its colour, 'she was called Natasha Graham?'

'Look, Em, can we just drop this?'

'Well, no, not really,' she said, biting her lip. 'When I told you last night that a cold caller had called, I was lying.'

'*What?* Why?'

'Because you have enough on your plate already, I didn't want to bother you with something I thought was trivial, something I thought I could sort out.'

'So who *was* on the phone?'

'Natasha Graham.'

26

'Dad, can I go and pack my bags now?' Seren came into the kitchen. She looked even smaller than usual. 'We should hurry.'

'Yeah, fine.' John waved his hand dismissively, without argument. He was sorting through loose paper from his box of stuff, including student loan statements, concert tickets, high street receipts and MOT certificates.

When Seren turned and wandered back into the lounge, Emily, her voice low, asked him, 'Do you think she'll drop the whole Megan thing when you get home?'

'I bloody hope so.'

Pulling her long ponytail over her shoulder, Emily began to fiddle with it, looking almost sheepish. 'So you, er...you definitely don't think there's anything in it then?'

John narrowed his eyes. 'Anything in it?'

'You know, anything *unusual*.' She reached over and picked up one of Seren's drawings from the dining table. It showed a heavily crayoned figure in a long black dress. 'It's just all this talk of Megan then Natasha and that business with the mould on the ceilings. I mean I'm not being funny, John, but what mould comes and goes like that?'

'I wouldn't know, I'm not a mould specialist.'

Emily huffed. 'Oh come on, it's a bit weird you have to admit.'

'Well, yeah, it's *very* weird, but it's mould all the same.'

'Is it though?'

'Of course.' He looked up from an HMV receipt and shook his head. 'What are you suggesting it is?

Ectoplasm?'

'No. I dunno.' Emily riffled through the pages of his sketch book again, quickly so that each image was nothing but a fleeting impression on the eye. 'And what about Seren running off? That's not like her.'

'Exactly. Breathing in mould spores is probably sending us all doolally. It can't be healthy.'

'Maybe.'

'All the more reason to get the hell out of here I say.'

'Why don't you stay another night or two so you can get someone to come out and take a look at it? Get it sorted once and for all.'

'Seren won't stay another night.'

Emily's eyes were suddenly scrutinising. 'Seren won't or *you* won't?'

'What's that supposed to mean?'

'You're holding something back, I can tell. You're acting all edgy.'

'No I'm not.'

'Yes you are. Something's happened. *Have* you seen Megan?'

John dropped the sheaf of papers to the draining board and gave her his full attention. 'No, of course I bloody haven't.'

'So what's up?'

'I don't know what you mean.'

'You look ill, John. I'm actually really worried about you. What's got you so rattled?'

He dragged a hand over his face. It was true, he felt drained, on the verge of some sickness. And her talking like this wasn't helping. Emily was echoing all of his own unvoiced concerns, making them even more real.

'Tell me,' she urged. 'I know you're holding something back.'

He took a long, slow breath and, relinquishing, lifted the front of his shirt to reveal the angry purple welt on his chest. 'It's this.'

Emily looked momentarily confused, but then her eyes sparked with understanding. 'You mean, you think that's why Seren's acting up? You've been seeing someone new and...'

'No,' he interrupted. Whatever she thought she understood, she definitely didn't. 'There is no one.'

'So who did that?'

'I don't know, that's the point. I had this dream about Pam...about one of my mother's neighbours. She bit me and when I woke up, there it was as though she really had.'

'But, that's not even possible.'

'I know.'

Emily was quiet for a moment, while she took stock of things. 'So, let's see. Seren's talking about a woman who visits her room every night who very bloody randomly told her to call your ex. Then you've got some, God, I dunno, succubus visiting *your* room. We've got weird mould that comes and goes. And let's not forget the bloody awful smell that keeps wafting about the place. Something's not right. There's bad tension in the house, can you feel it?'

John could, but he wasn't about to admit as much. 'You're creeping yourself out, trying to sell yourself a ghost story. But there's nothing sensational going on, Em, and I dare say it's *all* related to the mould. I'll get Nick to sort it out. Or Norman's daughter. They can set some dehumidifiers up in the bedrooms, see if that solves the problem. But, either way, I can't stay here any longer.'

'Well I think that's a horseshit excuse. I don't think it is mould.'

'And how would you know? You're an expert all of a sudden?'

'No, doofus. But it doesn't take an expert to know that

mould doesn't jump off walls and give people love bites.' She waved Seren's drawing of the black-haired woman in front of him. 'Something out of the ordinary is going on here, whether you'd care to admit it or not.'

John shook his head, disregarding the picture. 'So what, you think a *ghost* is causing all of this?'

'Yes, well…maybe.'

'Whose ghost?'

Emily bit her bottom lip and looked thoughtful for a moment. 'Okay, so this is just a thought right? But Seren says that Megan looks like me.'

'So?'

'So who do I look like?'

John looked at her and shrugged. 'Olive Oil?'

'Don't be a dick.'

'I dunno. Dad?'

'Yes. *And?*'

'And what?'

'*You!*'

'So?'

'So what if Megan is your daughter?'

John was stunned by the suggestion, the fact that it could even *be* a suggestion. 'She was just a baby, for fuck's sake.'

'Who says spirits don't age?'

'Who says they *exist?*'

'What if she's trying to warn you? She keeps telling Seren to leave. What if the bad woman is your succubus?'

'Have you heard yourself?'

Emily's chest heaved with an impatient sigh. 'You said the baby never had a name, why is that?'

'She was stillborn.' John had become visibly agitated, his demeanour prickly.

'Stillborns have names,' she challenged.

'For God's sake, Em.'

'Tell me what happened.'

'No.'

'Why not?'

He turned his back to her and looked out of the window. A pinky-beige dove was sitting on the fence post, its scrupulous black eyes watching him. He felt as though he had an audience, like this was his five minutes on the podium because the world suddenly wanted to hear him declare what a bastard he was, wanted to hear the words from his own mouth. And there was no backing out now, he realised, Emily was too persistent and the strange things that had been happening meant that the past needed to be explored at least.

'When Natasha gave birth to our dead baby,' he said at last. 'I left her.'

It took Emily a few moments to register what he'd said, then she gasped, 'You *what?*'

He spun round to face her, his jaw tight. 'I've lived with the guilt for the past eighteen years. Please, spare me the look of disgust.'

'But, didn't you hang around at least for a while? Till the baby was buried.'

'No.' His fists were bunched up by his sides and his eyes had clouded in a fugue of darkness that Emily didn't recognise.

Almost too nervous to press him further, but needing to know all the same, she asked, 'Surely you and Natasha discussed names though?'

A long silence stretched out. Eventually John sagged against the counter, his expression softening. 'We agreed we'd decide on a name when we saw the baby.'

'So, given the circumstances, Natasha must have given her a name.'

'And you're suggesting Megan?'

Emily shrugged. 'I'd say you've got to find out.'

'How?'

'Call Natasha. Ask her.'

'I can't do that.'

'Think about it, John.'

'I am! I couldn't do that to the poor woman. What would she think?' The thought of speaking to Natasha made him feel sick with shame. But then it occurred to him that she might already know Seren was his daughter, she'd called his mother's number so surely she'd remember it from the past.

Oh God, what must *she think?*

Maybe it *was* time he apologised. Maybe this was his opportunity to repent.

'How do you fancy taking Seren and the dogs out for some fresh air?' he asked.

Emily nodded, obviously sensing what he had in mind. 'Sure, but can I just ask one more thing?'

'If you must.'

'Why did you leave her?' She was looking at him as if he might be a complete stranger. As if what he'd told her had revealed an aspect of him that she didn't know and didn't like the sound of.

Before he could lose the respect of his little sister altogether, John pulled out a chair and sat down at the dining table, indicating that she should do the same. 'Okay, I'll tell you what happened.' He fiddled with his fingers and avoided her gaze, he couldn't cope with her judgement right now. 'But you have to understand that I wasn't myself for a long while afterwards. I lost the plot. I mean *really*. Natasha was the one I was going to spend the rest of my life with, and we wanted that baby *so* much.'

'So what changed?' Emily asked. 'What changed about the way you felt about Natasha?'

'Nothing. Nothing at all, that's the hard part. I never stopped loving her and I don't know how I'll explain this to you. It's awful and you'll hate me for it.'

'I'm sure that's not true…'

'After the baby was born I felt dead inside. Instantly. Seeing her perfect face but realising that she wasn't crying or moving, I can't put into words how terrible that was. And then I could hear other babies crying, elsewhere in the hospital, and it didn't seem fair. I know it sounds awful, but I actually resented their parents. I begrudged them the new lives they were embarking on because me and Natasha had been robbed of ours.'

'That's only natural, it doesn't make you a bad person to have thought that way. Anyone would after losing their own.' Emily put her hand on top of his, to show her support.

He smiled sardonically, wondering how long it would be before she removed it because that was the part of the story that at least warranted some sympathy. 'When I left the hospital that was the last time I ever saw Natasha. By the next morning I knew that I couldn't face her again. Not after what I'd done.'

27

When Peter Graham came to take his daughter Natasha home, minus his granddaughter, John had left the hospital. He went to the beach banks where he sat on a ledge with a bottle of vodka, berating the world for his loss. Darkness was setting in and nobody knew where he was. And nobody but Natasha and her dad knew the tragic news yet. He wasn't ready to tell people that despite how perfect his daughter had looked he'd been denied the joy of fatherhood.

On his grassy perch he swigged neat vodka from the bottle, sobbed a lot and got angry every now and then, shouting obscenities to anyone or anything that might be able to hear, because he didn't know how else he should be venting his emotions. He didn't think he'd known such sadness or rage existed within him.

To the north a solitary star shone, its brightness intensifying as the lilac sky turned to violet and then deep purple. At one time John might have thought it symbolic of a higher power that was looking down on him, offering comfort from the heavens, but now, on this night, the star was nothing more than a ball of gas suspended in the same galaxy as him. He'd renounced all hope of a sentient God the moment he'd held his daughter in his arms. Tonight, going forth, he was faithless.

It was the North Sea that provided John with all the unintrusive company he needed for the next few hours. Its foaming movement, way below, where he could see and hear it, was a constant in a world where babies were allowed to die without rhyme nor reason. It listened to his rebukes against life. And it stayed there till he was done.

By the time he went home everyone else was in bed. Nick was living in student digs and his dad had long since been kicked out, but Chris still lived there and his girlfriend Toni was staying over. John had seen her shoes by the back door. On the landing he heard his mother snoring, but all was quiet from behind Chris's door. He crept into his own room, not wanting to wake any of them.

He'd been lying in bed for only ten minutes when his bedroom door opened and Toni walked in. At first John thought she might be sleepwalking and had come into his room by accident, but then she closed the door behind her and said, 'Hey, I heard you coming in.'

Toni was a large girl, each of her thighs as big as Natasha's waist pre-pregnancy, but standing there in a short, tight nightdress she didn't look nearly as big as usual. Her long brown hair was black in the gloom and her massive breasts were squeezed together beneath a large crown printed onto the cotton fabric of her nightdress.

John grunted, unsure how else to respond, and watched, dumbfounded, as she walked to the bed and climbed under the duvet next to him.

Sitting upright, he jolted away from her, rubbing his tear-swollen eyes. 'What the fuck are you doing?'

'Aw poor baby,' she said, edging closer and running her fingers through his hair, the gesture more sexual than it ever should have been. She then pulled his head down so it rested against her chest and continued to stroke his hair. 'There, there, I know what happened. Poor, poor baby.'

He sat there stunned, in a grief induced vodka fugue, listening to her heart over the noise of his own, all too aware of the softness of her breasts against his cheek. The soft, soft comfort.

'Tell me all about it,' she urged. 'Go ahead. Cry.'

'But…how did you know? Who told you?'

'I didn't have to be told.'

'What're you talking about?' He pulled away from her.

'Hush now, I know you.'

'No. No you don't. You don't know me at all, you're my brother's girlfriend. You shouldn't even be in here.'

'Oh but I do and I should. I know you better than you know yourself.' And then she kissed him on the mouth and touched him in places she really shouldn't have.

28

'I still don't know how she knew,' John said.

Emily was regarding him with a look of horror. He could only hope that she was trying to find some valid excuse for what he'd done, so that she wouldn't have to think any less of him.

'I know I should have turned her away, refused her,' he went on. 'But it was like I just couldn't stop myself. As though someone else was controlling me. I can't even explain.

'The next morning I decided I had to leave. I couldn't face Natasha again, I felt sick thinking about what I'd done. I couldn't even look Chris in the eye. And Toni. She came downstairs and acted like nothing had happened. She looked me square in the eye and asked how I was. She said she hadn't seen me in over a week, then had the audacity to ask how Natasha was doing and when the baby was likely to be born. I mean, how cruel can a person be? I packed my bag and left. I was so full of shame and disgust and loathing for myself, I went for a drive not knowing where I was going or what I meant to do. I wound up at a friend's place in Manchester and ended up staying there. All I could think at the time was that Natasha deserved better than me.' John laughed scornfully. 'Christ, I was such a selfish little prick.'

'Shit, John,' Emily said at last. 'Why didn't you just confess?'

'Well, yeah, that would have been the most logical thing to do. That's what any *normal* person would have done. But I was consumed by these really dark thoughts and I was acting far from normally. Looking back I can see I had absolutely no regard for anybody. And that's what confuses me, Em. I'm not like that. I'm really not.'

'I don't know what to say.'

'I guess you don't have to say anything, what I did was inexcusable. I *hate* myself for it. You're the first person I've told any of this to.'

'Wow.'

'Wow indeed. Now you know what a bastard your big brother is.'

'Was.' She put her hand back on top of his.

...

John found Seren in the lounge. She was sitting on the floor in front of the television.

'You all packed, kidda?' he asked. 'Aunty Emily is gonna go for a walk with you and the dogs while I…'

Seren turned to him, her eyes wide and fearful, and whispered, 'Dad. She's here. Right. Now.'

'Aunty Emily? I know she is, dafty.'

'Not her. *Her.*' She tilted her head back and pointed to the ceiling.

John looked up. Red streaks veined the ceiling, a tangle of arteries bloodying the white. He gasped and, at the same time, a quick stabbing sensation brought him to his knees. It felt as though an invisible hot poker had been rammed through his chest, scorching flesh, muscle and tendon. His body instantly became stiff and his eyes rolled back. He could hear and feel the sea in his head, red waves creating white surf behind his eyes.

I know you. I know you. I know you.

'*Dad?*' Seren jumped to her feet and gripped his arm. She tried pulling, her face frantic as she urged him to get to his feet. But he dropped on all fours and hissed in pain, so she let go and ran from the room. 'Aunty Emily! *Quick!*'

John watched the lounge door slam shut after her. He

knew Seren hadn't done it. The ruckus of plywood against the doorjamb was as deafening as a gunshot and he imagined the furniture in the house next door would be trembling. He splayed his hands on the carpet and began to crawl towards the closed door, inch by agonising inch, with his back arched and teeth ground together. He had to get out. His temperature was soaring, pitching him into some red fever where the room all around him throbbed and undulated with the flow of blood. Whose, he didn't know. But he suspected if the ceiling were to split he'd drown in it. When eventually he reached the door and clenched its handle in his clammy hand, he found that it was jammed fast.

'Emily?' The pain in his chest made his voice sound terrifying, even to himself. '*Emily!*'

'What's happening, John?' She was on the other side of the door, her voice a crescendo of panic.

He could feel pressure on the handle as she also tried to get the door to open. 'I dunno, just get me out of here.'

'Alright, hang on I'll...' She screamed; a primal, horrible sound that made gooseflesh prick the back of John's neck. His pain then dissolved to nothing and the door handle turned easily in his grip. The door clicked open.

Staggering into the kitchen, barely upright, he found Emily cowering by the table, her hands cupped to either side of her head like blinkers, and Seren by the back door with both dogs.

'What happened?' he asked, gripping the back of a dining chair for support.

'I...I saw her,' Emily whimpered. Her eyes didn't seem to focus on him, even though she was talking to him.

'You saw who?'

'Megan. Over there. Next to Seren. She was pointing.'

'At what?'

'That.' Emily looked at the Quaker Oats box on the draining board. Her hands were trembling. 'And Seren was right, John. She was *so* right.'

'Right about what?'

'Megan. She looks just like me.'

29

Natasha was yet to hear from Lee. She'd sent numerous text messages, to which he hadn't replied. So when her home phone started to ring, she expected it to be him. It wasn't. John Gimmerick's old number was showing on the display. She faltered for a moment, contemplating whether or not to answer. In the end curiosity won through. 'Hello?'

'Natasha.'

That voice she hadn't heard for so many years made her gasp before she could stop herself. She took a deep breath. 'What do you want, John?'

'Listen, I'm so sorry about this…about everything in fact…I just…I don't know what to say.'

'You've waited almost eighteen years to say you're sorry?' Natasha could feel anger swelling in her chest, threatening to break through the calloused husk of her heart.

'No. I mean, yes. I mean, I've wanted to say sorry so many times before but I didn't know how.'

'So why now? Is your conscience finally too heavy for you to carry around? Is it such a burden on your otherwise happy life that you need to offload some of the weight?'

'Natasha, please…'

'No. Don't. You got your daughter to call me,' she spat. 'That's really warped, even by your standards.'

'No,' he said. 'I had no idea. Why would I get her to do that? She's only six for chrissakes.'

'The same reason you'd do anything I suppose. And I'm not interested in hearing your bullshit excuses by the way, you sick bastard.'

'I swear I didn't know. I have no idea where you are or how you're doing. How would I even get your number?'

'Same way your daughter did. Look me up online.'

'Tash, I'm so sorry. You have no idea…'

'Oh believe me, I have *every* idea. And don't you dare ask me to forgive you if that's what this is about.'

'No, no, no. I'm not going to ask for your forgiveness, I wouldn't expect that of you. And I wouldn't intrude into your life for the sake of redeeming my own conscience. I have more respect for you than that.'

Natasha laughed, a humourless sound that conveyed the extent of her animosity.

'For what it's worth I would like you to know that I'm eternally sorry for what happened, for what I did,' he reaffirmed. 'But that's not the reason I called. The thing is, I need to ask you something.'

'What could you possibly want to ask *me?*'

'I'm sorry this is out of the blue and that it's insensitive and totally unacceptable, but, please, I need to know…what did you call our baby?'

The question was as good as a kick in the stomach to Natasha. Her eyes blurred from the impact. '*Why?* Why torture me with this?'

'I wouldn't have called if it wasn't really important. Please, Tash, tell me this one thing and I'll leave you alone. You'll never hear from me again.'

Tears had begun to seep from her eyes and she struggled to keep her voice even. 'We lost our baby then shortly afterwards I lost my mother. I went through hell and back, John, but you wouldn't know that because you just disappeared. You left me to sort everything. And now, all these years later, you have the gall to harass me? I *hate* you. I can't even put into words how much.'

'If I could change the way things happened I would in a heartbeat. I'd do *everything* differently. But, as I said, I'm not seeking your forgiveness. It's just, I'm in some strange trouble right now. So please, I'm begging you, what did you call our baby?'

Natasha was now openly sobbing. 'Why should I tell you? You don't deserve to know her name. You never cared. As I recall you weren't there to pick out her coffin or choose a headstone. In fact you probably don't even know there is a grave, do you? Because if you did you'd know her name. You'd know where to find her.'

John fell quiet and Natasha could hear choked sobs on his end of the line. The sound of his pain made her feel in some way avenged, but nowhere near enough. She wanted to hurt him even more, to keep twisting and plunging the knife till his heart fell out of his chest, a pulp of unfixable mulch.

'Of course I cared,' he said eventually. 'I still do.'

'Keep telling yourself that, one day you might believe it.'

'You think I don't remember when her birthday is every year? That I didn't, and still don't, grieve her death? And that I don't think about all the different milestones, like when she'd have left school and the fact she'd be coming up eighteen? That she might have a boyfriend to fetch home by now or that I might be teaching her to drive. Each year on her birthday I *still* don't know whether I should be celebrating the memory of her or commiserating the fact she isn't here. So don't tell me I don't care, Tash. I might have been the lousiest shithouse of a boyfriend, but she was my daughter.'

'Sounds wonderfully sentimental. But, still, you never even knew her name.'

'Angel. She was always Angel to me.'

'Cute. So why change that now?'

'Because now I need to know her official name.'

'You don't deserve to know.'

'Please, Natasha, I'm begging you. If you won't do it for me, then please do it for my little girl's sake. Do it for Seren. She's six and I think she's in danger.'

'Oh my God, I can't believe you're pulling a stunt like that. What danger could your daughter possibly be in that has anything at all to do with *my* daughter?'

'It's not a stunt, Tash, I'm being serious. Tell me this one thing and you'll never hear from me ever again. I promise.'

'You better mean that.'

'I do, I swear.'

'Megan. Her name is Megan,' Natasha said. Then before terminating the call she told him, 'I hate you, Gimmerick. I really, truly despise you.'

30

John tipped the box's remaining contents out onto the counter. Two soggy photo albums and a plastic wallet full of old car documents slid across the formica and onto the floor. Something clanged against the stainless steel draining board three times before falling into the sink. It was a cameo brooch that came to rest in the plughole, face up, too large to fit through the slots. John picked it up, confused as to why it should have been amongst his stuff. His fingers brushed the aged enamel and he studied the milky profile of a lady on its terracotta-coloured background. Her wavy hair was swept into a Victorian updo and her thin-lipped mouth curved upwards. The roundedness of her face and thick neck suggested a high-end, sedentary lifestyle of fine dining, whereas the area where her eye had once been was worn to a dark socket. There was something unavoidably sinister about the contradictory cherubic skeletal image, and she wasn't smiling so much as leering, John thought.

A loud clatter from somewhere overhead made him jump. He pocketed the brooch and hurried upstairs to find that the loft hatch had swung open, taking a gouge out of the doorframe to his mother's bedroom. His stomach lurched when he saw familiar dark tendrils creeping from the opening in the ceiling, spoiling the artex with shadowy branches of mould that loomed over him.

'Megan? Is it you?' John kept his voice low. He listened. There was a stillness to the house, but he could hear nothing but the ticking of a clock somewhere and the hum of an electrical appliance. 'Tell me what you want me to do.'

Still nothing.

This is crazy.

As soon as Emily returned with Seren and the dogs it was time for them to leave, he decided. He felt bad for running out on his kid sister, especially since he'd hoped to offer her more than just a few days of high drama and the sort of head-fuckery that would give social services every good reason to come knocking on his door.

He went to his old room to pack his stuff together. When he opened the door he was taken aback by the smell that wafted out. It held the sourness of stagnant water in a vase of dead flowers, stinging his eyes with all its pungency. John gagged, automatically looking up, and saw the ceiling was laced with bulging grey veins which threaded down onto the walls, turning the room itself into some postmortem-like ventricle.

He marched to the window and threw it wide, to get rid of the stink, and saw that around thirty dead flies had collected on the sill. He frowned. Using the back of his hand he tried to sweep them outside, but most of them got stuck in the groove of the window frame. He'd need to pick them out.

Shit, shit! Fucking shit!

'Dad?'

The voice was a simple plea that brought with it a chill that swept over John, freezing him rigid and killing his fury. Then slowly, expectantly, slowly he began to turn, afraid of what he'd see but too afraid not to look.

Standing by the door was a hazy version of Emily. Only, it wasn't Emily. His sister's lips were fuller and happier. This girl was too pale, her face shrouded by deathly woe and her blue eyes lacklustre. Dark hair fell down to her waist and a long black dress looked at one with the darkness that must surely keep her. She was an image of pure torment.

'Megan?'

Her responsive smile was instant but wistful. 'You remember me?'

John was almost floored by a rush of emotion, tears blurred his eyes and he thought his knees would give out. He wiped at his cheeks with the heel of his hand and told her, 'I never ever forgot.'

She started moving towards him but suddenly stopped, fear etching a harrowing piteousness onto her ghostly face. She looked up, as though she'd heard something.

'What is it?' John asked, matching her move and stepping closer. She held out her hands to stop him, her eyes wide and fearful, and he saw that she faded around the edges at such proximity. He immediately jolted back, afraid she might disappear altogether.

'The brooch,' she said, her voice as delicate as distant memories inside his head.

He took the cameo from his pocket, holding it out, but not taking his eyes off her. 'What about it? What is it, Megan?'

'It's Her link to you. Her link to the children.'

'Whose link to me? What children?'

Megan lowered her voice and backed away till she was out on the landing. 'She's very close. And strong. If She catches me talking to you She'll punish me. I must go. Now. And so must Seren.'

'But…' There was a crackling sound, like dead beetles underfoot, and John watched, horrified, as skeins of mould left the landing ceiling to dangle like vines before wrapping themselves around Megan's arms and torso. *'Whose link to me?'* Desperation made his voice frantic and he lurched forward to try and stop her leaving. To break her binds somehow. But instantly she paled to nothing, her sad eyes lingering with him, and he heard her voice in his thoughts: 'Don't leave me again, Dad. Please don't leave me alone with Her.'

31

'I'm going to hang up and then I'm going to phone the police,' Natasha threatened, her voice a low hiss so as not to attract the attention of her customers.

'No. Please. Don't.' John's voice was thick with upset. 'You're the only person I can turn to. I know I said I'd leave you alone, but…something's happening, Tash.'

'I'm the *only* person you could turn to? Ha! I'm the *last* person you should turn to.'

'You're right. But I need your help making sense of something.'

'Where were you when *I* needed to make sense of things?'

'I know, I know. I have no right to hound you like this and I wouldn't if it wasn't so serious.'

Natasha sighed, her initial anger reducing to a wearied frustration. 'Okay, I'll humour you one last time. One. Last. Time. What is it?'

'I take it from your number that you're not living locally anymore?'

'If by living locally you mean Horden, then no, of course not.' After considering what he'd said some more, she asked, 'You weren't actually thinking of suggesting we meet up?'

'Well, yes. If you were in the vicinity at some point it might have been easier to explain this face to face.'

'Well I'm not.'

'And there's no chance I could come to you?'

'Absolutely none.'

'Okay, if that's the way it is.'

'It is. And you'll have to be quick, I'm busy.'

John paused for a moment, then asked, 'Can you

remember a cameo brooch at all?'

'No. Should I?'

'I don't know. I found it in a box of my old stuff.'

'And so you thought it might be mine?'

'Yeah, maybe.'

'Are you for real?' The outrage had returned to her voice. 'You call me up at work sounding like you've got some sort of emergency situation going on, but really you just wanted to ask if I'd mislaid a brooch some years ago?'

'No, it's not like that. I just needed to know if you remembered it, that's all. It's orange with a cream face…'

'I know what a bloody cameo looks like. Why *should* I remember it?'

'Because something's going on. Strange stuff has been happening and I think it's all related to the cameo.'

'Strange stuff like what?' Now she sounded sceptical.

'I'd rather not say. It's not exactly rational.'

'I'd rather you did say, so that I can know why it is you seem intent on making my life a misery.'

John sighed. 'Seren seems to think someone's coming for her. At first I thought she was being difficult, but now I'm starting to believe she might actually be in danger.'

'And who do you think is coming for her?'

'I don't know.'

'Why don't you call the police if you're so concerned?'

'Because it's not like that.'

'So how is it?'

'Oh never mind, it doesn't matter.'

'Obviously you think it does, else you wouldn't have bothered calling me.'

'I know, I'm sorry for bothering you, I just…'

'John. Tell me what's going on.'

Again there was a brief silence, then he said, 'It's like whoever's coming for Seren isn't real.'

'What the hell's that supposed to mean?'

'That there's possibly something supernatural going on.'

'Are you deliberately trying to mess with my head?' Natasha could feel her anxiety increasing again.

'No, not at all. Forget I called. You answered the question, that's all I wanted to know.'

'Wait. You can't just call me up, ask cryptic questions about a brooch and then expect to leave it at that. Why would you think that something supernatural is going on? For once in your damn life be fucking straight with me, Gimmerick.'

'Alright, alright.' He paused again then said, 'I've seen her.'

'You've seen who?'

'Megan. Our daughter.'

32

Father Murray was escorted to the room by Kevin. He looked nice enough, handsome that is, but Sissy Dawson was sure he would prove to be inadequate, much too young and inexperienced to deal with matters such as hers. The men exchanged mumbled words at the door then Kevin left, closing the door behind him.

'Ah, Mrs Dawson,' Father Murray said, striding to the bedside with a white-toothed greeting. He removed the black felt fedora from his head, a gesture of considered gentility, she thought, but didn't bother ruffling his dark brown hair back into place. It lay lank and fine against his head, the weight of the hat having defeated any oomph it might have had. He wore a fitted black shirt, complete with white dog collar at the neck, and skinny black jeans. On his feet a pair of black, ornate cowboy boots. He tossed his hat onto the dresser and took the liberty of dragging an armchair closer to the bed, uninvited, then sat down. His shoulders were broad, squared and sturdy and he sat with his legs wide apart. Obviously a man comfortable in his own skin, confident in his own abilities.

'Father Murray,' Sissy said in acknowledgement. She raised an eyebrow at his forwardness, half smiling at his atypical persona – he wasn't what she'd expected at all. He smelled of cigarettes and aftershave and there was a cheeky, defiant gleam to his eye that wasn't standard for anyone of the cloth she'd ever met before. There was a silver band on his wedding finger which instantly made her wonder about his wife, what a woman who utilised those broad hands, thinking they were hers alone, would look like.

'So then,' he said, clapping those hands onto his thighs. 'Young Kevin tells me you've been fretting. That right?'

Father Murray could only be a couple of years older than Kevin himself, if that, Sissy observed, yet he'd assumed the role of dominant male in the guise of fatherliness. She smiled and said to him, 'She'd have a field day with you, young man.'

'She would?'

'Mmm hmmm.'

'She being who exactly?' Father Murray leaned forward. His eyes were patchy. Green or brown, depending on which angle the light caught them.

'The nameless, faceless one.' Sissy saw no point in faffing around with the niceties of proper introductions, preferring to get straight down to business.

Father Murray's handsome face looked vague for a moment. He swiped a hand through his hair, which made no difference whatsoever to its limp composition. 'She sounds rather ominous. I'd sooner she didn't have a field day with me if I'm honest.'

'Wise words, Father Murray.'

His whole demeanour seemed to smile, an arrogance that shone through as if she'd just validated something he expected was always the case. 'Indeed.'

'But, of course, I don't believe you,' she added.

This seemed to disconcert the vicar for a snatch of a second. His eyes appeared anxious and his lip twitched, but he recovered himself well enough. Anyone else, apart from Sissy, might not have noticed at all.

'Now, what's this all about?' he asked, coughing into his hand, by way of diversion 'What is it that's got you so troubled?'

'Oh, you know.' Sissy wafted her hand, the one not in the plaster cast, in the air. 'This and that.'

'Let's start with the this then, shall we?'

'Very well. God won't speak to me. I fear I've offended Him too much.'

'Nonsense.' Father Murray shook his head reprovingly. 'Now what about the that? We'll come back to this.'

'Okay. She's returned after a long spate of silence and Her ghosts have come to haunt me.'

'Are you referring to yourself in the past tense, Mrs Dawson?'

'Of course not, what kind of nutter would I be to do that?'

Father Murray laughed. 'Then forgive me, Mrs Dawson, but I'm not quite sure I understand. That is, I understand the this but not the that. Can we start from the beginning? Tell me who this mysterious *she* is.'

'No. It doesn't matter, not to you. I've already tried fighting Her with all the love for God I've ever known, but it's never been enough. And now She must have found a new host because She's getting stronger and stronger. Maybe She's even got a new child or children to prey on. I do hope not.'

'Ridiculous. God's *always* enough when it matters,' Father Murray scoffed. 'And we're all His children, so if any of us should stray I'm sure we'd find our way back to Him in the end.'

'You mean, that's what you hope.'

'It's what I know.'

'Are you really certain about that, Father?'

'Of course.'

'What about those who never had any choice?'

'They'll find their way eventually.'

'I'm not so sure. What will happen when the ghost children grow old and He can't, or won't, save them? Will they die all over again? And what about me? When I die will I be an unclaimed ghost who is haunted by the ghosts of ghosts? It's a cycle I fear might never change if

I were to get into it, but there's no alternative that I can see.'

If Father Murray was confused he didn't show it, he simply nodded his head as though she'd said the most rational thing. 'I can assure you that God *will* be waiting to welcome you into His loving arms when the day comes. Fear not, Mrs Dawson.'

'Oh I fear alright. And perhaps you should too.'

'What specifically is it that you fear?' Father Murray asked. 'Death?'

'Not at all.'

'Then what?'

'We are all treading where the saints have trodden before, are we not?'

'Indeed we are.'

'But that doesn't mean we get to join them in their final resting place when we grow tired, for not all of us are saints.' Sissy fixed him with a hard stare.

Father Murray shifted in his seat and sat back, his expression dubious. 'But we're all God's children nonetheless and He doesn't expect us *all* to be saints.'

'Hmmm, I do hope you're right. For both of our sakes.' Sissy turned her head away and closed her eyes. 'I think you'd better leave now, Father. She draws near and, as I already said, She'd have a field day with you.'

'Nonsense. I don't fear this woman, whoever she may be.'

'Then you're a wilful fool.'

'Now that's not altogether polite, is it, Mrs Dawson?' Father Murray said, his eyes showing amusement rather than offence.

'Nor will She be, She doesn't indulge in subtlety.'

'Nor do I.' He laughed. 'I'm not exactly known for my delicacy or softness, I can assure you.'

'Yes, and that's why She'll eat your cock as soon as look at you if you're still here when She arrives. And I swear to God She'll enjoy every inch of it.'

33

Emily found John sitting at the top of the stairs, his face even paler than usual. He didn't seem to notice that she was standing in the hallway looking up at him.

'John?'

When he still didn't acknowledge her she rushed up the stairs, two at a time. 'What happened?'

'I can't leave,' he said, adrift in his own thoughts. 'I have to stay here and work it out.'

'Work what out?' She shuffled in next to him on the top stair, so their shoulders were touching.

'I found this in the box.' He opened his hand and showed her the brooch. 'It's relevant to everything that's been going on.'

'Relevant how?'

'I dunno, that's what I've got to figure out.' He'd been staring at a section of the wall beneath the window but finally turned to look at her. 'Listen, if I give you some money will you take Seren away for the night? I dunno if there's a hotel nearby or…'

Emily clicked her tongue and nudged him hard. 'Hotel my arse. I'll take her home with me if you don't want her here. She can share my bed and hang out with the boys.'

'Are you sure?'

'Of course I am, doofus. A houseful of miscreants might do her good.' She nudged him with her shoulder again, trying for a smile.

He obliged.

'Seriously, though,' she said, 'there'll be plenty of eyes to keep tabs on her.'

'Thanks, Em.'

'What about you though? I won't lie, I'm not happy about you staying here alone.'

'I won't be alone. I've got the dogs.'

Emily sighed but didn't bother arguing, she could tell he'd made up his mind. 'You do nothing but worry me sick, you know that, dickhead?'

He smiled thinly. 'Sorry, but I need to do this.'

'Then I'm coming to check up on you first thing in the morning.'

'Alright, Mam.'

...

John felt strangely calm once he was alone again, just knowing that Seren was out of harm's way was a huge relief. He had no plan of action, but knew that, whatever happened, he couldn't leave his mother's house, not until whatever danger Megan was in had been resolved. Although not hungry, he prepared himself a stir fry and ate in silence, hoping to be receptive to any message Megan should want to convey. Occasionally he even spoke to her. But no answers came.

It was just after eight when the garden gate creaked. Otis and Mindy ran to the kitchen and shortly afterwards there was a knock at the back door.

Oh God.

Pamela Tanner was the last person John wanted to be dealing with. Perhaps she had seen Emily leave with Seren and knew of his vulnerability, the fact that he was home alone. The very idea filled him with dread, but that quickly turned to outrage. He was in no mood for her games. How dare she keep imposing on him, intruding into his life and making things even more complicated than they already were. He stalked through to the kitchen and threw open the back door, ready to face her down, but instead was stunned into silence.

Natasha Graham had aged well. She looked just as surprised as he did, even though she must have anticipated seeing him. Her hair was now caramel blonde and her face more slender than it had been. Fine lines around her eyes and mouth didn't make her any less attractive, but a large bruise on her forehead was a juxtapositional flaw that wasn't good at all. She wore a cream chiffon shirt tucked into skinny blue jeans and exuded a more adult sophistication. After recovering from the initial shock of seeing him, she took on an expression that John could only interpret as loathing. She stood there, waiting for him to do something, and he could tell she wasn't going to make this easy.

'Tash.'

'John.' Her entire countenance was solemn, and there wasn't an ounce of warmth or welcome to be found in her eyes.

He moved aside and pulled the door open further. Gesturing with his hand, he said, 'You'd better come in.'

She glanced down the drive for a moment, which made him wonder if she was worried that someone might see her there, or whether someone was waiting for her in a car. But then she nodded and stepped into the kitchen.

'Thanks for coming.' John pulled at his shirt, a subconscious effort to straighten it, but really it was his insides that were all twisted up and knotted. 'It, er, means a lot.'

'I'm not here for you,' she said, bending to stroke one of the dogs. 'I came because I wanted to…I thought that…if you're telling the truth, I want to…'

'See her?'

She nodded and straightened up again, allowing their eyes to meet. 'And I remembered something about the brooch…'

34

Natasha's stomach clenched. John wasn't the same John. She'd expected he would be, just older. But he wasn't and seeing him like this stirred all kinds of emotions. She wanted to hate him. Should have been satisfied to see that his mesmeric eyes, still beguiling in their intensity, were now haunted. That his lean physique was now too angular and thin, his complexion marred by the hint of illness. But, strangely, the sight of him ailing didn't give her any sense of recompense. In fact it surprised her to find that, if anything, it hurt her to look at him. On the drive north from Whitby she'd imagined standing where she was now, yelling. She had plenty she wanted to say to him, she'd even thought she might slap him. But instead she just stood there, saying not much at all, uncertainty quelling eighteen years' worth of built-up rage.

John ran a hand through his thick hair, his full-lipped smile weary. 'Would you like to come through?' He gestured towards the lounge.

'Only if I'm not interrupting anything, I'd hate to…'

'No, not at all. Emily's taken Seren away for the night. There's just me.' John urged her to lead the way and, once in the lounge, he seemed compelled to explain, 'Emily's my kid sister by the way.'

'Oh?' Natasha sat on the edge of the couch, clasping her hands together, her shoulders rigid.

'My dad's big scandal,' John explained, easing down into the armchair opposite.

'Right, I see. There were a couple of Gimmerick scandals that year as I recall.' She tried to intimidate him with a hard stare, but her voice lacked its intended venom.

John's face reddened, nonetheless, and he averted his gaze. 'Can I, er, get you something to drink? Tea? Coffee? Something cold?'

'No, I'm fine thanks.' She looked around. 'So, this place has changed quite a bit.'

'Yeah. It's been a while.'

'How come you're staying here? Is your mam…'

'On holiday. She asked me to mind the place while she's away.'

'And your little girl?'

'Yeah she's been staying with me too. Only, not tonight.' He shuffled back in the armchair, perhaps to give the illusion of ease, but he looked anything but comfortable. 'So how about you? What's back in Whitby? Husband? Kids?'

Natasha shook her head and said, 'This isn't a social call, John.'

'Yeah. Sorry. I just hoped to hear that things are going well for you.'

'To ease your guilt?'

'Something like that.'

'Longterm boyfriend,' she sighed. Then for reasons she didn't understand, she felt compelled to lie. 'We're going to be married.'

'Nice. Congratulations.'

'What about you?' She felt obliged to ask, though, admittedly was curious to know the answer.

'Usually home is Leeds. Just me and Seren.'

'Does she still see her mother?'

'No. Amy passed away. Three years ago.'

'Oh. I'm sorry.'

'It's okay.'

Natasha shuffled about. She felt awkward. They had way overstepped some privacy boundaries they had no business overstepping. He didn't know her and she didn't know him. They were strangers, alienated by a troubled past. No amount of chit-chat would fix that. 'Listen, let's cut to the chase eh?'

'Yeah,' he agreed, sitting forward again. 'I don't think it's nice for either of us, especially you, for all this to be…dredged up. I really didn't mean to upset you on the phone. I'm sorry. It's all been hard for me to swallow. That is, this latest business with Megan…'

Natasha hadn't known what to think when John had told her on the phone that he'd seen the ghost of their daughter. And sitting here now she worried about his mental stability. But, still, she had to see for herself. Had to know for sure. 'So, what was she like?'

'All grown up. Beautiful.'

Natasha's eyes felt hot with tears and she clamped her teeth together, the last thing she wanted to do was to cry in front of John Gimmerick. He rocked forward as if to get up and go to her, then relaxed back as if having thought better of it.

'And where was it you saw her?' she asked.

'Upstairs. In my old room.'

'Is that the only place?'

'Yeah. But Seren's seen her all over the place. And Emily saw her in the kitchen.'

'You've *all* seen her?'

'Yeah. And now that you've come all the way from Whitby, I hope you do.'

'Me too, I certainly didn't come all this way to see you.'

John frowned. 'No, given the choice I imagine I'm the last person you want to see.'

'You're not wrong.' This in itself was another lie. In truth she'd longed to see him, if only to be reassured that in the long run he'd done her a great service by leaving her. She needed closure. She'd hoped to find that John Gimmerick was an irritating waste of space, someone she could continue to loathe, but the reality was very different. If anything she felt pity towards him, which was a totally unexpected development. This meeting was turning out to be a different kind of therapy altogether. But perhaps a better one. Who needed a constant source of anger? Life was tough enough.

'Are you sure I can't get you something to drink?' John asked.

Her shoulders relaxed a little and she managed a wan smile. 'Well, only if you're having one.'

'Tea? Coffee?'

'Tea would be great thanks.'

'Or a glass of wine maybe?'

'I'd better not, I'm driving.'

'You could always stay. I mean, not like that or anything. God, obviously not like that. Wow, I'm sorry, that sounded weird. I just meant...she might come to you if you do.'

Natasha pondered the offer and surprised herself by accepting so readily. 'Alright then, I will.'

John disappeared into the kitchen and came back with two crystal cut glasses full of red wine. 'I can't promise you will see her,' he said, handing her a glass. 'But I hope you do. I really want you to.'

'Thanks.' She took the wine and sank back, allowing the sofa's cushions to mould around her. A faint beeping alerted her to a text message. She took her mobile from her handbag and saw she had a message from Lee: **You busy?**

She looked at John, who was watching her with what she thought was bewildered awe. 'Sorry, just got to reply to this,' she said, her finger already tapping out a reply: **Yes, sorry. Long story. Will explain tomorrow.**

She balanced the phone on her knee and took a sip from her glass. 'So, did Megan say anything to you at all?'

John tugged on his bottom lip, pondering his answer, then just as he readied himself to speak her phone beeped again. Lee: **Don't bother calling. Going away for a while. Need to get head in order.**

What?

How long was a while? A day? A week? A month? Eighteen years?

So, he intended to leave her hanging for an indefinite amount of time?

No chance.

She put the phone back into her bag without responding. She didn't have the emotional capability to do so sensibly. It was taking all of her resolve to keep a neutral face, what she wanted was to excuse herself and go to the bathroom so she could lament in peace. Lee had as good as sealed the fate of their future.

'Everything alright?' John asked, obviously sensing her upset.

'Yeah, yeah.' She waved a hand dismissively, aware that her demeanour probably made it clear that everything wasn't. 'So, you were about to say?'

John nodded, his face reflecting his quiet concern, but he was careful to respect her situation and avoid causing embarrassment. 'Megan spoke of another person, someone female. But she wouldn't say who. She said that the brooch was this other female's link to me, and to the children. Does that mean anything to you?'

'Not specifically, no, but I do remember the brooch. It came to me suddenly after you'd been on the phone. Do you remember when…'

35

'Do you think she'll recognise me today?'

'I dunno.' John squeezed Natasha's hand. 'Try not to get too upset if she doesn't though.' It wasn't often that he went to Eden Vale with Natasha to visit her mother. It was a depressing place full of elderly and sick people. It highlighted his own mortality and reluctance to grow old. Also, he felt like an intruder getting in the way of Natasha's time with her mother. Diane Graham never remembered who he was so he would just sit there quietly, on standby, ready to offer emotional support to Natasha should she need it. Today Natasha had specifically asked him to go with her because she wanted them, together, to tell Diane Graham that she was going to be a grandmother. Even though they'd told her four times before.

Pushing through the entrance swing doors and stepping into the dowdy foyer, John and Natasha were greeted by the smiley receptionist, Angie. She was an attractive woman in her mid-thirties whose permed, lacquered hair and slouchy Arran cardigans made John think her sense of style might have come to a halt at the onset of motherhood some ten years before. He wondered if the same thing would happen to Natasha. Looking at her now, though, with her 'Rachel' haircut and a cropped denim jacket worn over the top of a stretch midi dress, which hugged her baby bump and curves, he didn't think he'd mind at all.

'Afternoon,' Angie said, beaming at the sight of Natasha. 'Look at the size of you now. How long?'

'Five weeks and counting.' Natasha smiled, rubbing the mound of her belly. 'Is it okay for us to go up, Ang?'

'Yeah, sure. I think she might be in the communal room, probably watching Countdown or some such. Richard Whiteley seems to perk the lot of them up. I think it's his ties.'

Natasha laughed and climbed the stairs to the first floor alongside John.

Eden Vale smelled stale, of too many sick people being cooped up together over too many years. The carpet throughout was navy with a repetitive yellow-gold pattern somewhere between crooked tree and fleur-de-lys. It felt flat underfoot and was just as cheerless and dispiriting to look at. Striped blue and cream wallpaper adorned the lower half of the walls and dividing it from the stark plain whiteness of the upper half was a pink floral border. The walls clashed with themselves, as well as the carpet. And with the regular passage of wheelchairs and tea trolleys by the looks of it. Numerous wall-moustaches had been added to the wallpaper's vertical stripes where wheels and hard edges had scuffed past.

In the communal room Diane Graham was sitting in front of the television on a brown leather three-seater. Next to her was an old woman in a lilac pointelle jumper, her fat ankles were the colour of corned beef and angry with water retention. At the other end of the couch an old man in a bobbly grey cardigan sat with his mouth open. All three of them looked engrossed in some celebrity chef's witticisms on screen, but most likely none of them were listening to a damn word he said. In the corner of the room three men and a woman were playing cards and a thin grey-haired woman paced the floor on slippered feet. 'It's no good,' she kept saying to nobody in particular. 'No good at all. We need to get out.'

John and Natasha pulled up plastic chairs which reminded them both of being back at school, and sat down by the side of the couch.

'Mam?' Natasha touched the back of her mother's hand.

Diane Graham remained facing the television, unresponsive, but the woman in the lilac jumper turned and hushed Natasha with vexed eyes. So Natasha and John waited thirty minutes in uncompanionable silence and watched as the celebrity chef and his panel of guests diced veg for a Mediterranean stew, then cooked and ate it. Eventually Natasha shook her head at John and stood up. It was one of those days when Diane Graham just wasn't responsive at all and no amount of sitting with her or talking to her would change that. John cleared their chairs away while Natasha said her goodbyes, then the two of them made for the door. Before they got there the old woman who had been pacing the floor stood still and shouted, 'A baby. A beautiful baby girl!'

The four card players stopped what they were doing and looked up.

'I've got a baby,' one of them said. He was an overweight man, in his forties, who had alopecia. His skin looked dewy and radiant.

'Give your head a shake, Barry, no you don't,' said another of the men, before taking a lengthy draw on the end of a biro. He looked considerably older than the fat man, with thin brown hair and lenses in his glasses that looked as dense and discoloured as the bottoms of empty coffee jars. He tapped his finger against the pen, knocking invisible ash off onto the table. 'You're a right crackerjack you are, lad.'

'I *do* have a baby,' Barry argued. 'Her name's Martha and she's the sweetest thing. Oh aye. I've got most of the hearts an' all. I'm gonna win this time.'

'Don't be daft,' the pen smoker said. 'You're nowt but a cheat and a bloody big liar. I can see you're hidin' something up your sleeve there.'

Barry slammed his arms hands down onto the table and blushed profusely.

'Eee now here, Bazza, you better not be hiding the Queen of Spades.' The woman card player stood up, her voice shrill and phlegmy; nauseating like teeth on wool. She jabbed her finger in Barry's direction to demonstrate her disapproval, the loose skin of her upper arm flapping about like an offcut of meat. 'Nev, is that what he's got? Is it? Is it? Can you see? Bloody disgrace if you have mind, Bazza. Bloody disgrace.'

Barry stood and whipped a card from his shirt sleeve. He slapped it down on the table, his face glowing with rage and the embarrassment of being caught out. Without another word he turned and stomped towards the door.

The slippered old woman cackled and called after him, 'Fairness fades the Queen of Spades, but you oughtn't hide her, you know. Keep her in your hearts, she'll do well. She *always* wins.' She then returned her attention to Natasha and crooned, 'Baby girl.'

Something about the way the old woman grinned unsettled John. Her eyes looked cunning, not befitting the confused state of mind she had at first appeared to keep. In fact he thought there was a sharp level of awareness about her, an intellect that was crude and calculating. He kept his hand on Natasha's arm.

'We're not sure what sex the baby is yet,' Natasha said, smiling politely. 'We'll have to wait and see.'

'I'm telling you,' the old woman said, moving closer. 'It's a girl.' She dropped her hand into the pocket of her cardigan then pulled something out and offered it to Natasha. 'Here, for the baby.'

'That's very kind of you,' Natasha said, 'but no thank you.'

The woman's arthritic hand uncurled, revealing an antique brooch. A lady's head and shoulders in cream enamel contrasted against a burnt orange background, surrounded by ornate brass filigree. 'Please. Take it.'

'No really,' Natasha said, edging away. 'I couldn't take your belongings from you.'

'But I insist.'

'It looks expensive, and I'm sure it must have sentimental value. You keep it.'

'No! Here…' The old woman lurched forward but John was quick to intervene.

'Look, missus,' he said, his hand closing around hers so that her bony fist kept the brooch, 'it's very kind of you, but we can't take your stuff.'

At first the old woman looked startled, but then her eyes mellowed and she smiled. 'Ah, the baby's father?'

'Yes.'

She looked at Natasha and winked. 'Very nice indeed.'

Natasha, in turn, looked at John and raised her eyebrows.

'Such pretty eyes,' the old woman said. 'She's quite partial to young men, especially them that's got pretty eyes.'

'Who is?'

'She is.'

'Alright, well it was nice meeting you.' John squeezed Natasha's arm, a prompt to get her moving.

'Young men, so full of haste and hormones and no experience,' the old woman said. 'She finds that irresistible.'

'I'm sure she does,' he said moving off.

The old woman grabbed the sleeve of his hooded sweater, the fabric bunching tightly in her fist and her fingers digging into the skin of his forearm. 'Wait!' she rasped, pulling him to her.

A warm stink like blocked drains emitted from her mouth and John reeled from the fetid impact as it hit the back of his nose. He tried to shrug away from her raptor-like grip, nauseous because of her breath and confounded that she possessed so much strength. 'Let go of me please.'

She released her hold but took his hand and pressed the brooch into it. 'Here, for the baby,' she said. 'Take it. *Take it!*'

Everyone in the communal room turned and looked, Diane Graham included.

'Okay, okay, I'll take the damn thing,' he said, shaking his head despairingly.

Natasha put her hand in his and they both hurried from the room.

Downstairs, at reception, John showed Angie the brooch. 'Hey Ang, some old lady gave me this. I didn't want to take it, but she was adamant...'

Angie started to laugh. 'Oh that'll be Sissy. She's always trying to give that thing away.'

'She seemed like a bit of a handful, so I didn't want to argue too much,' John said, putting the brooch on the counter. 'Could you give it back to her please?'

'Gosh no, she *is* a handful and she'd have a dicky fit if I took that back up to her. No way. My advice is to just take it. If she asks for it back, I know where to find you. But I'll bet you a million pounds she won't.'

36

John went to bed with a heavy heart and a loaded conscience. What did the brooch from Eden Vale have to do with Megan? Had the old woman, Sissy, cursed him? Was it her fault that he and Natasha had lost Megan? Moreover his *own* fault because he was the one who'd taken the brooch. The idea made him feel physically sick. He'd left Natasha downstairs, sleeping on his mother's couch. They'd both been in a state of melancholic shock by the time they'd finished discussing the brooch and all it might mean. Just days earlier John had thought his life could only improve, that things could get no worse, but now he realised he'd been wrong. This was a new level of torture that he'd been totally unprepared for.

He'd felt awkward about leaving Natasha in the lounge, but she'd declined the offer of a bedroom; probably uncomfortable about the entire situation, but curious enough to want to stay the night if only for a glimpse of her daughter. John felt wracked with guilt in case he'd built her hopes up unfairly, in case Megan didn't reveal herself. But then he reasoned with himself that Natasha had a right to know what was going on.

The brooch itself was on the kitchen table. Tomorrow they'd decide, together, what they should do with it.

He lay entangled in sheets. It was a cool night but the window was cracked open, his escape route to the outside world, should he need it. He stared at the ceiling thinking that he wouldn't be able to sleep at all, but at some point he must have drifted off. When he awoke again it was still grey enough for him to know that it was nowhere near morning, and he could hear the undeniable creak of floorboards out on the landing. Not from the cooling or heating of wooden boards as the house settled, but actual footfalls. Someone was out there.

Surely it couldn't be Natasha. Why would she come upstairs? The bathroom was downstairs and she knew that. Unless she'd seen Megan and was coming to tell him. But somehow he very much doubted she'd want to share that experience with him.

Or maybe it *was* Megan.

Or Pamela Tanner.

He eased up onto his elbow and watched with nervous apprehension as the door handle moved.

Please not Pamela Tanner.

Please not one of those *nights.*

When the door was fully open he was stunned to see Natasha standing there, wrapped in the gold chenille throw from the couch.

'Tash?' He sat up fully, self-conscious enough to cover his bare chest with the duvet. 'Is everything okay?'

'Yes. Well, no.' She shuffled to the bed. 'I can't sleep at all. I don't know what I'm doing here.'

John didn't know if it was a generalised statement about her staying in his mother's house or if she was being more specific about being in his bedroom. 'You're upset. It's been a lot to take in.'

She sat down on the edge of the bed, the soft throw that was around her brushing against his arm. He could feel her heat.

'Funny how things turned out,' she said, looking down at her hands.

'How do you mean?'

'All our dreams for the future. All the promises we made. It's hard to believe we were deliriously happy once.'

'Is it?'

She looked up at him and smiled. 'Yes, it is.'

'I never forgot about you.' He tried to rest a hand on her shoulder, but instantly she shied away from the contact.

'Good,' she said. 'I'm glad you never did. I hope in all these years you've been *consumed* by thoughts of me.' Her eyes and body language were frosty and John could sense an argument in the offing.

'It's late,' he said, not knowing what else to say.

'Does it matter?'

He thought for a moment then sighed. 'No, I don't suppose it does. I expect you want to shout at me, to say your piece, hit me even, but you've had a drink. Do you really want to do this right now?'

'You think that's what I want?'

'Well what do you want?'

'An explanation.' He saw now that he'd been mistaken. Her eyes resounded with hurt, not anger.

He closed his eyes and applied pressure to them. Sighing inwardly, he knew he had no choice but to confess. She deserved to know. 'I did something terrible. I felt that I had to go.'

'What was so terrible that you had to shun me?'

'I slept with Chris's girlfriend. *That* night. She came to me. I didn't ask her to. I didn't want her to. But I didn't stop her.'

If Natasha was shocked by the admission she didn't flinch or give any outward sign.

'I'm really sorry, Tash,' he said. 'It meant nothing, nothing at all, and I know I should have told you instead of just running away. I still can't believe I did...*any of it.* Just so you know, I'll never forgive myself. And I don't expect you to either. I don't expect anything from you.'

'You don't?'

His eyes narrowed. 'What could I possibly expect from you?'

She lifted her arm and traced a finger along the

knuckles of his left hand. 'There's always been a part of me that never stopped thinking about you, John.'

For a moment he couldn't speak, taken aback by the fact she was touching him. But, also, he was now sceptical about her motive. He expected she'd blow at any minute. 'I'm sure that's the wine talking.'

'And I'm sure it's not. I only had two glasses.'

He relaxed his grip on the duvet, exposing his chest, and pivoted round so that his body was facing her. Whatever she had planned he wanted to get it over and done with as quickly as possible. He accepted that he deserved every single bit of her wrath, so he'd let her do whatever she needed. 'What are you doing here, Tash? Why did you come to my room?'

'Because I want you.'

That was the last thing ever he'd have expected her to say. Astounded and perplexed, he shook his head. 'No. No you don't.'

'There were times when I really, really hated you, when I wished you dead. But seeing you tonight, I dunno, I remember now how vulnerable you always were. I knew you had issues, I always knew you were different. But that's what I liked most about you, aside from your eyes of course. I always loved your eyes.' She twisted round and climbed onto the bed, so that she was kneeling beside him, staring intently into his eyes. Her skin was flawless in the dawn's grey tones and he wanted to reach out and embrace her. He wanted to hold her tight against him until she could *feel* his heartfelt apology pouring out, because he was sure he could make her *know*, not just hear, how sorry he was for all he'd put her through.

She let the chenille throw slip down around her shoulders and reached out to touch the side of his face. Her fingers were so gentle but her words were scathing: 'You really don't know how much I've missed you,

Gimmerick.'

John tried not to look down at her lithe body, but he couldn't help it. She wore nothing but black lace underwear. He hardly dared to breathe. 'I…I really don't know what to say, Tash. Is this some sort of trick?'

'Why would you think that?'

'Because a few hours ago you couldn't berate me enough.'

'That's my prerogative. I can change my mind whenever I like, *you* gave me the right to do so.'

'But what changed it?'

'Seeing you again.'

'Even after what I just told you?' He was astounded. 'It's not right. Let's talk tomorrow, in the cold light of day, when we're both sober.'

'I have to go home tomorrow.'

'Exactly, which is why *this* is a bad idea. We'd be opening a can of worms.'

'For me the can was never closed. I still dream about you, John.' She moved her thumb lightly over his bottom lip. He still expected she might slap him at any moment. Maybe even land him a full blown punch to bloody his mouth.

'What about your boyfriend?' he asked, desperate for her to stop toying with him like this.

'What about him?'

John shuffled backwards. 'I'm not comfortable with this, Tash. Seriously. Please, go back downstairs. Sleep it off.'

'I'd rather stay here.'

'Then fucking shout at me,' he demanded. 'Go ape. Get angry. Do something!'

Her eyes sparkled at his frustration and she leant forward and made as if to kiss him. But he was quick to avert his face.

'Go back to bed, Tash! *I don't want you.*'

She sat back, her expression wounded as though he'd slapped her. 'You're rejecting me? *Again?*'

'Yes. Well, no. Definitely no. But I can't do this. It's not what you really want.'

'How would you know what I want?'

'I don't. But I don't think you do either.'

'Shall I show you what I want?' She stuck her hand beneath the duvet and grabbed hold of him.

He closed his eyes and leant back and this time, when her mouth closed over his, he responded to her kiss. She ripped the duvet away, her hands were all over him and she pulled his hair so it hurt. He gripped hold of her and spun her round so she lay on the mattress beneath him, then he held her closer than he thought he'd ever held her before. His shoulder was soon wet with her tears and they both cried as they made love.

Eventually, when they were exhausted by one another, she lay in the crook of his arm. She closed her eyes and slept while he hugged her close and kissed the top of her head. By the time John fell asleep he was content.

37

John awoke to the sound of rain and a fresh breeze blowing in through the open window. His heart sank when he looked to the empty space in the bed next to him. Natasha was gone. He rolled over onto his back. The moderate daylight in the room stung his eyes and hurt his head with all the intensity of a bad hangover, even though he wasn't hungover. He squinted and lay still, thinking about the previous night. He wondered how he and Natasha would proceed from here. The fact she wasn't still next to him now probably meant she regretted what had happened between them. He expected an onslaught of some emotional outburst when he went downstairs. *If* she was still around and hadn't gone home to Whitby already.

When, eventually, he'd psyched himself to face whatever needed to be faced, he sat up. Every part of him ached. His head pounded with white heat and his guts churned, saliva a sudden tang in his mouth as though he might throw up. He waited a moment for the feeling to pass, then peeled back the duvet. It hurt to do so, his limbs weak and shaky. His fever seemed to have worsened tenfold overnight and the bruise on his chest, he saw, was now worryingly blackish in colour and extremely tender to touch. His feet felt like dead weights as he moved them to the floor and he groaned as he stooped to pick yesterday's clothes up; every movement an arduous, painful effort.

Traipsing down the stairs, every step pounded his head and jolted his aching joints. He went straight to the bathroom and took a piss, then looked at himself in the vanity mirror. He looked like a corpse. Purple bruising of fatigue discoloured the areas beneath his eyes and his lips were anaemic. His hair was tousled and wild, and two-day stubble reminded him he needed to shave, else he'd lapse back into old ways.

Once the toilet cistern had refilled and fallen silent, he stood listening. Elsewhere in the house he couldn't hear a thing. He hoped Natasha had left, letting herself out like Pamela Tanner had done.

Only one way to find out.

He went through to the lounge and found Natasha Graham sitting on the couch, fully dressed. Her hair had been combed and she was wearing fresh make-up. She looked discomfited in a sense, but certainly not highly charged with any type of emotion.

'Shit, are you okay?' she asked as soon as she saw him. 'You don't look too good.'

'I think I might be coming down with something. Want a cup of tea? Coffee?' He moved off to the kitchen without waiting for a response, keen to have a task in hand for when things turned awkward.

Natasha stood up and followed him through. 'Certainly looks like you might be getting something. Did you sleep okay?'

Holding the kettle under the running tap, he looked at her curiously. 'Er, yeah. No. I mean, I'm not sure. You?'

'Yeah, surprisingly well actually. I was out like a log.' Her mouth then became slightly downturned. 'No sign of Megan though.'

'Oh. I'm sorry.' John set the kettle down in its cradle and flipped its switch. Running his fingers through his hair, he took a deep breath. He *needed* to know what was going on. 'Tash, did you come up to my room last night?'

She looked instantly horrified. 'Why the hell would I have done that?'

'I, er, hmmm…' He pulled out a chair and flopped

down at the table, cradling his head in his hands.

What's happening to me?

'John?' Natasha moved to his side and regarded him warily. 'Should I call for a doctor or something?'

'No, I'm fine,' he said. 'You're sure you didn't come upstairs?'

'Never more sure of anything in my life.'

'Seriously?'

'Jesus, John, why are you pressing the issue? Why would you even think that?'

'I'm not. It's just...I dunno. It must have been a dream.'

'You had a dream about me coming to your room?'

'Yes. But...Look, is it okay if we drop this? It's a bit...'

'Weird?'

'Yes.'

'Alright. It's dropped. But for the record, just so we're both clear, I didn't leave the couch last night.'

'Good.'

'Good.'

'Okay.' He reached across and picked up the cameo, which was mocking him with its presence; the cream-faced Victorian woman seemed to know something he didn't, her smirk too deliberate. 'I've got a bad feeling about everything we talked about last night,' he said. 'I've been feeling increasingly shit since I arrived here, and strange things keep happening around the house. Maybe this thing *is* cursed.'

'Strange things like what?' The kettle had boiled and Natasha took over making the tea. She poured hot water into two mugs then went to the fridge to find milk.

'There've been some awful smells upstairs that I can't even describe, and a fly infestation in two of the bedrooms, usually wherever I've been sleeping.'

Natasha paused from dunking teabags. 'Thought about

taking a shower?'

'Funny as ever.'

'Hmmm. Carry on.'

'There are strange markings on the ceilings that come and go, usually wherever Seren's been. And my dreams and waking life have merged into one, so half the time I don't know what's real and what's not anymore.' He didn't go as far as to tell her he'd been hallucinating too, because by now she was giving him that look again, as if he might be losing his mind.

'Okay, it certainly sounds bizarre,' she said, placing the teaspoon in the sink. 'So what happens in your dreams exactly? They might be a clue as to what's going on.'

'I hardly think so.'

'But it's possible. What did you dream about last night? What did we do?'

'I'd rather not say.'

'Jesus.' Natasha plonked a cup of tea before him. 'You had a dirty dream about me, didn't you?'

'No! Well, yes. Maybe. I suppose.' John's face coloured, but only to the extent that his complexion looked normal.

She pulled out a chair and sat down next to him. 'Shit, and that's why you asked because you really thought we'd actually…'

'Hey, I was just as appalled by the idea,' he interrupted.

'Sounds like it.'

'Hey, I might have been in love with you when I was nineteen, but you didn't exactly stir up old feelings when you walked in here last night, so don't flatter yourself.'

'Well it seems like I stirred something up,' she said, her eyes now seething.

John knew he'd spoken out of turn, retorted too defensively. He took a sip of tea and said, 'Look, I'm sorry. I didn't mean that. Well, I did, but...never mind. It's just that, well, it's not just you.' He pulled a face of distaste. 'I keep dreaming about one of my mam's neighbours too.'

'You mean in the same context?'

'Yes. But if you saw her you'd understand why I take such issue with it.'

Natasha raised her eyebrows. 'Explain.'

'Let's just say she's got to have twenty years on me. I mean, don't get me wrong, she's alright for her age and all, but I certainly wouldn't go there.'

This time Natasha looked embarrassed. 'So *is* any of this actually relevant? I thought something weird was going on in your dreams, in an out-of-the-ordinary sense. When I drove up from Whitby last night the last thing in the world I thought I'd be doing was counselling my estranged ex on a few smutty dreams he's been having about people he really shouldn't be having them about.'

John cocked an eyebrow. 'I'm not some hormone-riddled teenager, Tash, I'm pushing forty for chrissakes, I *was* actually getting to the point.'

'Which is?'

'I dreamt that Pamela Tanner, my mam's neighbour, bit me, then when I woke up I had this.' He pulled his t-shirt up to show her the bite.

Natasha sucked in air through her teeth and grimaced. 'Ugh. That looks infected, maybe that's what's making you feel unwell. You should get it checked out.'

'Maybe.'

'So how did it really happen?'

'I just told you, I dreamt about it and then there it was.' He could see the disbelief in her eyes and when she opened her mouth to speak, he said, 'Don't bother suggesting it was self-inflicted or give me that look you keep giving me as if I'm losing the plot. Emily saw it before it turned black, there were *definite* teeth marks.'

'I don't know what to say to that, John.' Natasha drank from her cup, her eyes cautious, watching him.

'I don't think you need to say anything. In fact, it's probably best if you just go home once you've finished your tea.'

'No way.' She slammed her palm down on the table, making both of the dogs jump. 'I'm involved in this now.'

'But I don't want you to be. I want you to go.'

'Megan is my daughter, you bastard. I showed interest in your dreams because I've had a couple of odd experiences myself lately.' She reached up and touched the bump on her head.

John's uptight manner eased in an instant. His shoulders slumped and he nodded. 'Okay. So what do you suggest we do?'

'Go to Eden Vale. See if Sissy's still there.'

'Seriously? You really think she might still be pacing about? After all these years? She looked old then, she'd be ancient now.'

'We won't know till we check, will we? And I'd say it's the best starting point we've got.'

'Okay. Let's go to Eden Vale.'

John went off to shower and shave. He changed into clean clothes and put on some aftershave. On his way back to the kitchen he saw Emily and Seren walking down the garden path. He opened the back door for them and Emily called, 'Hey, you survived the night then?' When she stepped into the kitchen she saw Natasha sitting at the table and her eyes widened. 'Oh, I didn't realise you had company.'

'It's not what you think,' John said.

'Far from it,' Natasha echoed.

'Alright, if you say so, but I didn't get time to think *anything*,' Emily said, kicking her shoes off.

'Did you have a good night, kidda?' Seren came in

behind Emily and John ruffled her hair.

'Mmm hmmm.' Seren dropped her overnight bag on the table and took an instant interest in Natasha. 'Are you the lady I phoned?'

Natasha nodded and smiled. 'Yes, I'm Natasha.'

'Good. Megan says that you and Dad need to sort yourselves out. Settle your differences.'

Natasha eyed John suspiciously.

'I'm not sure Megan would have said anything of the sort,' John said, reproachfully; mortified that Natasha might now think this whole thing had been orchestrated for his own warped purposes.

'She did though, Dad,' Seren insisted. 'She says you left home because of something you didn't really do.'

Again Natasha looked at John for some sort of validation.

His face became even more ashen. *'What?'*

Seren shrugged. 'I dunno, that's all she said. I thought you'd know.'

Clutching the back of an empty dining chair, he closed his eyes and clenched his teeth. He wanted to shout and scream and swear and cry, all at the same time, but he just stood there, silently.

'Er, is everything okay?' Emily was now refilling the kettle. She turned her head and looked at John, her expression grave. 'Is that the stuff you told me about yesterday?'

John didn't respond, remaining statuesque for another minute or two, his scrunched face pained. When eventually he did open his eyes again, he said, 'Em, would you be able to watch Seren this morning for a while? Me and Natasha need to pop out.'

'Sure. Yeah. What are you up to?'

'We've got some business to sort. Some old bitch has a *lot* of explaining to do.'

38

Eden Vale loomed before them, a redbrick, two storey relic that packed all the emotional clout of time-weary funerals and rainy afternoons spent moping about the house, reflecting too much on misfortune. The building could be pigeonholed with everything bad that had ever happened in their lives, because it instilled uncomfortable memories and it wasn't a nice place to be. Its stained wooden window frames were peeling and the guttering was well-worn and mossy in places. Aesthetically it didn't look as though it had had much time or money invested in it over the past eighteen years and, perhaps because of this, it harboured a certain air of menace. John wondered if people who had no former connection to Eden Vale detected a portentous gloom at first sight, or if to them it appeared to be no more daunting than any tired-looking residential care home that promised mediocrity at best. A row of jackdaws was perched along a section of guttering on the eaves above the entrance, ominous little guards, watching, their silver eyes curious.

Natasha pulled her red Golf into a vacant space in the small car parking area and switched off the engine. 'Right,' she said, without taking her eyes off Eden Vale's brooding facade, her forehead lightly creased. 'Let's get this over and done with.'

'Are you sure you want to do this?' John said, fraught with concern. He could only imagine the nostalgic trauma it must be causing her to be here again. 'I can go in on my own if you like...'

'No, I need to do this,' she said, popping her door open and taking the keys from the ignition. 'I *have* to do it.

For Megan.'

Inside the foyer navy carpet had been replaced by the sort of grey carpet squares found in corporate offices and the reception desk was different too, a beech top with white panelling down the sides made it more contemporary and business-like than the mahogany one years ago. A woman in her twenties was sitting behind it, tapping away on a keyboard. Her thick-rimmed red glasses and jaunty hairstyle denoted a chicness that far exceeded the job, and she didn't even bother to look up at John and Natasha. She was definitely no Angie.

'Morning,' Natasha said, resting her elbows on the counter. 'I wonder if you could help us?'

'Just a sec.' The receptionist, whose name badge read: BRIONY, finished what she was typing before looking up. 'Is it an overview of prices and facilities you want?'

'No actually, it's something different altogether,' Natasha said. 'My mother was here back in ninety-seven and one time when we visited her we met another resident, a lady called Sissy. I was wondering if you might have any information as to whether this lady might still be here or…well, if she's still alive.'

Briony raised her neatly stencilled eyebrows, managing to exude a certain amount of attitude. 'And are you related to this other woman?'

'Well, no, but…'

'Then I'm sorry but I can't give out that type of information.'

'Why not? Surely there's no harm…'

'It'd be a breach of client confidentiality to discuss any such matters with non-relatives.'

'So she *is* here?'

'I didn't say that. I wouldn't know from the information you gave me.'

'Look, I appreciate what you're saying,' John said, clenching his hands together, 'but we don't actually want to discuss *anything* confidential about this woman, we just want to see her. She gave something to us, something we've only just rediscovered, and it looks like it might be quite valuable. We were very young at the time, we...'

'That might well be the case,' Briony interrupted, adopting a fiercer glare that was surely meant to intimidate him. She tapped her manicured, square nails on the desk, a *rick-tick-tick* that emphasised her impatience on the matter. 'But it seems you're just going to have to hold onto whatever it was she gave you, because there's nothing I can do for you.'

'But surely you could just...'

'No, I couldn't. I couldn't just anything. Now, if that's all, I'm busy.'

Such was his bad mood, when John pulled open the swing door to leave Eden Vale, he failed to see the middle-aged woman who was entering at the same time. He barged straight into her, knocking her backwards.

'Christ, I'm so sorry,' he said, lurching forward and grabbing hold of the woman's arm to set her straight before she could fall onto the pavement.

'Bloody hell, lad,' she said, her voice a cigarette-hardened bark. 'You're on a mission, aren't you?'

Natasha rushed outside to help ensure the woman was steady on her feet. 'Are you okay?'

'Yeah, yeah, no harm done. That's usually how *I* leave the place if I'm honest, like a blinking bat out of hell.' The woman was wearing a blue polyester uniform and her predominantly grey hair, streaked with dark brown, was a neat short bob, swept to the side at the very front and fixed in place with a bobby pin. As she looked at Natasha a flash of recognition sparked in her eyes. 'Do I know you?'

Natasha's eyes narrowed as she tried to place the woman's face. Then it came to her. *'Norma?'*

'Natasha!'

John looked back and forth between the two women.

'This is Norma Fennel,' Natasha explained. 'She was one of the care assistants that looked after my mam.'

'Oh right. Hi,' he said. 'Sorry again for walking into you like that, I wasn't paying attention.'

'Obviously,' Norma said, smiling. The apples of her cheeks were thread-veined and rosy, somehow affirming John's impression that she was a good-natured, good-humoured person. 'And, of course, I remember you as well. Can't for the life of me remember your name, but yours are a set of eyes I wouldn't likely forget.' She stood back a little and regarded John and Natasha. 'Lovely couple. Always were.'

'Oh no,' Natasha said, shaking her head. 'We aren't together.'

Norma frowned, as though genuinely saddened by this fact. 'Ah, now there's a shame.'

'Hmmm.' Natasha cocked an eyebrow, but then looked suddenly hopeful. 'Actually, Norma, you might be able to help us. You must still work here?'

Norma laughed. 'Well I'm certainly not wearing this outfit for the fun of it, lass.' She pulled at the hem of the blue shapeless top she was wearing. 'What do you need help with?'

'Remember when my mam was here? There was another woman called Sissy…'

'Oh yes.' Norma was already nodding. 'Sissy Dawson. I know her.'

'You do? Is she still here?'

'Well, yeah, but what the heck do you want with *her?*'

'She gave us a brooch and we hoped we might be able to return it.'

'Oh I see.' Norma shrugged. 'Well, if you like, I can give it to her?'

'The thing is,' Natasha said, 'we sort of hoped to be

able to see her ourselves. We'd like to ask her a little bit about it.'

'Hmmm.' Norma bit her lip and pondered this for a moment. But then she nodded. 'Okay. Why don't you pop back in about an hour or so? I'll get my morning rounds done then take you up to see her. In fact, gimme an hour and a half, that'll be even better, I'll check with Kevin to make sure she's alright for receiving visitors.'

'What about Briony?' Natasha asked, 'I'm not sure she'd let us get past reception.'

'Oh don't worry about that little madam, she wouldn't dare challenge me.' Norma shook her head and rolled her eyes. 'I'm friendly with Rob, the manager, known him since he was a kid. So long as Mrs Dawson is well enough this morning, I can take you up to see her no problem. It'll be fine. Old dear probably hasn't had visitors in donkey's years, would probably do her good.' Checking her watch, she reaffirmed, 'See you back here in about ninety minutes then.'

John and Natasha went back to the car.

'Where to? Your mam's?' Natasha turned the key in the ignition and the Golf purred to life.

Although still feeling unwell for the most part, John had perked up a little since leaving his mother's house. He had no inclination to rush back. 'Why don't we pop into town for a coffee?'

'What about Seren? Shouldn't you get back to her?'

'Nah, Emily's got it covered.'

They ended up in a cafe in Peterlee's shopping centre, an independently run greasy spoon that held no pretensions about where or what it was. They chose a formica table by the window and John told Natasha to sit down while he placed their order. A few minutes later he returned with a pot of tea, a mug of latte and two large wedges of flapjack.

'Sorry, I didn't make us any breakfast this morning,'

he said, sitting down opposite her and pushing the plate of flapjack towards her. 'You must be starving.'

'Funnily enough, I'm not. All this business has got me on edge.' Still, she broke a corner from one of the oaty squares and put it in her mouth.

'Same here,' he said, sipping at the latte.

Natasha regarded him. 'I don't mean to speak out of turn, but you look like you should try eating more than this.' She pushed the plate so that it was in the centre of the table where they could both reach it. 'You don't look well at all. Are you looking after yourself properly?'

He licked froth from his top lip and shrugged. 'I guess not.'

Pouring tea from the small stainless steel teapot into her mug, Natasha frowned when it leaked from the spout and dribbled onto the table. 'So,' she said, reaching for a serviette, 'what do you do for a living these days?'

'IT consultant.' John's expression wasn't in the least bit enthusiastic. 'I won't bore you with the details.'

'Fair enough. Is Leeds nice?'

'Not bad. What about you? Where do you call home?'

'Well, as you know, I run a boutique in Whitby. Live there too, about ten minutes' walk from the shop. I set up the business with some of my inheritance money, after my dad passed away.'

'Oh. I'm sorry to hear that, about your dad.'

'Hmmm.'

They sat for a moment, contemplating all they'd just said. John reached for a square of flapjack and took a large bite; he chewed slowly before asking, 'What about your boyfriend? Sorry, fiancé. What does he do?'

Natasha looked down and began fidgeting with an empty sugar sachet. 'Lee's a software technician.'

'Another IT bod.' John smiled, a forced gesture that didn't feel right, but he wasn't sure what else to do. He wasn't even sure why he'd asked the question. What business was it of his who her partner was or what he did for a living?

Natasha returned his smile, nonetheless, and nodded. 'So, what about you? Anyone special back in Leeds?'

'No. My head's not in the right place if I'm honest.'

Her mouth pulled to the side in what looked like sympathy. 'At least you've got Seren though, eh?'

'Yeah, I suppose.'

Natasha drank from her mug, her eyes fixing on his. 'Must be amazing.'

'What?'

'Having a daughter.' There was no hint of scorn in her voice to suggest she begrudged him this, only subdued regret, which her eyes also projected.

John set the remainder of his flapjack down on the plate, too discomfited to finish it. 'Did you, er, decide you didn't want children in the end?'

'Far from it, I always wanted kids. I was too scared though, after what happened. Near enough destroyed me.' She looked away and feigned interest in a woman outside the cafe who was fiddling with the straps of her sandals, the conversation becoming too personal, too emotional. He could see that her eyes had glazed over.

John frowned. 'God, Tash, I'm really sorry.'

'Me too.'

She continued to gaze out of the window while biting the edge of her thumb, so John sat back in his chair and took the opportunity to look at her properly without feeling too self-conscious about doing so. Her mouth was serious and she had two frown lines between her brows, like the number eleven. Her large brown eyes were still appealing, but now lacked some of their former optimism. He suspected he'd robbed them of some of that. Her hair, now several shades lighter, was shiny and complemented her complexion, and she wore it in a style similar to the one she'd had all those years ago, only longer. Before it had skimmed her shoulders, now it reached down past her shoulder blades. John was finding it surreal that she was sitting here, directly in front of him. She was a significant part of his life, one that had been suppressed but, over the years, never truly got over or forgotten about, and although they weren't on the best of terms they were conversing with such civility that he never would have imagined. He would even go as far as to say that he was enjoying her company. And moreover, quite worryingly, was still attracted to her.

'What's that look for?' she said, turning to face him, perhaps having caught him staring at her in some reflection in the window.

'What look?' he said, becoming visibly flustered and looking down at the frothy dregs of his latte.

'Never mind.' She stood up abruptly, chair legs scraping across the floor so that two women nearby turned and looked. Lifting her handbag, she swung it over her shoulder and said, 'Come on, Gimmerick, the quicker we get this sorted the quicker I can go home.'

John eased to his feet. 'Yeah. Sounds good.'

At Eden Vale Norma was waiting for them outside the main entrance, the last bit of a cigarette held between her fingers. 'Ready to go up?'

Natasha nodded. 'Yeah.'

'Mrs Dawson's not faring too well, mind.' Norma took one last draw before flicking the cigarette butt to the floor and grinding it out under her foot. 'Had an accident this week, broke a wrist and hip while trying to get out of bed. Kevin reckons she's been a bit flighty lately, but if you keep your visit brief I don't see any harm in me taking you up to see her.' She pushed through the entrance door and held it open for them.

All three of them breezed past reception. Briony didn't look up, but John could feel her eyes burning into the back of them as they began their ascent up the main staircase.

'What's Sissy Dawson's story?' Natasha asked Norma as they reached the first floor landing.

'I don't know much about the old dear to be honest,' Norma replied. 'By all accounts she used to be a midwife back in the day. No living husband or kids. That's about the extent of what I know.'

'A midwife?' A shiver ran down John's spine as Megan's words came back to him: *It's Her link to you. Her link to the children.*

'Yeah, at Thorpe Hospital.'

'That's where I was born,' he said.

'Me too,' Natasha chimed in.

'Not on Mrs Dawson's watch you weren't.' Norma looked at John, her eyes smiling. 'Sissy will have worked there in the fifties or sixties, way before your time.' She motioned for them to follow her to the left, down a corridor that looked much the same as the one to the right and the one straight ahead. Beige carpet bore a grey runway strip of wear and tear and ingrained outside dirt from countless visiting feet. The skimmed walls were pastel blue, cold and uninspiring, and chrome wall lights flickered and dimmed as they walked past, making Natasha look to John nervously. At the same time John could feel his heartbeat thumping in his head, a stabbing sensation accompanying it. He was woozy and tired again, his fever reactivating so that his skin felt chilled despite his veins melting beneath the surface.

Norma came to a stop and pointed to a door on the right. 'In here.' She proceeded to open the door without knocking and called inside, 'Morning, Mrs Dawson, you've got some visitors.' She stood to the side and motioned for John and Natasha to enter.

John waited for Natasha to go first, then followed her into the dreary bedroom of Sissy Dawson. A stale smell of stagnancy pervaded the room, coating his airways with an unpleasantness that wouldn't shift till he was back outside breathing fresh air. A quick sweep of the room and its contents revealed it as an impersonal space with nothing of the old woman's on display; no photographs, trinkets, books, jewellery or items of clothing. A television mount was affixed to the magnolia wall opposite the bed but it held no television. Instead, a small portable sat on top of a set of drawers. A cheap wall clock, like those found in waiting rooms, hung on the wall above the bed and beneath it, in the bed, was a skeletal woman with thinning hair that was just as white as the plaster cast on her arm. Her eyes were barely open, gluey in the corners, one of them blackened, and her mouth was a sunken pit. It was hard to tell if it was the same woman they'd met pacing around the communal room all those years back.

'Who are you?' Sissy Dawson croaked. 'God's agents? Have you come to take me away?'

'We've come to talk,' Natasha said, her tone sharp but not entirely unfriendly. 'We met a long time ago.'

'We did?'

'Yes. Me and John, we were very young then.'

Sissy's eyes widened a fraction and she tilted her head to the side. 'I don't remember.'

'Let me remind you.' Natasha walked to the bed, so she was standing just a couple of feet away from the old woman. 'I was pregnant. You gave something to us.'

Sissy Dawson's expression didn't change.

Natasha unzipped her handbag and rummaged around. After a few moments she looked at John. 'Did you fetch it?'

John patted the pockets of his jeans, even though he already knew they contained nothing more than his wallet and house key. He sighed. 'Shit, we must have left it on the kitchen table.'

At this news Sissy Dawson seemed to relax.

Moving to the bed, and standing next to Natasha, John bent over the old woman and said, 'It was a cameo brooch. You remember giving it to me, don't you?'

'No.'

'Think harder because I think you do.'

'I don't know what you're talking about.'

'Yes you do,' he insisted. *'We lost our baby!* I want to know what's wrong with that fucking brooch because my six-year-old daughter is in danger.'

Sissy's eyes grew even more moist and she shook her head. 'I'm sorry,' she said, trying to cover her ears with her hands. 'I'm sorry, I'm sorry, I'm sorry. I didn't want…it was *Her*…She made me. I wanted peace, I wanted Her out of my head…but…but I never would have…I didn't want…She *made* me do it.'

'Who did?'

'Don't you know?'

Natasha and John looked at each other.

'Alright, alright,' Sissy Dawson whimpered. 'I'll tell you. I'll tell you everything, if it'll bring me peace.'

39

10th November, 1955 – Thorpe Hospital

Sissy Dawson passed through the open gates, staying close to the grass verge. The redbrick building which served as the houseman's residence, immediately to her right, rested in darkness. A cold blustery wind made her walk a little faster than usual and as she scurried along the road she glanced warily at the storage building to her left. Back in the 1800s, when Thorpe was built, and up until just six years ago it had been the hospital's morgue. In those days Thorpe had been a specialist hospital for those inflicted with infectious diseases. It had been known locally as Fever Hospital; an establishment that had known its fair share of pain, suffering and death. Sissy didn't care much at all for the old morgue building during daylight, never mind at night. The number of bodies it must have stored over the years inspired uncomfortable thoughts, and the idea of going inside was enough to quicken her pulse. A keen imagination always saw to it that dead eyes watched her pass at the beginning and end of each shift, fevered eyes belonging to those that would never leave because they'd succumbed to some nasty ailment or other. Henry, her husband, had always said she was too flighty for her own good.

Once inside Ward Three, the delivery section of the hospital, Sissy, a state enrolled nurse, began a lengthy nightshift alongside Mrs Rogers, a midwife from Grants Houses. Mrs Rogers was a blunt but not unfriendly older woman with coarse, greying hair and the beginnings of a moustache. She'd delivered countless babies and was adept at overlooking the gruesome aspects of the job and doling out empathy where applicable. Their first delivery of the evening began not twenty minutes after Sissy had arrived, when a young woman from Easington Colliery declared her waters broken. The birth wasn't an easy one. At first Mrs Rogers suspected the baby was breech and Sissy imagined she'd need to go and wake the houseman, but in the end Mrs Rogers managed to help the young woman deliver a healthy baby boy. Then just half an hour after that mother and child had been taken to Ward One, another woman started with labour pains.

After six hours on her feet helping to deliver two babies, sterilising equipment and administering gas and air, Sissy eventually went to the break room. She found Muriel Beasley, a fellow SEN, there, nibbling on a triangular sandwich.

'Busy night for you?' Muriel asked.

'Dead on my feet,' Sissy said, plonking herself down on the padded seat of a wooden chair.

'Ha! Imagine that.' Muriel swiped crumbs from her lap, then dabbed at the sides of her mouth with an embroidered floral cotton handkerchief.

'I don't have to try very hard.' Sissy smiled wearily and rested her head against the wall behind, closing her eyes.

'Are you planning to have a nap?'

'No, just resting my eyes.' Sissy sat up straight again and looked at her friend. 'I'm tired, but much too awake to sleep, if that makes sense.'

'Only too well.' Muriel winked, her dark eyes small behind the lenses of her brown thick-rimmed NHS glasses. 'Say, why don't we do something fun? Wake ourselves up a bit.'

'Something fun? *Here?* Like what?'

'Contact the dead. Get *them* on their feet.'

'What dead?' Sissy already didn't like the sound of

Muriel's idea.

'Just think of all the people who've died in this place,' Muriel said, sitting forward excitedly. Her brown hair was curly, styled close to her head, and when she fidgeted it hardly moved. 'If we try to make contact we're bound to reach someone.'

'I'd rather we didn't.'

'Lillian Grey and Jeannie Todd have tried before. Right here. In this room. They got some old man come through, said he'd died of scarlet fever back in nineteen-oh-two.'

'That's silly,' Sissy scoffed, fussing with the hem of her white uniform in a bid to look bored and unimpressed with what Muriel was saying. 'It's just an old building with a bit of history, that's all.'

'Oh come on, spoil sport. It'll be a laugh.'

'I'm not sure it would be at all. I mean, *should* we be dabbling?'

'Crikey, it's just a bit of fun. All we need to do is write the letters of the alphabet onto paper, with numbers from one to ten across the bottom along with the words yes and no, then we ask the spooks to answer our questions. Easy peasy, lemon squeezy.' Muriel already had a piece of paper and pencil in her hand.

'But what if Sister Howard was to catch us?' Sissy complained, desperate to find a way out of Muriel's mischievous plan.

'Sister Howard rarely comes in here, you know that. Now stop being such a scaredy cat.' Muriel used a small wooden table to rest on while she fashioned the sheet of paper into a makeshift Ouija board, then beckoned for Sissy to pull her chair up beside her. 'What shall we use as a planchette?'

'What's one of them?' Sissy asked, defeatedly dragging her chair over to the table.

'The thing we move about on the board. Or should I

say, the thing the *spooks* move about the board.'

'I dunno, what sort of thing do you usually use?'

'Anything I suppose. Got a coin?'

'No.'

'Me neither.' Muriel pointed at the cameo affixed to Sissy's cardigan. 'What about that?'

'I'd rather not, it was my grandmother's…' But Muriel was already unclipping it. Sissy objected but the other nurse batted her hands away and placed the cameo on the paper.

'Okay, put your finger on it and let's make a start,' Muriel said.

Sissy sighed loudly but did as instructed.

They both sat still for a moment, Muriel grinning and Sissy frowning, then Muriel, taking on a mock-sinister tone, asked, 'Is anybody there?'

They waited.

Nothing happened.

Sissy breathed out, realising she hadn't expelled the air from her lungs in a while, nervous anticipation having held it there.

'Are there any spirits that would like to make contact with us?' Muriel persisted.

Again nothing happened.

'Oh, I knew this was silly,' Sissy said after a few silent moments had passed. She took her finger away from the brooch and sat back, relieved that nothing had happened. 'Spirits indeed!'

The brooch, still beneath Muriel's finger, then slid across the paper and came to a stop on the word YES. Muriel gasped and pulled her hand away.

Sissy regarded her friend with narrowed eyes. 'Muriel Beasley you're nothing but a tease, full of devilment. You moved that!'

'I really didn't.' Muriel shook her head and there was something about her paled expression that Sissy didn't like one bit.

'Yes you did.'

'I swear, I didn't.' Muriel was quick to regain her composure and she put her finger back on the cameo. 'Come on, let's try again.'

Sissy stared down at the paper, her mind whirring. She didn't move.

'Go on! *Hurry*,' Muriel insisted. 'We'll lose whoever it is.'

Tentatively Sissy brought her hand back up to the table, her index finger coming to rest on her grandmother's cameo.

'Are you still there?' Muriel raised her face as though whatever spirit might be lingering was floating above their heads near the ceiling.

Nothing happened.

'See, I knew you'd done it,' Sissy chided.

Muriel gave her friend a warning glare then looked again to the ceiling. 'Are you an old patient of the hospital?'

Wind spattered rain against the window pane and shrieked through gaps in the wooden frame. Sissy shivered. The brooch then moved to NO with such force she yanked her hand away and stared at it.

'Put your finger back,' Muriel hissed. She looked excited now, her initial fright waning.

Sissy, still sceptical but persuaded enough to be scared, whined, 'I'm not happy about this, Muriel. At. All.'

'Oh don't be such a big girl's blouse.'

Tight-lipped, Sissy touched the brooch again, her hand trembling. She listened to the low moan of wind outside. It was a lonely sound, like the separation anxiety of a pack animal left alone for too long.

'Could you tell us your name?' Muriel asked.

They waited and the brooch slowly scraped around the

paper in a big circle till it rested on NO.

'Can't you spell it out for us?'

Again NO.

Muriel was frowning now. 'Are you a man?'

NO.

'A woman?'

NO.

'A boy?'

NO.

'Girl?'

NO.

'I don't think whoever it is wants to communicate with us,' Sissy said. But Muriel hushed her with an impatient scowl and asked, 'Are you an animal?'

NO.

'Then what are you, for pity's sake?' Muriel blurted.

The brooch began to move again, but this time it moved around the letters of the alphabet, halting on certain ones. Muriel snatched up the pencil with her left hand and made a note of each: T.H.E.O.N.E.T.H.A.T.H.A.S.N.O.N.A.M.E.O.R.F.A.C. E.

'What in the world does that mean?' she muttered, looking down at her own scribbled handwriting once the brooch became still.

'The one that has no name or face,' Sissy read.

'Is that who you are?' Muriel asked the space beneath the ceiling. 'The one that has no name or face?'

YES.

'How bizarre.'

'Very,' Sissy agreed, growing increasingly intrigued by the whole charade despite herself.

'But if it's not a man, woman, boy, girl or animal, what else could it be?' Muriel complained. 'What on earth is nameless and faceless?'

'An alien?' Sissy suggested.

Muriel laughed, a nervous sound. 'Whoever heard of an alien making contact via the Ouija board?'

'There's a first time for everything, I suppose.'

'*Are* you an alien?' Muriel looked up at the ceiling.

NO.

'Oh I give up,' she said, removing her finger from the brooch. 'It's impossible. Like a game of charades with my senile granny.'

But Sissy, now enjoying the puzzle too much, kept her finger in place and asked, 'Are you male?'

NO.

'It already said no to that,' Muriel snapped, looking unreasonably cross.

'It said that it wasn't a boy or a man.'

'Same difference isn't it?'

'Not necessarily,' Sissy said. 'Are you female?'

YES.

'Aha!' She smiled, a little too smugly, at Muriel.

'A female *what* though?' Muriel sighed, exasperated.

'Are you a creature of God's good Earth?' Sissy asked.

NO.

'What about a creature of God's heavenly realm? Are you an angel, perhaps?'

NO.

'It's a maddeningly impossible puzzle, that's what it is,' Muriel complained.

But Sissy suddenly felt fearful, an idea forming in her head, bringing with it a creeping sensation of dread that clawed at her skin. She hardly dared ask but needed to know, 'Are you a creature of darkness? A...demon, perhaps?'

Muriel made to object, but the brooch jerked forcefully to YES. Both women shrieked and pulled their hands away. At the same time the wind roared, rattling the window in its frame.

'This isn't funny,' Muriel cried, looking anxiously at

the window.

'I can assure you I'm not laughing,' Sissy affirmed. '*You* said this would be fun! What have we done?'

Muriel looked sheepish. 'Maybe it's a harmless demon?'

'Is there such a thing?'

'I wouldn't know. Let's ask.'

Sissy shook her head. 'No, I don't want to. I don't want to ask it anything else.'

'Then I will, and then we'll stop larking about and get back to work.'

Sissy pondered this for a moment, then agreed.

'Do you mean us any harm?' Muriel asked, her voice small, lacking all of its former bravado.

NO.

She breathed out a lengthy sigh of relief and managed a smile. 'See, we were getting our pantyhose in a twist about nothing.'

Feeling none of the reassurance her friend gained from the reply, Sissy asked the supposed demon, 'What do you want?'

This time the brooch moved slowly amongst the letters of the alphabet, spelling out: H.O.S.T.

'Host?' Sissy asked. 'What does that mean?'

The brooch didn't move again in response. Both women waited a few minutes, the wind harrying the window and jangling their nerves, urging them to make a decision. Eventually Sissy huffed and picked up the cameo and pinned it back onto her cardigan.

'If I were you I'd get rid of that,' Muriel said, eyeing it warily as she stood up.

'It's a family heirloom,' Sissy retorted. 'It was my grandmother's, passed down to her from *her* grandmother.'

'Heirloom or not, I'd throw it away. Or bury it somewhere.'

'Whatever I *do* do I won't be listening to another word you say Muriel Beasley, that's for certain. It's your fault that all of this happened.'

The pair of them walked back to Ward Three in silence, and not another word was ever spoken about what they had invoked that night. Following her shift Sissy put her grandmother's cameo brooch into a box and hid it out of sight, at the back of her underwear drawer. During the following weeks she seldom spoke to Muriel Beasley, the pair amicably drifting apart. Sissy started attending church more often, and became introverted and unwilling to socialise in her leisure time. Her rosy complexion took on a pallid tone and her eyes carried shadows beneath them all the time, even when she felt well rested. A blackness had shrouded her life, intensifying over the months, like great crows' wings suffocating all of the wellbeing within her. She began hearing a voice inside her head, which she told nobody about, and she dreamt about a faceless female form each and every night. Sometimes she would forget large pockets of time throughout the day and Henry, her husband, would often imply that she had two personalities. He once wondered aloud whether she might be possessed.

When Sissy fell pregnant with their first child she snapped back to her former self at last, blooming and becoming a much better, joyous person. Life was great once again for Henry and her and when their daughter, Eleanor, was born it was the happiest day of Sissy's life. The worst day of her life followed three months later, when Eleanor passed away.

Her daughter's unexplained death caused Sissy to fall into a deep depression. Even when she fell pregnant again soon after, her spirits didn't lift, and the voice in her head came back louder than ever. Sissy miscarried the second child at four months, but within three months was pregnant again. The third baby, Elizabeth, who looked just like Eleanor, was stillborn. Doctors said the umbilical cord had asphyxiated the infant. Sissy's fourth and fifth babies ended in miscarriage at mid-way points during the pregnancies. Then her sixth baby, William, was born healthy; a vivacious little boy with whom she was scared to bond. By the time he reached the age of five months, Sissy was pregnant again and went on to have a healthy baby girl called Polly. The Dawson's spate of bad luck seemed to have finally run aground and, despite the pains of the past, their lives picked up for a brief while. Sissy and Henry started to believe they might enjoy a happy family life after all. But that wasn't to be. Henry came home one evening to find Sissy collapsed on the bathroom floor, the onset of some fever having taken its toll. Tragically she'd been bathing William and Polly at the time. Both children had drowned.

Sissy was never the same afterwards. Neither was Henry. He couldn't cope with the misfortune of having lost seven children, or indeed with Sissy's increasing level of paranoia and split-personality. Sometimes she was a nervous, withdrawn shell of a woman who couldn't be consoled nor communicated with and at other times she was a spitting, vindictive woman who wouldn't be reasoned with. Henry became more and more distant, working longer hours and spending long spates of time at the pub just so that he wouldn't have to be at home, and by the autumn of 1959 Sissy lost him too. She found him strung up in their front room, the cord of his dressing gown around his neck.

40

'Can you forgive me?' Sissy's voice was rough, her throat dry from having talked so much. '*Will* you forgive me?'

Anger surged inside John. Despite the old woman's story he couldn't feel pity towards her. He struggled to find any words; it was Natasha who replied, her voice despondent, 'How could I ever forgive what you did? From one mother to another, how could you have given that thing to me, knowing what would happen?'

'She made me do it,' Sissy sobbed. 'When I came here, to Eden Vale, after She'd ruined my life, She had no more innocence to take, She needed to get out.'

'What are you talking about?'

'Thorpe was perfect for Her, that's why She communicated with me and Muriel Beasley that night. She had all She ever needed there. She survives by taking the innocence of children, you see, and what better place is there to do that than a maternity ward? Infants have the purest souls, they keep Her alive. And She thrives on the corruption of humanity, seeking out the worst in the rest of us, manipulating and moulding those faults to the extreme. She's a malignant force and for years She dominated me, till I was no longer myself, till I ended up here. And there are, of course, no children in a place like this. But the day you came She saw an opportunity...Oh, I'm so sorry. So, so sorry for your loss. I would never have given you to Her...not on purpose.' Tears soaked the creases in her face and her small body shuddered. 'My soul's unclean now and the spirits won't let me rest. I can't sleep because they hound me day and night. Can't you see them? They're all the babies from Thorpe, the ones She stole, as well as my own little ones. She took them from me and I was Her device, Her direct link to them.'

John looked around the room but saw nothing. 'Then perhaps you should ask *them* for forgiveness,' he spat. 'Surely they are the ones to grant you the mercy you want. Not me or Tash.'

Sissy stopped weeping, enlightenment slowly registering on her face. 'Yes, perhaps you're right.' She glanced all about her, her eyes appealing to unseen faces. '*Will* you forgive me?' she beseeched, her voice trembling. 'Will you set me free so that I may be at peace? So that we all might be at peace? I know the error of my ways and the good Lord knows how much I've suffered for it in my own way. I didn't mean any harm to come to any of you, I swear.'

The ceiling light made a loud pinging noise as though the bulb had been flicked. Everyone looked up. John felt a sudden thickness of static on his bare skin and flinched as the bulb shattered with a loud pop. He and Natasha shielded their heads with their arms to avoid the shower of splintered glass, but tiny fragments rained across Sissy's unprotected face, lacerating her skin so that pricks of blood beaded on the surface. The set of drawers at the foot of the bed then began to shudder and a remote control danced across its surface till it crashed to the floor. At the same time the television on top of the drawers crackled to life. Some bearded evangelical preacher appeared in the multi-coloured snowstorm on screen and, with a southern drawl, promised: 'Ask for forgiveness and it *shall* be granted...' A jumble of images then flashed on the portable's screen and a mashed-up sequence of dialogue was created from various programmes: *'She is...The one...That can't be... Named...And never should be...She is the one...Everyone fears...And if you let...Her...In...She will!…Destroy you.'*

The television then settled to black and white snow and from somewhere amidst the frantic, buzzing storm the voice of Metallica's James Hetfield loudly declared, 'We're off to never-never land, ha ha!'

Sissy was now writhing on the bed, as though suffering a seizure of some sort. Her face contorted with pain and she reached out a clawed hand to John and Natasha. Neither of them moved, both too shocked by what was happening, stunned into non-action. When the television screen exploded, though, flames leaping outward amongst hot sprays of glass, they broke free of their stupor and Natasha ran to the door. 'Shit, I need to get help,' she cried.

John moved close to the bed and towered over Sissy, who looked likely to be fighting her last battle. He grabbed her by the shoulder. 'What am I supposed to do about the brooch?' he asked, now feeling frantic that she would die and leave him without a solution. 'How do I get rid of Her, Sissy?'

But the old woman didn't seem to hear.

He took her by both shoulders and shook her fragile body. 'What do I do? How do I save my little girl?' His face was right in front of hers and he could feel her breath on his mouth and nose.

'Get rid of it,' Sissy groaned, her eyes rolling back and her body rigid between spasms. 'Put it somewhere out of reach. Do it now. *Now!* Before She gets into your head any more than She is. She's growing powerful, I can feel Her. She's been feeding from you too much already, She wants you to be her host. Get rid of the brooch and take your little girl far away from it. But don't let anybody else touch it. Please.'

'Why not? What will happen?'

'She seeks to inhabit a body. She can do this easily with the young and naïve of heart, as She once did with me, but you're older than I was, you're proving more of a challenge. She *will* succeed though, eventually, and She'll take your child if you don't act now. She's almost strong enough.'

'What if I destroy the brooch?'

'No!' Sissy clawed at her throat, as if to talk suddenly pained her greatly. 'The brooch *contains* Her. If you destroy it you might free Her, then She would do untold damage. Think of all the children She might steal if She had no boundaries. Get rid of the brooch, put it somewhere that no one will ever find it, but don't destroy it.'

Footsteps pounded down the corridor and a nurse came rushing into the room followed by Natasha. The nurse was a young Asian lady whose face expressed astonishment at the mayhem she found in Sissy's room. 'What on earth happened in here? Mrs Dawson?' She regarded John suspiciously and reached out to inspect Sissy's bleeding face.

'Leave me be,' Sissy implored, shrinking away from the nurse's fingers. 'They're letting me go. This is my time, my time at last. I'm ready to face my judgement. Crowns and thrones may perish, kingdoms will rise and wane, but the church of Jesus is constant and constant it will remain. I'm tired of this life, so let me go. Let me go to Him.'

John stepped back and stood with Natasha. They watched in silence as the nurse tried to calm Sissy, but eventually the old woman stopped struggling and fell still. The nurse felt for a pulse.

'Is she dead?' Natasha asked, her voice conveying surprise even though she knew the answer.

'What happened here?' The nurse's eyes were stern as she looked about the room. Curls of smoke from the television veiled the room and tiny pieces of glass beaded the bedsheets.

'There must have been a power surge or an electrical fault of some kind,' Natasha explained, her whole body trembling and her face sickly white. 'The ceiling light and television set both exploded and the drama of it seemed to set Mrs Dawson off into some sort of fit. It was awful.'

The nurse nodded, her grave frown not loosening at all. 'I suspect you'll both need to stay and give a statement to the police. Could you go down to reception and wait there, it's no longer suitable for you to be in here.'

'Yes, of course.' Natasha was already moving towards the door.

John grabbed her arm and spun her round to face him. Something Sissy had said earlier suddenly inspired cold dread. 'Oh God, Tash, the brooch! I need to get home. Now!'

'Why? What's the urgency?'

'We left it on the table.'

'So?'

'Emily!'

41

John was out of the car before Natasha had pulled the handbrake on, running up the garden path and scrabbling in his jeans pocket for the back door key. All kinds of anxious thoughts whirred through his mind. Was there really a malevolent force attached to the old cameo brooch? Or was he just as crazy as Sissy Dawson for thinking there might be? And would he find Seren and Emily in the house? Safe?

No dogs greeted him as he burst into the kitchen. His heart sank. It sank even lower when he saw the brooch wasn't on the table.

Fuck.

'Seren!' He rushed from the kitchen to the lounge, then the lounge to the hall where he stood at the foot of the stairs and called, *'Emily?'*

There was no answer.

Taking the stairs two at a time, he sprinted up to the landing. He flung all of the doors open and found the three bedrooms were empty. Moments later, when he was thundering back down the stairs, Natasha was in the hall, her face racked with concern. 'Where might they be?' she asked. 'Any idea?'

'I dunno,' he said, raking his hair back. 'They've taken the dogs, so maybe the beach banks. Or the beach. Maybe the dene. God. I really don't know.'

'Should we wait here till they come back?'

'No, I need to find them now. Emily has the brooch!'

'Shit.' Natasha started gnawing at the skin around one of her fingernails. 'You could try her mobile again.'

John chewed on his lip and took his phone out of his pocket. He'd tried to contact Emily five times since they'd left Eden Vale, but each time the call had gone to answerphone. When he called her now, for the sixth time, a jingling sound upstairs announced that she'd left her phone at home. '*Bollocks!*' He ushered Natasha out of the house and hurried her down the path. 'Let's try the banks first, shall we?'

'Er, yeah, okay.' She pulled the gate open and looked east, towards the sea. 'Whatever you think's best.'

Suddenly remembering that Natasha Graham wasn't someone he might expect, or deserve, help from, John pinched the bridge of his nose and sighed. He touched her shoulder and said, 'Of course, you don't have to. You could go home if you want. I mean, this isn't your problem anymore.'

This time Natasha didn't shrug away from his hand, but anger flashed in her eyes. 'Thanks for the pardon, Gimmerick, I'm aware that I can leave any time I damn well choose. But do you honestly think I'd leave right now? Do you really think...'

'No. I don't know.' He shook his head. The intensity of her animosity stung more than a slap to the face would have done.

'Seren's not my daughter or responsibility, granted, but I do have a bloody heart.'

'I know, I know you do, I just didn't want to be presumptuous. I didn't want to drag you any further into this mess.'

'Fine. Let's find Seren, then I'll leave you to get on with it.'

They took up a jogging pace and headed over the railway bridge then along past the allotments, attracting a few suspicious glares from gardeners on the way. Neither of them was kitted out in appropriate running gear, so most likely it looked as though they were up to no good. By the time they got to the last few allotments in the row, John's lungs stung with every intake of air and he struggled hard not to wheeze. At the gap in the fence, which led onto the field, he hurdled over a cluster of tall nettles then turned to see if Natasha needed help, but she had already cleared them. Her face was flushed with exertion, he saw, and she was gasping for breath. She started out across the field without complaint and John accelerated faster now, despite the head-on wind which made progress even more demanding. The greenness of grass all around them seemed dulled by a dirty-white sky which the sun couldn't burn through and a couple of partridges took to the air, disturbed by John and Natasha's galloping feet. Off to the far side of the field an elderly man was out walking with a large furry dog, an Alsatian perhaps, but other than that there was no one else about.

John's legs were quick to discover a new rhythm, albeit one his respiratory system wasn't happy about, but when the edge of his foot dipped into the deep groove of a pothole he lost all coordination and was propelled forward, falling to his hands and knees with a violent thud. Upon impact with the ground his palms throbbed and a crushing pain from his left kneecap seared through his entire leg. When he tried to pull himself to his feet he felt Natasha's hands about his waist, helping him up, and he relished the concern apparent in her voice when she asked, 'Are you okay?'

'Yeah. Thanks.' Panting profusely, he wiped his earthy hands down the front of his jeans and squeezed his burning knee before taking off again at a hobbled jog.

Once at the top of the cliffs they looked down to the beach. The sea was a sulky grey and the sand looked bruised and dull, having taken the brunt of the sea's now receding mood.

'There! Down there!' Natasha pointed to two figures walking along the foot of the banks. One in red, the other purple. Scampering behind them were two dogs, one grey, one beige.

Cupping his hands around his mouth, John yelled, 'Seren! Emily!'

Neither of the girls looked up.

'They're too far away, probably can't hear you,' Natasha reasoned. She was standing close enough to John that her long mid-blonde hair whipped his face as the wind blustered all about them.

'Come on,' he said. Seeing a worn track on the bank's rugged, grassy face from which to climb down to the beach, he got to his hunkers, grasping a handful of grass for anchorage, and eased himself down past the initial three-foot ledge. He then turned to offer his hand to Natasha. She took it and lowered herself down next to him.

'Climbing was never my forte,' she admitted, dropping his hand, feeling somewhat awkward about their brief contact.

'Mine neither.'

'This should be great fun then.'

'Under different circumstances, I'm sure.'

Natasha cocked a caustic eyebrow but John didn't see, he was already making his descent. She scurried to catch up, not wishing to get caught in a tight spot up there on her own. The north-easterly wind was cutting straight through the flimsy material of her shirt as she chased John down the decline, but exertion and anxiety kept her warm. She slipped several times on the way down, each tumble small enough and resulting in no more than dirt patches on the seat of her jeans and scuff marks on the toes of her boots. John fared worse, however. When he lost his footing on a loose piece of earth he fell forwards and commando rolled a few metres down the bank's side, and it was as he flailed his arms in an attempt to correct his balance that a jagged rock he tumbled past gouged a chunk of skin from his wrist. When he came to a halt he sat in a grassy crevice for a few moments, dazed and bleeding. He told Natasha he was fine, but every time the wind sliced into the raw wound he winced and had to count to five.

After climbing down further, when they were nearing the bottom, they could see that Seren and Emily were now walking across the beach towards the sea. John came to a stop and tried calling to them again. This time Emily turned and looked. He raised an arm and waved, but she turned away and carried on walking, her pace increasing.

'Something's not right,' he said to Natasha. He skittered down the last few metres of the embankment till he was standing firmly on the pebbled edge of the beach and yelled, 'Emily, stop!'

This time Seren looked round and beckoned to him with outstretched arms, but Emily took hold of her hand and appeared to drag her along roughly.

'*Dad!*'

Hearing the urgent distress of his daughter's cry, John left Natasha standing in his wake. He raced down the beach, kicking up pebbles and sand behind him. His wrist throbbed with every heartbeat and his left knee scorched each time his foot smacked the ground, but he gritted his teeth and ran through the pain. He watched as Emily and Seren reached the shoreline. Seren tried to shake her hand free from Emily's grip, reluctant to go any further, but Emily stooped and bundled her into her arms, then began wading into the sea.

'Emily, wait! *No!*' John's cry was so ferocious it hurt his throat and he thought his lungs might have seared with the effort because each breath he took thereafter was fiery and hellish. He could hear nothing now, not even the sea, for the frantic thumping of his own heart as he watched his sister carry his daughter into the cold North Sea. The absolute absurdity of the situation made him hope he was dreaming.

Once hip-deep in the busy water Emily lay Seren backwards, holding the little girl half-submerged, then she looked up at John and grinned.

No, no, no.

He was close, so close. He had to be able to stop this. Couldn't let it happen. He carried on running, as fast as was physically possible, scuttling down the broken section of the shore's shale wall that Emily and Seren had used.

Don't you dare. DON'T YOU DARE.

Arriving at the shallows he ploughed ahead, thrashing through the frothy saltwater, and watched in horror as Emily thrust Seren's head underwater and held it there. His little girl's arms thrashed amidst the push and tug of the tide, her legs kicking furiously. Frightened but enraged by this, John thrust himself forward and knocked Emily backwards with an extended arm aimed at her throat. As Emily stumbled she was dragged further back by a receding wave and, as a result, her hold on Seren slackened. John, allowing himself to move with the water, seized his little girl and pulled her limp body away from Emily. Clutching her to his chest he looked down at her face, which was upturned to the miserable sky, and said, 'I've got you, kidda. Dad's got you, okay?'

She spluttered and her eyes cracked open, but she didn't answer.

'Give her back, she's mine!' Emily shrieked. She was standing chest-deep in the water only a few feet away, her face a distorted scowl.

John had never seen his sister look so feral. He turned and began to fight his way back to the shore, to get away from her, but Emily dived forward, using the swell of an incoming wave to her advantage. She grasped Seren by the arm and pulled, surprising John by how strong she was.

'Emily, stop this,' John pleaded, buffeted about in the current while holding onto Seren tightly. Saltwater stung his eyes and throat, making him cough and splutter. He refused to let go, even when it felt like Emily might pull the little girl's arm out of its socket. Once the wave had passed he swiped a clunky underwater kick at Emily's legs. Not the most effective of moves, but enough to knock her off balance again.

'Here, John.' Turning, he saw Natasha sloshing towards him, her arms outstretched. 'Pass her to me!'

Plunging forward, he handed Seren to Natasha just as cold, clawed fingers grabbed his hair from behind and yanked him backwards.

'Give her back!' Emily screamed, trying to force John's head underwater.

'Run, Tash,' he cried, before water came rushing into his mouth. He lashed about frantically, cold, salty water pouring straight into his lungs and making him spew when he resurfaced. Emily let go of his hair and he managed to regain his footing. 'Give me the brooch, Emily,' he spluttered.

She looked at him, her eyes darker and full of malicious intent. Her hair was black, pasted to her head, and she seemed much older than her seventeen years. 'Never,' she growled.

'Fight Her, Em!' he pleaded. 'Give me the fucking brooch.'

She sneered and lunged for him. But he was quicker. He grabbed a fistful of her cardigan and managed to spin her round so that her back was to him, he then wrestled her into a bear hug. Waves knocked him about as he manhandled her towards the beach. He was able to hold on, even when she dug her fingernails into his arms, worsening the wound on his wrist and making him feel dizzy with the pain. He managed to get to a place where he was only knee-deep in the water, but then she butted him in the face with the back of her head. A dirty blow he hadn't expected. He didn't hear the crackle of gristle in his nose above the noise of the sea, but he felt it. And he feared he might black out, such was the pain. He let go of Emily and managed to flounder his way back to the sand, where he dropped to all fours and spat a mouthful of blood onto the back of his hands. When he glanced up he saw Emily standing at the top of the shale bank, most likely looking in the direction of Seren and Natasha. He hoped they had managed to put enough distance between themselves and Emily to be safe.

Suddenly Otis came into view. The wiry-haired lurcher was growling and snarling at Emily. John felt weak and defeated but knew he couldn't give in. He dragged himself to his feet. Otis was diverting Emily's attention, creating the perfect opportunity, so he rushed up the shingle bank and knocked Emily to the ground. Pinning her arms to the sand, he said, 'Where's the brooch? I can help you, Em, just tell me where it is.'

His sister's lips curled into a vindictive grin and she laughed, a raucous sound he'd never heard before. 'Such optimism from a melancholic wreck, but you can't even help yourself. And don't forget, I easily rule you.'

'Shut up!' he hissed, spraying her face with red spittle. 'I'm not talking to *you,* I'm talking to Emily.'

'She can't hear you, I'm stronger than she is. And I'm stronger than you. I always was. You've been so receptive, letting me tap into your wants and desires. You've helped me to grow so strong.' She licked his blood from her lips, a crude gesture meant to throw him, and chided, 'You very much enjoyed my take on Pamela Tanner, didn't you?'

'Fuck you.'

'No, you, I'm sure.' She laughed. 'Pamela Tanner wasn't as good as Toni though was she, John? Oh you enjoyed your brother's girlfriend. What a fun night that was.'

'Hardly, it was your undoing as well as mine.'

'Hardly.' Her brow bunched angrily.

'When I left Horden I left you behind.' John's tone was scathing and the tip of his nose almost touched hers. 'You were stashed away in a box, forgotten about because you didn't have my bad traits to feed off anymore and there were no children in the house for you to take.'

'Nevertheless, I have all the time in the world to wait. And here you are now.'

'Yes, exactly, here I am now. You're nothing without me. *I* rule *you*.'

Emily's initial response was one of stunned frustration, but then she quickly became furious. She drew her lips back to reveal straight, white teeth and thrashed about beneath his weight. 'You could *never* rule me! I know you better than you know yourself.'

'Bullshit!' John pressed down on her a little harder, her arms thin in his grip. 'Sissy Dawson invoked you all those years ago, a woman not long into adulthood, not so different to my sister.'

'So?'

'So you only prey on the young. You aren't as powerful as you'd like me to think you are. If you were then I'd be your host, not Emily. As it is you have absolutely no power over me because I'm neither young nor weak.'

'Of course you're weak,' she crooned. 'You're a man. You couldn't resist me, even if you wanted to.'

'You're so wrong, I see what you are now. You're *pathetic*. And this body you've chosen to steal is my sister's, you sick fuck, you have *no* control over me!'

Emily grinned nonchalantly, although her eyes betrayed her irritation at the fact that he was right. 'On the contrary, you've already given me everything I need. I'm done with you now John Gimmerick. Your child is mine to take and your sister is my new chosen host. You're as good as dead already. Want to know why? You'll drink yourself into oblivion. It was always going to happen. You'll carry on this guilt-infested existence in which you'll push everyone even further away and go madder than you already are. Oh yes, I know you. I created all of that in you. I. RULE. YOU.'

'No, that'll never happen,' he hissed through gritted teeth. 'None of it.'

Writhing underneath him she tried to butt him in face with her head, but he was quick to draw back. At the same time her cardigan draped open and he saw the cameo pinned to her t-shirt. He instantly released his grip on her left arm and tore the brooch free. At this, Emily cried out in rage: a guttural sound that John felt in his bones. She flipped him onto his back and landed a weighty punch on his cheekbone, then tried to tackle the brooch from his hand. John cast it away, watching as it sailed through the air and landed some distance away amongst sand and stones at the shore's lip. Emily screamed again and punched him in the mouth. The taste of new blood was strong and when he touched the back of his front teeth with his tongue they felt slack. Before he could retaliate, Emily had straddled his chest and grabbed him by the hair. She then proceeded to whack his head against the ground. Furious and barbaric, she meant to kill him.

'Why don't you show yourself to me?' he cried. White snow danced before his eyes in a flurry of semi-consciousness. 'Why hide in a seventeen-year-old kid? Are you scared of me?'

She let go of his hair and slapped his face. Laughing, her eyes dark with malice, she said, 'If you thought me to be some red-bodied demon, right-hand to Satan, sent from the fiery depths of hell then you're very much mistaken. I'm much, much worse than that. I'm all of the dark aspects of the human psyche. I'm all that is wrong with the world. Your worst nightmares, your grimmest of fairy tales. But I have no physical form, you fool. The hell I come from lies right here.' She jabbed a finger at his forehead and tapped it hard.

John's vision was blurred and his skull ached. He rolled his head to the side to escape the pressure of her fingernail, which was now screwing into his flesh, breaking the skin, and it was then that he noticed a pocket of sea fret drifting towards them. At first he thought his eyes were deceiving him, because the fret was rolling the wrong way, heading towards the sea instead of inland, but after blinking several times he decided that he could definitely make out a white mist, floating about five feet above the ground, heading in their direction.

The sea crashed nearby, but other than that John was aware of an eerie silence. There were no gull, crow or pheasant calls and no wind noise. He continued to watch the band of sea fret with interest and soon he realised there were figures inside the mist. The figures *were* the mist. Swirling faces and limbs that grew closer and closer. Emily looked up to see what had got his attention and when she saw the fog bank she frowned in troubled bewilderment.

And then John was laughing. He felt delirious.

'What's so funny?' Emily spat, her fingers tightening in his hair once again.

'If I can't beat you, they will.'

'Who?'

'Them. All the innocent lives you took.'

Emily tore at his hair till strands pulled out at the roots. 'Impossible, they're *mine!*'

'They were never yours, certainly not to keep. Now

they're free. Look. And in forgiveness they have an ally.' The mist was almost upon them. It smelt of clean air and was so cold it prickled John's skin. 'Sissy Dawson has led them to you.'

'No. I'm more powerful than any of them.'

'You're wrong. For every bad deed there's compassion and empathy. They *forgave* her, which enabled her to forgive herself. That's more powerful than anything you ever stood for. Forgiveness. It's what we all seek at some time or other. It's what you don't understand.'

Emily's hands wound their way around his throat and she squeezed tight till his face purpled. 'If that's so then you'll never have yours.'

'Stop!' A small transparent figure emerged from the mist and regarded Emily with stern, unafraid, eyes. 'I inflicted you upon all of these lives and now I will remove you. You belong to me, not the other way round. This ends right now.'

Emily's eyes became wide, uncertain. Her hands loosened around John's neck and she began to back away. But the fog of spirits gathered round, forming a circle so that she couldn't escape.

John coughed, rubbing at his throat, and watched as the spirits' white vapours began to pour into Emily's mouth and nostrils. Her body convulsed and her eyes rolled back, so the blue of both irises was no longer visible. John reached out to her, but the ghost of Sissy Dawson laid a quick, cold hand on his arm to stop him. She shook her head and said, 'Let them do what they need to, they won't harm your sister, I promise. They need release from Her just as much as she does. They need to take back all that She stole from them.'

Falteringly John retracted his arm, his eyes never leaving Emily. 'What about you?'

'I'll answer for all I'm answerable for. That is all I can do.'

Soon grey vapours started to seep from Emily's nose and mouth, like dirty cigarette smoke, and her flaccid body flopped to the damp ground with a slap.

'I must go now.' Sissy Dawson's face was pained as she spoke to John. 'Please accept my heartfelt apology for the hurt and suffering I've caused you and your family. You're a good man, John. Stick to the path you've chosen, you'll find your way.'

John merely nodded in acknowledgement.

Her form then condensed into a mist and merged easily with the rest. As a whole, the entire mass of spirits began to spin, an opaque whirlwind, faster and faster, whipping up sand round about. John covered his face, but couldn't not watch. Eventually a blackened cloud, like a puff of coal smoke, rose from the top of the vortex then shot down into the brooch that lay on the ground some five metres away. Next to the brooch John saw the fleeting image of a small red-haired boy wearing shorts and a cheeky grin. He'd wavered away to nothing by the time John had blinked once.

Petey Moon?

The remaining mist was now brilliant white and had slowed to a calming swirl. John lay and watched it dissipate, drifting skyward like water evaporating in the heat. Once it had disappeared, John rested his head and closed his eyes.

Rest in peace.

The next thing he was aware of was someone running towards him, shouting.

'*John?* John, are you okay?' It was Natasha.

'Seren?' He tried to sit up, but he did so too fast. His brain created a painful flash of strobe lighting behind his eyes, making him crash back down onto his back. 'Where's Seren?'

'She's safe. She's fine.' Natasha dropped to her knees beside him. Holding his arm and supporting his shoulders, she helped to ease him up into a sitting position.

'But where? Where's…?'

'Shhh. She's with the paramedics. She's okay, I promise. Help will be here soon, look.' Natasha pointed off into the distance. 'You'll be with her shortly.'

John could see two figures in green overalls approaching at a jogging pace.

'Is it over?' Natasha asked, her eyes searching his. 'Is it finally over?'

'Yeah. Sissy Dawson came. She ended what she started.' Using Natasha as a support John managed to stand. When he saw Emily lying nearby, her body limp and lifeless, he groaned. Rushing to her, he ignored the blinding pain in his head and stooped to pick her up.

'John, no. Put her down.' Natasha was by his side again, prising his hands away. 'Help's here.'

Before leaving the beach with Natasha and Emily and the two paramedics, some ten minutes later, John hobbled down to where the cameo brooch was and kicked it with the toe of his shoe. When no black smoke emitted from it, he picked it up. It felt normal against his skin. Not wanting to maintain direct contact with it for any longer than was necessary, he pulled back his arm and hurled it into the frothing abyss of the North Sea.

Let that be the last of it, you evil bitch.

42

John was sitting at Seren's bedside, stroking her hand, when a nurse popped her head into the room. 'You have a visitor, Mr Gimmerick.'

He sighed. 'Police again?'

'No, a Miss Graham.'

John brightened. 'Could you send her in please?'

'Of course, she's right here.'

Natasha was wearing fresh clothes: a floor-length red floral maxi dress and black cotton shrug. Her hair was tied back now and her makeup was newly applied. She carried a holdall into the room with her and gave John a tired smile when their eyes met. 'Hey.'

'Hey.'

'How is she?'

'Out for the count. She has a high temperature and possible chest infection. Owing to the circumstances they're gonna keep her in for a short while. Maybe overnight.'

Natasha went to the bed and touched Seren's forehead with the backs of her fingers. 'Poor little thing.'

'Yeah. And on top of everything, she lost her favourite glasses in the sea. She's not gonna be happy about that.'

'Oh dear. Well, let me know if there's anything I can do.' Natasha looked down at the holdall and held it out to him. 'Actually, when I checked in on the dogs I sorted some stuff out for Seren. I hope you don't mind, I mean, I didn't nose about or rummage or anything, I just thought that if she needed some pyjamas and toiletries it might help if I…'

'Yes, of course. Wow, thanks, Tash. That was really thoughtful.' John took the holdall and unzipped it. When he peered inside he took a sharp intake of air. 'Where did you find *that?*'

Natasha's mouth became pinched and she looked at him worriedly. 'Find what?'

He pulled out a plush triceratops. 'Geller. Where did you find him?'

'Oh sorry, is it not Seren's? It was on top of the bed, I thought…'

'No, no, it is hers and it's great that you brought him, she'll be over the moon. It's just, he went missing for a while.'

Natasha shrugged. 'He was just sitting there looking all cute when I found him.'

John laughed. 'I don't believe it. Petey-bloody-Moon.'

'Sorry?'

'Never mind.'

Natasha pulled up a chair and sat down next to him. 'How's Emily?'

'Stable. Also sleeping. I'll go along in a while and check on her, I just thought I'd be better off staying here with Seren for the time being. You know, till they decide what they're going to do with her.'

'Of course. I'm sure the nurses will let you know when Emily wakes up.' Natasha studied his face. He looked dreadful. A swelling on his cheek was beginning to blacken the area beneath his eye, a split in his top lip made it look like it was painful for him to talk and a large scab on the bridge of his nose was angry red around its base. And that was just what she could see, she was sure he must have obtained more injuries. 'So, how are *you* feeling?'

'Ah, who cares?'

'Don't push it, Gimmerick, I wouldn't have asked.'

'You're being polite.'

'To you? No chance.'

John inhaled deeply, his whole body tensing with the

strain of pent up emotion. 'God, I made such a fuck up of everything, didn't I Tash? Then I had to go and involve my daughter and kid sister as well.'

'Involving Seren and Emily wasn't your fault. You weren't to know.' Natasha reached over and touched his hand. 'But it's over now. For all of us.'

He looked into her eyes, unsure what to make of the burning intensity he saw there. 'Hey, thanks for everything,' he said. 'I couldn't have done this without you.'

Smiling, she looked away, her cheeks colouring. 'Listen, do you want a cuppa?'

'Don't you need to get home? Won't your fiancé be wondering where you've got to?'

'I wouldn't dream of leaving right now. Not like this.'

'You're a better person than me.'

'I know.' She stood up. 'Still one and a half sugars?'

'Yeah.' He didn't bother correcting her. He smiled because she'd remembered, happy to have his tea sweet.

Once she'd left the room, John turned to Seren. She was still sleeping. He leant forward, placing Geller beneath her arm, and said in a low voice, 'Hey, kidda, I'm not sure Petey Moon will be back to see you anymore. I think he's gone to a happier place. Not that he wasn't happy with you, you understand, he just didn't belong here. Remember when you told me some people get trapped? Well he's not trapped anymore. And your mam, your mam was never trapped. She got to where she needed to be and she's happy. That's why she's never been to visit. But that doesn't mean she doesn't care. She still loves you just as much as she ever did, and she knows that someday in the future, a long, *long* time from now, you'll go to that same happy place and you'll meet again.'

Seren murmured, her arm tightening around Geller, but she didn't wake. John stroked her hair and bit his lip.

When Natasha returned with polystyrene cups filled with sour-tasting tea, she and John sat by Seren's bed in silence; a comfortable silence that didn't need filling.

Eventually John asked, 'Are you heading back to Whitby tonight?'

Snorting in a mock offence-taken kind of way, Natasha said, 'Bloody hell, Gimmerick, desperate to get rid of me aren't you?'

'No, not at all. In fact, I was kind of wondering if maybe...Hey, Emily!' He pointed to the door.

Natasha turned her head and saw Emily looking at them through the door's glass panel. When Emily saw they were both looking she smiled and raised a hand to wave, then walked off.

John jumped to his feet and rushed to the door. Natasha followed him. Out in the corridor Emily was nowhere to be seen.

'Maybe she went back to her room,' Natasha suggested.

'Yeah.' John started limping down the corridor, leading the way, his knee causing him great pain. 'She's probably not meant to be out of bed, truth be told.'

When they got to Emily's room they found her lying under starched white sheets, pulled tight around her lower torso. A nurse was standing to the bottom of the bed reading paperwork attached to a clipboard. At their arrival the nurse looked up and asked, 'Can I help?'

'We just came to see how's she doing,' John said, pointing at Emily.

'Same as before. Stable and resting.'

'But we saw her out in the corridor not two minutes since...'

'Unlikely,' the nurse said, her eyes narrowing. 'I've been here for the past five minutes and she hasn't moved once.'

'Oh.'

'Rest assured we'll let you know as soon as she's awake. And don't you worry, she'll be fine.'

John and Natasha excused themselves. In the corridor two nurses bustled past them, the sound of their plimsolls on the lino squeaked into the distance. When they were alone again, Natasha looked at John, her eyes glazed, and said, 'It was Megan, wasn't it?'

John's jaw immediately tightened and his brow creased with building emotion. He couldn't speak.

Biting her lip in an effort to control her own mounting tears, Natasha insisted, 'Our daughter came to say goodbye, didn't she?'

This time John nodded and the glassiness of his eyes spilled down onto his cheeks. Unsure if it was the right thing to do but needing to do it anyway because if he didn't he felt he would crumple to the floor and never get back up again, he reached out and pulled Natasha into his arms.

She didn't resist and began crying freely against his chest. Her body shuddered and she surprised him by reciprocating the hug, squeezing him back just as tight. They stood like that for a long time, both needing the contact. Both needing the comfort.

'Now I know our baby's safe,' she said eventually, between sobs, 'I hope I can let go of all the bad stuff.'

John closed his eyes and tears continued to track a course down his cheeks. 'Yes, I think everything will be alright from now on.' He kissed the top of her head so softly he doubted she'd notice.

'I think so too,' he thought he heard her say.

Epilogue

Jess Overton was bringing up the rear, making sure none of the children dawdled too much. She was a twenty-year-old classroom assistant, out on her first field trip with Mrs Farrow's Year Sixes. 'This place used to be full of coal when Horden colliery was open,' she heard Mrs Farrow, up ahead, saying. 'I doubt we'll see any today, but let's see what other treasures we can find.'

'Treasures like what?' asked a little boy who was walking directly in front of Jess.

'Let's find out, shall we?' Jess said. 'All sorts of things get washed up by the sea.'

Acknowledgements

I'd like to thank Hannah Thompson for the time she spent copy-editing *Emergence* and the wonderfully helpful suggestions she made.

Thanks, also, to Easington Writers, especially Mary Bell and Mavis Farrell for telling me tales about when they used to work at Thorpe Hospital, the place I was born. Those Thursday afternoon ghost stories got my mind ticking.

Thanks to my childhood friend Kelly (Dodds) Philpott for sending me information on Thorpe Hospital and to Mary Bell for allowing me access to her photograph collection.

Thanks to my mam and dad for going on field trips with me, refreshing my memory and taking me back to all the places in Horden I loved best as a child: the beach banks, the beach, the dene and, of course, the formidable cundy.

Thanks to fans, friends and family who offered words of encouragement throughout. There are too many to name individually, but you know who you are!

And, as ever, thank you Derek!

R. H. DIXON

About The Author

R. H. Dixon is a horror enthusiast who, when not escaping into the fantastical realms of fiction, lives in the northeast of England with her husband and two whippets.

Visit her website for horror features, short stories, promotions and news of her upcoming books: **www.rhdixon.com**

IF YOU ENJOYED READING THIS BOOK, PLEASE LEAVE A REVIEW ON AMAZON. THANK YOU!